Knight's Gambit

by

Kevin G. Robinson

This is a work of fiction. Names, characters, places and incidents are
either the product of the author's imagination or are used fictitiously.
Any resemblance to actual persons, living or dead, is entirely
coincidental.

Knight's Gambit

Copyright © 2021 by Kevin G. Robinson

ISBN: 9798599264439 (Paperback)

This book is dedicated to all my family and friends who have helped and supported me over the years on this journey to realise a dream.

CHAPTER ONE

Atop the central headquarters of Knight Technologies, inside the chief executive's office, Adam Knight's close friend LJ called out to him to get his attention. It'd been a very long, trying and emotional day, and Adam had said little since they'd got back from the memorial service, preferring to remain buried deep in his own thoughts.

'What did you say, LJ?' asked Adam. His voice was devoid of animation in acknowledging her presence for the first time in hours.

'I said I'm about to leave. Are you sure you're going to be alright on your own? You know I can stay as long as you need me to.'

'No, I'll be fine. I'm going to sit here a while longer and watch this impending storm play out.'

'Okay. If you need anything, don't hesitate to call me, Cormac or Calypso. We'll come straight over, no matter the hour.'

'Thank you, LJ. Before you go, would you mind turning on my radio for me? And LJ' – he turned to look at her – 'could you let me know when Johnny's flight from Lima gets in? I want to be there for him when he lands. He's taken the news very hard, especially having missed today.'

'I'll call you an hour before his plane lands and we'll go pick him up together. Until then, try to get some sleep; you'll feel better for it. Goodnight, Adam.'

Adam didn't reply. LJ presumed that he'd retreated into his thoughts. She switched on the radio and tuned into Adam's favourite jazz station. As she left the office, she hoped the music would lift his spirits from the darkness she knew he would slip into, knowing in her heart of hearts she could bring no more comfort to him. She headed towards the lift, her footsteps echoing against the polished granite floor. She pressed the button and pulled out her phone to dial Calypso's number.

'Hey, I've just left him. He's not in a good place. I could almost see the wheels turning inside his head, desperately searching for answers.' Saying the words out loud made LJ realise just how deeply concerned she was. 'Anyway, what time does Johnny's plane land at Heathrow?'

'He gets in at around 4.30 a.m.'

'Okay, let me know when his plane is an hour from landing. I promised Adam we'd go pick him up together. I think we need to be very watchful of them both over the next few days.'

'You suspect he's up to something?'

'I don't know for sure. My instincts are telling me that Adam is cooking up some scheme, given the circumstances and the many unanswered questions he has. I just don't understand what drives a man like Colonel Monroe to turn traitor and betray his men, his friends and his country.'

The lift doors opened and LJ stepped inside.

Adam sat listening to the smooth jazz playing in the background as a crack of thunder and lightning streaked across the sky. He took a large sip of his double vodka on the rocks. The glass which he'd been cradling for the last half hour was damp to the touch with condensation from the melting cubes of ice. He stared out in an almost dreamlike state at the storm-battered city. Although the rainwater pouring against his office windows was a reflection of the tears he wished to shed, he couldn't cry. Suppressed anger and questions filled the numbing void where his loss and grief should be, and Adam feared if he were to let out everything he was feeling, he wouldn't be able to contain the fury burning inside him. So for now, silence, contemplation and alcohol would have to suffice as his comforters.

He set his glass down on the small side table next to his chair, loosened his black tie and undid the top button of his white cotton shirt. With his eyes closed, he snatched up his glass and downed the rest of his drink. The remnants of the ice cubes clinked against the glass as the coldness of the vodka made his entire body shudder from its sharp but silky taste.

Resting the empty glass on his knee, Adam reached into his top jacket pocket and pulled out a small silver knight chess piece. He peered down at the inanimate object and grasped it tightly to his chest. It was as if the ground had opened up beneath him and he was falling further into the dark abyss. He would have continued his dark descent had it not been mediated by a sharp ping of yet another text message. His first thought was to ignore it; after all, he'd been getting messages all day from acquaintances, colleagues, friends and distant relations, and right now all he wanted was for them to leave him alone.

He fished the phone out of his trouser pocket and glanced at the anonymous message from a number he didn't recognise. Another well-intentioned but unwelcome condolence message from someone he'd long forgotten about. Annoyed, he went to place his phone on the armrest of his chair when it pinged again. The second message was from the same anonymous number but its tone was more forceful this time.

Don't ignore me, Adam.

Who the hell is this? Adam wondered. He scrolled down the first message and shot out of his chair, sending his empty glass flying and shattering on the mahogany floor. Adam couldn't take his eyes off the message's contents or the king's chess piece insignia at the end, which gave away the anonymous messenger's identity.

The late evening news broadcast began.

'Good evening, London. This is Devin Marques, live from Broadcasting House. Here are the headlines. A small private ceremony was held today in the City's Temple Church to commemorate the lives of six British special forces operatives killed in an alleged illegal and unsanctioned covert operation in Afghanistan three weeks ago. The families of the men and women of Unit Six—'

Electrical static from the storm caused a break in the broadcast. Adam pried his eyes away from his phone and glanced over at the radio as it fought to continue transmitting. He stuffed the phone back in his pocket, grabbed his overcoat and rushed out of his office, slamming the door behind him.

Adam's Ford GT roared into life like a silvery grey ocelot. Slipping the car into gear, he slammed the accelerator to the floor and sped out of Knight Technologies' driveway. The wheels of the car sprayed a thick mist of rainwater into the air as Adam raced out into the cold, stormy night. He switched on his car radio to hear the rest of the news broadcast. He turned onto the main road and crossed Tower Bridge with speed. Passing the Tower of London and turning left on

Tower Hill Road, Adam proceeded to take an obscure route to his destination as instructed by the text message; a precautionary measure to shake off any potential tails.

The news broadcast came back on air.

'Our apologies for the interruption to our programming. In related news, the security services are seeking Colonel Arthur Monroe, former commanding officer of Unit Six, who escaped from custody twenty-four hours after his initial arrest. Colonel Monroe is wanted for treason and questioning concerning his actions and his unit's unsanctioned and illegal mission, which resulted in their deaths at the hands of Mahmud Al-Kabir. The colonel is described as six foot two with white hair, blue-grey eyes, and a scar on his left hand. If any member of the public should see him—'

Adam flicked off the radio and peeked at his watch.

Half past twelve.

He shifted into a higher gear and increased his speed. Reckless in these wet conditions, but he didn't care. London's towering concrete and glass maze of streets was eerily quiet as he raced towards his destination.

CHAPTER TWO

Satisfied that he'd lost any potential tails, Adam reduced his speed as he drove across Waterloo Bridge. Dropping into a lower gear, he entered the Strand and drove into the Savoy hotel's famous entrance and came to a grinding halt. Steam rose from the car's vents as the accumulated rainwater began trickling down through them, cooling the hot engine. Adam reached into the glove compartment of his car and pulled out a small semi-automatic pistol he kept for protection. He stuffed it inside his coat pocket and got out the car. The rain battered his face as he tossed his keys to the approaching valet and darted into the foyer of the hotel.

'Good evening, sir. How may I help you?' asked the night concierge.

'I believe you have a Mr King staying here. I've an urgent appointment with him,' Adam gasped, dashing the excess rainwater from his coat.

'Yes, sir, Mr King is expecting you. You'll find him in Suite 221. Here's the key card.'

'Thank you very much.'

Adam was heading for the lifts when the night concierge called out, 'What name shall I say for the guest register, sir?'

'Just put me down as Mr Jack Queen from London.'

'Very good, sir. Have a good night.'

Adam stepped out of the lift onto the second floor. The air was perfumed with jasmine from the countless vases of flowers that lined the corridor. His heart was beating a little faster with anxious anticipation as to what awaited him in Suite 221. The message he'd received had promised answers, and at this point nothing else mattered except being met by Mr King, or, as Adam knew him, Colonel Arthur Monroe.

Adam's eyes flickered from room number to room number as he rushed past the many doors, searching for Suite 221. A few minutes passed by before he found himself outside the suite. As he paused a moment to gather his thoughts, a crippling pang of fear gripped him. What if Colonel Monroe hadn't sent that message? What if this was an elaborate ruse? A set-up by the security services to see who would aid the colonel, and then use them to draw him out in the open? Adam knew he was being overly paranoid again, but it was something to consider. Either way, he had to know. His hand holding the electronic key card shook as it hovered over the electronic lock. As an extra precaution, Adam used his other hand to pull out the small semi-automatic pistol in his pocket. If he was walking into a trap, he wasn't going to make it easy for them.

Taking a deep breath, he slotted the key card into the lock, pulled down on the handle and pushed the door open. The lights from the corridor flooded the suite which had been shrouded in darkness. Adam cautiously stepped inside. Closing the door behind him, a streak of blue lightning illuminated the room as he turned on the main lights.

'Hello? Arthur, are you here? It's me, Adam,' he called out, moving further into the suite, but there was no response. The suite was empty.

Puzzled and disappointed, Adam wondered what had happened to Colonel Monroe. He'd said in his message he would be here to explain everything. He began searching the rest of the suite. Perhaps the colonel had left a message for him to find, asking him to meet elsewhere. His gaze eventually fell upon the coffee table, where a crisp white envelope emblazoned with a knight's chess piece lay. Adam pocketed his pistol and went straight over.

He ripped open the envelope and found a DVD with a note that simply said *Play me*. Adam turned on the suite's plasma screen TV and slotted the DVD into the inbuilt player. After taking off his coat and throwing it to one side, he sat down on the sofa and waited for the disc to play. After a few seconds the screen sprang to life, revealing a dishevelled-looking Colonel Arthur Monroe.

'My God, Arthur.' Adam was shocked to see him in such a state. It had been three months since they had last seen one another in person, and only three weeks since the tragic incident.

The colonel's white hair was matted and uncombed; his blue-grey eyes once full of authority were now drawn and shifty. He looked like he hadn't slept or shaved in weeks, and he was out of uniform. A regimentally pristine man as a rule, his civilian clothing seemed at odds with the man Adam knew.

'Hello, Adam, my old friend. If you are watching this recording, then it means that I still have your friendship. It also means that I've used the last available channels left open to me to get you here. At the moment the entire country believes me to be a traitor who sold out his unit, but this is not true. Trust me when I say I was framed, and that what I tell you now is the whole unedited truth of what really happened three weeks ago.'

Adam didn't move a muscle. The rest of the suite faded into obscurity as he stared into his friend's face, completely transfixed by his words.

'First, I want to make it absolutely clear to you that our covert operation, Guardian Angel, was sanctioned at the highest level by the Prime Minister and, as far as I was aware, was not illegal.'

'Second, the mission was to rescue a local Afghan tribal leader and his family. They had been of considerable assistance to us in gathering and providing us with vital intelligence on a terror cell that was working in the area, headed by a ruthless insurgent commander by the name of Mahmud Al-Kabir. Adam, you've got to believe me when I say that everything about this mission seemed routine, but what happened in the hours after our final briefing will haunt me forever.'

Colonel Monroe paused for a moment to regain his composure. His face was contorted and Adam could tell he was burdened with tremendous regret, guilt and shame. He felt sorry for the old man, and he knew that what the colonel had to say next was going to be very painful for them both.

CHAPTER THREE

Bishop's Abbey was a small, picturesque village in the charming county of Surrey. It was a picture postcard of idyllic English country life, surrounded by rolling fields and hills. It was here at Mitre Hall, the village's former manor house, that Colonel Monroe conducted his secret operations and planned Unit Six's overseas assignments. Unknown to the villagers, Mitre Hall had a secret. An underground concrete bunker – a relic from the Cold War – had been brought back into full operational service at the turn of the century. The bunker was on full alert and the atmosphere inside was a dense mixture of quiet confidence and uneasiness. Colonel Monroe sat in the main control room with his support staff, monitoring Unit Six's progress on the main viewing screen.

'Any developments from Echo team yet, Corporal Narendra?' he asked, checking the international clock times between London and Afghanistan.

'Not since their last check-in, sir, before they went dark, but I'm keeping my ear out for any radio chatter,' she replied. 'I should also point out, sir, that our satellite is moving out of visual range, but we'll still be able to track the team on locators.'

'Thank you, Corporal. I'm going to my office. Notify me right away the moment Echo team re-establish contact with us.'

'Yes, sir.'

Colonel Monroe sat down at his desk and rubbed his temples. He could feel the onset of a stress headache, which wasn't surprising given the amount of pressure he and his unit had been under for the past seventy-two hours to get this mission off the ground. Yet despite his unwavering confidence in his unit's abilities, he sensed that it was going to be a long night. Waiting for news on missions such as this was worse than that split second of tension before a dentist extracts a tooth. Even worse for the colonel were his own private feelings of fatigue and weariness. Age had begun to creep up on him despite his best attempts to hide it beneath his regimental and pristine façade. Pretty soon he would have to retire, after a long and distinguished career. Raising his arms above his head to stretch and shake off some of that fatigue, Colonel Monroe yawned deeply and sat back in his chair, resting his legs up on his desk. He tilted his head to look up at the ceiling and was about to close his eyes when the bunker's emergency alarm started screaming. Shaken from his lethargy, Colonel Monroe sprang from his chair like a coiled viper and rushed out of his office, back into the main control room.

'Corporal, what the hell is happening?' he said. 'And someone shut that bloody alarm off.' The alarm pierced through his ears like hot needles being inserted into his eardrums.

'Sir, the entire system went haywire. We've a Code Hades situation in progress with multiple casualties. I'm trying to make contact with Echo One and Two,' Corporal Narendra replied.

'Keep trying to establish contact with Echo One and get him to confirm Code Hades and give us a sitrep on their status.' Colonel Monroe looked up at the main viewing screen which was flashing *Code Hades Protocol Activated*. Hades was the last thing he or anyone in the bunker wanted to see on the screen during any mission. He surmised that the situation on the ground must be dire. To his horror, he also noticed that only two of his unit were still alive – if the information on-screen from their tracking implants was accurate.

'Sir, I've got them. Echo One is transmitting but the signal is fragmented. Their radio may be damaged,' said Corporal Narendra, handing over her headpiece.

Between the heavy static and breaks in communication, Colonel Monroe and his support staff could hear a fierce firefight being waged in the background, along with faint screams from what they concluded to be civilians. In the foreground a faint but firm voice was trying to break through.

'Echo On … Papa Al … do you read me?'

'Papa Alpha to Echo One, we're receiving you. Can you hear us?' said Monroe.

There was no response.

'Corporal, boost the signal. We need to cut through this bloody interference.'

There was a brief pause.

'Try now, sir.'

'Papa Alpha to Echo One, please respond, over?'

Explosions and heavy machine-gun fire ripped through the Afghan town of Teshkat-Alim-Zur. The last two surviving members of Unit Six burst into a derelict government building on the outskirts of the ruined town and barricaded themselves inside on the top floor. Echo Two darted across the room to a broken window and rained down suppressive fire on the enemy insurgents of Mahmud Al-Kabir, while Echo One responded to Colonel Monroe's continuous hails.

'Echo One to Papa Alpha, receiving you. I say again, we are under heavy attack from multiple hostiles, over,' he shouted, as Echo Two fired off a couple more rounds, killing two advancing insurgents.

'Echo One, understood. Give me a sitrep and confirm status of unit,' Monroe replied.

Echo One covered the street below while Echo Two reloaded his SA80.

After a few moments Echo Two started firing again and Echo One responded to the colonel's enquiry. 'Confirm Code Hades protocol. Echo Two and I are the only ones left alive. Objective and mission were a set-up. Repeat: set-up. Our primary and secondary targets were already dead, and the enemy were lying in wait for us, sir.'

A huge explosion from a rocket-propelled grenade ripped a hole in the side of the building, shaking its fragile foundations and knocking them both to the ground, covering them in sand, dust and debris. Brushing himself down, Echo Two scrambled to his feet and took up another position to lay down more suppressive fire as the enemy insurgents advanced on their position.

'Whatever they're doing at base, tell them get their arses out of their heads and think of something to help us, fast. We're sitting ducks up here and our ammo isn't going to last forever,' he shouted over to Echo One, a hint of panic leaking into his voice as a few rounds of bullets peppered the brickwork.

'Papa Alpha, we need options now, and fast.'

'Do we have any support options under DIDO conditions?' asked Colonel Monroe, futilely hoping one of his support staff would have an answer.

'You know there are none, sir. Deep Infiltration Dark Operations are carried out in complete secrecy with no ground or air support. Even if we could scramble jets, drones or support units, they wouldn't get there in time,' someone called out.

'I agree with that assessment, sir. Echo One and Two's only chance is to escape, lie low and make it to a safe extraction zone,' said Corporal Narendra, her voice full of regret.

Colonel Monroe grasped the radio mic tightly. He didn't like the assessment of the situation given by his support staff, but he couldn't fault their logic either. He faced one of the worst scenarios any commanding officer could face – the loss of his entire unit – which made him sick to his stomach. The only solution was pretty much suicidal, but there was a small chance, nonetheless.

Echo One's voice cackled over the radio, demanding updated orders.

'Lieutenant … Jamie, I am ordering you and Sergeant Beckett to escape by any means necessary and lie low until we can find you a safe extraction zone for evac, over.'

Colonel Monroe's message cut Echo One and Two to the core. They were on their own with a fanatical enemy surrounding them and pummelling the building they were held up in.

'It's impossible to evac, sir. The bastards have us surrounded,' Echo One replied, looking across at Echo Two.

With a thunderous noise that felt like the heavens themselves were collapsing in, several RPG explosions blew out a section of the top floor where Sergeant Beckett had been positioned, killing him instantly. Jamie was thrown against the other wall, sustaining severe shrapnel wounds to both his legs. He let out an agonising scream and watched helplessly in slow motion as his friend's lifeless body was engulfed by flames and disappeared into the street below.

'They got Ryan. Ryan's dead, sir,' Jamie shouted over the radio.

Colonel Monroe tried to calm Jamie down but it was no good. A cold realisation had now descended over Jamie like an avalanche. He was going to die. Nothing could prevent that now, and he wasn't in any position to make a run for it. In his mind, there was only one last course of action to take.

'It's been an honour to serve with you, Colonel. Find out who betrayed us. Promise me that.' He swallowed hard, the pain increasing with every word. 'Tell my family I love them and that my last thoughts were of them, over and out.'

Jamie threw down his radio mic, picked up his machine gun and dragged himself over to a better position in direct line of sight of the barricaded wooden door. Propping himself up and desperate not to fall unconscious, he watched as the door was ripped open from the outside. He took aim as the sound of death grew closer and closer. 'The moment I see their faces …' he muttered to himself through gritted teeth.

'Come on then, you bastards!' he shouted, in one last act of defiance.

The door gave way. Jamie took one last breath and aimed his weapon.

Back in the bunker, Colonel Monroe and his entire support staff listened powerlessly as they heard a hail of machine-gun fire over the radio, followed by an explosion of what sounded like a grenade.

'Echo One from Papa Alpha, come in, please?' said Colonel Monroe, clutching his radio mic.

Radio silence.

'Echo One, this is Papa Alpha … Jamie?'

* * *

Several cracks of thunder boomed outside the windows of the suite. Adam leant back into the sofa, speechless. He turned his head away from the screen as several tears escaped his eyes and streaked down his cheeks. He couldn't breathe as an even greater pain plunged deeper inside his already broken heart.

'I'm so sorry, Adam. There was nothing more I could have done to save them. It will haunt me forever,' said Colonel Monroe. 'There's more, and you must brace yourself for this next part, but their deaths and my own predicament could have been avoided if only I hadn't been too blind to realise there was another sinister agenda at play.'

'Adam, we were sold out and betrayed by our own Prime Minister and members of his cabinet.'

CHAPTER FOUR

The events of the last few hours had taken their toll on Colonel Monroe. He was in a daze as his mind kept replaying the conversation he'd had with Jamie in those last few desperate minutes, over and over again. Had they really been set up and betrayed? It was a question that made him sick to his stomach. Command had its privileges and burdens and losing anyone under your command was dreadful and regrettable. But losing your entire unit to a relentless enemy because of a turncoat who had tipped them off was almost too much to bear.

Officially under DIDO conditions, Colonel Monroe was under strict instructions not to report to the PM until 0700 hours the next day. However, given the night's catastrophic events, and out of loyalty to his fallen unit, he felt compelled to make his report earlier than expected to contain the situation and make arrangements to retrieve their bodies as soon as possible.

The drive from Bishop's Abbey to Downing Street had gone by in a flash. Colonel Monroe checked his watch – 0245 hours – and rubbed his hands over his face to stem his fatigue. Despite the lateness of the hour, he knew Prime Minister Brooks would be up as he seldom went to bed until late. Lingering for a moment outside Number Ten, Colonel Monroe reflected on the number of times he'd been here in the past seventy-two hours. Prime Minister George Brooks had demanded constant reports on their progress in person, which had annoyed him no end. He'd always hated bureaucratic interference from politicians, but this time it would be different. The fallout from this would be a quagmire of anger, resentment and reproach, both publicly and privately, and no doubt a lengthy and painful public enquiry would be held by the Defence Select Committee.

Colonel Monroe mounted the small stone steps and entered through the famous black door to be greeted by Ludlow, the night doorman. 'Good Evening, sir.'

'Good evening, Ludlow, is the PM still awake? I'm not expected but it is most important that I speak with him,' said Colonel Monroe.

'Sir, I'm sorry, but if you're not expected you won't be able to see him. He left orders not to be disturbed as he's with the Foreign Secretary in his private study.'

'What I have to report can't wait. It's a matter of national security.'

'Very well, I'll get someone to announce you're here to see him then, sir.'

'No, thank you. I'd prefer to go unannounced. Say, it's very quiet here tonight. Where is everyone? What's going on?' Colonel Monroe had noticed that Number Ten looked almost deserted.

'No idea, sir. All I know is that the PM ordered a skeleton staff to be on duty tonight and gave everyone else the night off, the lucky devils.'

'I see. Well, thank you, Ludlow. I can find my way from here.'

Colonel Monroe proceeded down the corridor towards the PM's private study. He took a slow walk to gather his thoughts and prepare for the onslaught of questions that were sure to come. What was he going to say? And what was the PM going to make of Jamie's accusations of a set-up and betrayal? His chain of thoughts soon evaporated as he approached the PM's study. The door was ajar and he could hear laughter emanating from inside. Peering through the crack in the door, Colonel Monroe could see the imposing figure of Prime Minister George Brooks and an anxious-looking Foreign Secretary, David Miller, who sat with his head bowed, swirling his drink. They were having what appeared to be a conversation on a secure comms link with the bespectacled Defence Secretary, Richard Ashworth, the cigar-smoking Home Secretary, Eric Jackson, and, most sickening of all, the militant and battle-scarred figure of Mahmud Al-Kabir. There were very few photos of Kabir on file, but thanks to the joint intelligence they'd gathered over the years, it was definitely him.

Colonel Monroe took a step back from the door, full of revulsion and disbelief. He felt like he was going to throw up at what he'd witnessed. How could he have been so blind? Jamie was right. A rotten apple – or in this case, several – had betrayed them, and it had come from the very top of the proverbial tree. Even more horrific was that they'd used Kabir and his insurgents to carry out the attack, knowing full well that his unit had killed Kabir's brother fifteen months ago in another operation.

A dark poison swelled within every fibre of Colonel Monroe's body. He had never felt such anger or rage as he felt now. He wanted revenge. He wanted to burst into the room and kill Brooks and Miller right there and then, and go after Ashworth, Jackson and Kabir. But what would it achieve? His unit would still be dead, and he'd just witnessed four of the most senior politicians in Britain collaborating with an enemy of this nation. He owed it to himself, and more to his fallen unit, to gather as much incriminating evidence as possible and bring the whole sordid affair out in the open. It took all the self-restraint and composure he could muster, but Colonel Monroe stepped back to the study door, peered through the crack and listened in to every word that was being spoken.

'Lastly, gentlemen, I would like to raise a toast to a job well done. I trust we have held up our end of the bargain to your satisfaction, Mahmud?' said Prime Minister Brooks, finishing with glee what had clearly been a long-winded speech.

'I'm most appeased that my brother has been avenged,' replied Mahmud, delicious self-satisfaction written all over his scarred face.

'Quite. So where are the bodies now?'

'We left them to the elements. You can send another team in to come and collect what's left once we've moved out.'

'Good. I trust you will hold up your end of the bargain and relinquish control of the region to us and offer no more resistance against British interests in that part of Afghanistan?'

'As long as you pay what you owe us to compensate for the loss of revenue and our opium fields, my men and I will honour the agreement and vanish like ghosts in the sand.'

'Consider it done. The money will be in your account by sunrise. Now, gentlemen, one more toast: to us, for a most amicable, one-off partnership.' Prime Minister Brooks raised his glass and together all five men drank their glasses dry.

The main viewing screen went blank.

Brooks took Foreign Secretary Miller's empty glass from his warm, sweaty hands and refilled both glasses with generous amounts of Scotch. He passed Miller's glass back to him and clunked their glasses together genially, then sat down opposite.

'What's wrong with you, Miller? You haven't said much all evening except when asked directly for your input, and even then it felt forced.'

'It's nothing, Prime Minister. I'm very pleased with the outcome of your excellent plan and I offer my congratulations again most heartily; but did the soldiers have to die so violently? I mean, what are we going to tell their loved ones? And do you really trust Al-Kabir to keep his mouth shut and keep his word?'

'Now, David ...' said Brooks

Outside in the corridor, Colonel Monroe had seen and heard enough. By using his Christian name, no doubt the PM was trying to be empathetic to Foreign Secretary Miller and alleviate his feelings of guilt. He was shaking with anger and ready to burst through the door and lay into them both when he heard the click of a hammer from a semi-automatic pistol draw back. The cold metal of a gun barrel was pressed hard into the back of his neck.

'Oh Colonel, you really shouldn't be listening at the door to private conversations. Now put your hands up, open the door and walk inside,' said the voice.

In an act of defiance, Colonel Monroe kicked the door open with a bang, taking Prime Minister Brooks and Foreign Secretary Miller by surprise. For that small act of defiance Colonel Monroe received a smack to the back of his head from the butt of the pistol of his captor, who then pushed him inside, making him fall to his knees.

'Dominic, what is the meaning of this?'

'I'm sorry for the interruption, Prime Minister, but we found Colonel Monroe lurking outside the door listening in to your conversation. Ludlow decided he wasn't comfortable with you being in the building unannounced, and informed us,' Dominic replied, looking down and pointing his gun at Colonel Monroe, who was soothing the back of his head.

Colonel Monroe glared up in anger at the imposing figure of Prime Minister Brooks, who was now towering over him and looking straight back into his eyes. His facial expression remained neutral, as if Colonel Monroe's unannounced presence was nothing more than a minor inconvenience.

'Where's Paul?' Brooks asked, enquiring about his other bodyguard.

'He's taking care of Ludlow and the security systems, sir.'

'Good. So, Colonel, tell me, how much did you see and hear?'

'Enough to go public with and have you all arrested for treason, you treacherous bastard.'

'Calm yourself, Colonel.' Prime Minister Brooks let out a defiant laugh. 'I realise you're angry and upset, but your unit had to die. Their deaths were necessary to keep us in the game and our interests secured.'

Colonel Monroe went to savage Brooks for his chilling, inhuman remarks but was thwarted by Dominic who pressed the gun hard into the back of his neck again.

'Have you no conscience at all? You murdered my entire unit for your own warped ends. You let them be slaughtered by that slime of humanity, Al-Kabir, who will betray whatever bargain you struck.'

'I don't think so, Colonel. You see, Al-Kabir won't be alive for much longer. I intend to give him and his terror cell up to the Americans, who will end him once and for all and tie up a nice loose end,' said Brooks, retrieving his glass of Scotch. He took a long, satisfying gulp.

'You're more of a fool than I gave you credit for, Brooks. You won't be able to cover this up. I'll make such waves that everyone will know what you've all done.'

Prime Minister Brooks put his glass down on the table and walked back over to Colonel Monroe. He grabbed his face harshly, forcing him to look up. 'You seem to have overlooked your current position, Colonel.'

'What do you want done with him, sir?' Dominic interrupted.

'Do you really have to ask, Dominic?'

'Prime Minister,' said Foreign Secretary Miller, speaking up for the first time.

'What, Miller?'

'Sir, we can't kill him—'

'He's right, Brooks. My support staff know I'm here, and their loyalty to me is infinite. If you kill me, they will ask questions—'

'And will their loyalty be as infinite when they discover it was you who betrayed them?'

Colonel Monroe took another swing at Brooks but was once again forced back into his kneeling position by Dominic. He watched the Prime Minister look across at Foreign Secretary Miller and, turning his head slightly to see Miller's reaction, he watched in disgust as the cowardly and weak-natured Foreign Secretary clammed up and averted his eyes from Brooks's cold, frustrated and scowling gaze.

'Miller, I don't want to hear another peep out of you until we settle this. The colonel's seen and heard too much. He has to die, but I will concede he shouldn't be killed here.'

'Even if you kill me, Brooks, the truth will come out in the end.'

'Trust me, Colonel, it won't once I tell everyone that it was you who betrayed your entire unit in this unsanctioned and illegal mission. You and Al-Kabir cooked up this entire plot. You came here tonight to kill me and Foreign Secretary Miller, and, having failed, you took your own life, dying in disgrace.'

'No one will believe you or your crazy cover story, Brooks.'

'I grant you, Colonel, it needs a little polishing, but I'll make it work.'

***

'The next thing I remember, Adam, is waking up in the back of a Range Rover, in a clearing, miles from anywhere, surrounded by trees. The back of my head was bleeding a little from where Dominic had knocked me out. Thankfully, neither he nor the other bodyguard, Paul, bothered to tie me up, which gave me my one chance. I killed them both and made my escape in their Range Rover.'

Adam stopped the DVD again. He sat, dejected, trying to process all the information Colonel Monroe had divulged. His eyes filled with more tears, and the rage that had been bubbling away inside of him all day finally spilled out. He picked up the small coffee table and threw it against the wall with an almighty crash, smashing a vintage art deco mirror. Breathing heavily, he managed to regain some self-control and collapsed onto the floor. He was reluctant to watch the last part of the DVD but knew he had no choice.

He picked up the remote and hit play.

'Adam, I know this is a great deal to take in and Lord knows I can't imagine what you must be feeling, but I must ask something of you. I've known for a number of years now, thanks to some reliable sources, that you still hang around with a small, trusted circle of friends, all of whom, including yourself, pulled off some of the most spectacular white-collar crimes some years ago. I want you to restart your extracurricular activities and use your collective talents to expose Brooks and his government's betrayal and crimes.'

Adam was taken aback by his old friend's candour. He looked back on that part of his life with great fondness and fun, but he'd covered his tracks well – or so he'd thought. He never for one moment believed that anyone would ever find out.

The colonel continued to speak. 'I've left a briefcase in the wall safe of your suite, containing all the relevant information I could gather. Use it well. Brooks erased everything on their secure ghost drive apart from the SIS file, as far as I know. The combination to the safe is 1605. Do not try to find me, Adam; I'm a dead man walking. I know that Brooks is looking for me, and I don't expect to live long. If I'm to die, I will die happy in the knowledge that I did my best to right this wrong and that you will see it through to the bitter end. I wish you good luck. Goodbye, my friend.'

The DVD went blank.

Adam was numb. He picked himself up off the floor, wiped his eyes and composed himself, taking in a deep breath. He walked over to the wall safe, entered the combination and took out the briefcase as instructed. On opening the lid, he found a dossier of documents. A quick glimpse revealed they were intelligence files containing information on a man known as Aree, as well as some of the colonel's personal computer files and a few other interesting trinkets.

Another crack of lightning danced across the late-night sky.

Adam locked the briefcase and walked over to the window. He stared out across the storm-battered city. Shutting his eyes, he heard the colonel's words pound like a jackhammer in his head. When it became too much to bear, his eyes opened, but they were no longer filled with tears. They were ablaze with silent retribution.

CHAPTER FIVE

One year later

Inspector Sonia O'Shaughnessy was halfway through her dreary night shift duty at the Garda station in Letterkenny, County Donegal, writing up her reports for closed and ongoing cases, when her phone rang. She checked the screen and was relieved to see it wasn't another call-out but an old friend from London she affectionately called Aree – a nickname her friend had acquired from his initials when they'd worked closely together on the border during the troubles as his real name was considered too English.

'Aree, it's lovely to hear from you. It's been a while.'

'Hello, Sonia, it certainly has. I wish I could say this was a social call, but my time is limited and I need a favour. I promise I'll owe you big time.'

'Same old Aree ... I can forgive you this one time, I suppose, and being owed a favour from you is definitely worth it. What can I do for you?'

'Sonia, you're a gem, and I promise when I'm over in a few weeks we'll go for dinner and reminisce about old times. Now, I need you to go to Rathmullan for me. A body has been discovered inside the old Carmelite friary ruins,' Aree replied with what sounded like a flicker of nervousness in his voice.

'Yes, I heard about that one over my police radio. One of our team is up there now dealing with it.'

'Brilliant, I need you to get up there and be my eyes and ears. We don't have much time as your men have already run his prints, but I need you to confirm if the deceased remains are that of Colonel Arthur Monroe.'

Sonia was taken aback by the potential name of the victim. She knew of Colonel Monroe and his alleged crimes from the Europol collective intelligence reports on their most wanted suspects. The fact that this particular individual, if indeed it was Colonel Monroe, had somehow evaded capture and settled in Rathmullan under a probable assumed identity was a testament to his resourcefulness and training as a former military intelligence officer and soldier.

'I'll leave right now. It'll take me half an hour to get there,' said Sonia, picking up her car keys from her desk.

'Thanks, Sonia. Contact me when you can and let me know if any Whitehall suits turn up. They're liable to take possession of the body without causing too much fuss. If they do, don't resist above the normal objections a police inspector would make. These men are ruthless and not to be trusted.'

'I don't like the sound of that, Aree. You know I don't like going in blind. What aren't you telling me?'

'Trust me, it's better that you don't know right now. I'll send you the colonel's profile and description en route.'

'Okay, we'll play it your way for now. I'll call you back when I have something definite.'

The seaside village of Rathmullan lay on the Fanad Peninsula on the western shores of Lough Swilly. This hidden gem was a beautiful, safe haven from the world where someone could forget their troubles and escape the trappings of modern life. At least, that had been the case until tonight. Inspector O'Shaughnessy pulled up to the police cordon where there was a flurry of activity. She'd made good time, having taken the R247 at some speed. The full moon illuminated the entire village, the friary ruins and the lough, beyond which a veil of mist floated ominously above the water. Death had certainly passed through and taken another poor soul to the next world, she thought.

Presenting her identification to the officer on guard, Sonia ducked under the police cordon. A throng of lush green ivy covered the friary ruins, making it almost impossible to see what was going on inside. The only clues that anything was amiss were the bright forensic lights that illuminated the white tarp, and the occasional shadows moving about inside. A small crowd of villagers had gathered on the other side of the road, held at bay by uniformed officers. They were all a flutter with rumour and speculation. Clearly this had been one of the most stirring incidents to have happened since the Flight of the Earls in 1607. Pulling back the white tarp, she stepped into the friary's shell of an interior.

'Good evening, Sergeant Brady, Dr Maher.'

'Evening, Inspector, I didn't expect to see you here,' said Sergeant Brady.

'It's a slow night, so I thought I'd pop by to see how you're getting on and what progress you've made on the case and the deceased.' Sonia looked down at the dead body, which was covered with a blood-stained sheet.

'May I look at the deceased?'

'Certainly, but I warn you; it's not a pleasant sight,' replied Dr Maher.

Squatting down next to the victim, she pulled back the bloodied sheet and was unsettled by the state of the deceased. Despite the severe bruising to his face and the injuries he'd sustained to his body, he fitted the profile and description that Aree had sent her. It was definitely Colonel Monroe. His blue-grey eyes, once full of life and authority, were glazed over by the stone-cold stare of death.

Surreptitiously, Sonia pulled out her phone and took a few shots of the colonel's face and half-naked body to send to Aree later.

'What do we know so far? Does he have any identification on him?'

'Yes, but here's the strange part, Inspector: the ID found in his wallet says his name is Ronan McCarthy, a retired civil servant from England. Been here about a year, and by all accounts was a pleasant enough fellow who kept to himself, according to some of the villagers. He has a small house on the other side of the lough which we are going through now,' said Sergeant Brady. 'However, given his severe injuries, we ran his prints to make a positive ID and found that his identity is fake. His real name is Arthur Monroe, former colonel of military intelligence and the very same treacherous Arthur Monroe who sold out his entire special ops unit last year.' Brady had an air of disdain in his voice. Sonia knew that Sergeant Brady had served some years ago and so took a very dim view of anyone betraying their own side.

'Dr Maher, what was the cause of death?'

'My preliminary examinations suggest he was murdered. I'd say he's been dead for at least four hours. There are multiple lacerations and defensive wounds to his face and body, indicating he struggled with his attacker. There is also strong evidence to suggest he was tortured, but what killed him were the two gunshot wounds to his chest, grouped close together around the heart. Death would have been instantaneous.' Maher had that calm, robotic tone that almost every forensic doctor acquired after years of seeing dead bodies.

'I will, of course, know more and confirm my preliminary examinations once I get him back to the morgue to perform an autopsy,' he continued.

'Who found him?'

'A couple of loved-up teenagers who were looking for a quiet romantic spot, if you know what I mean,' replied Sergeant Brady with a smirk on his face.

'And neither they nor anyone in the village heard any gunfire or got a glimpse of him or his attacker?'

'Apparently not. The evidence suggests the colonel and his murderer were using suppressors to muffle the sound of their gunshots. We found bullet holes and spent cartridges all over the place, and the colonel's gun was found next to his body, with a suppressor attached.

'The old devil must have given his murderer a run for his money, though. We found some blood that doesn't belong to him over by a window. We also found this grab bag near to his body. Probably stashed a few of these bags around the village in case he needed to get out quick; a resourceful soldier to the end, even if he was a disgrace to his uniform,' Brady continued acidly.

'Okay, Sergeant, that'll do. The man is dead, after all, and we have a—'

One of Sergeant Brady's men came rushing in and whispered something into his ear as the white tarp covering the entrance was pushed back and two well-dressed men in suits appeared. From their appearance, Sonia surmised that these must be the men from Whitehall Aree had warned her about. She felt a cold chill emanating from their direction.

'Sergeant Brady, I presume?' one of them said.

'Aye, that's me. What can I do for you?'

'My name is John Hyde and this is my colleague Arkwright Jones. We are representatives of Her Majesty's Government.' The two men presented their identification cards. 'We are here to take charge of the deceased, Arthur Monroe, and any and all evidence relating to this tragic case of suicide.'

'Suicide? This man has been violently murdered,' said Sergeant Brady, his voice full of scorn as Dr Maher looked on in amazement at the cover-up that was unfolding before their eyes.

'You're mistaken, Sergeant. Colonel Monroe died four hours ago by his own hand. That will be the official verdict and the end to a rather sordid affair that has caused deep embarrassment to my government,' Hyde replied, unmoved by Sergeant Brady's protests.

'What authority do you have to take over like this? You've no jurisdiction or authority over the border,' Sonia interjected before Sergeant Brady or Dr Maher could reply.

'Ah yes, you must be Inspector Sonia O'Shaughnessy. We were told you might be here. The paperwork in my colleague's hand gives me all the authority I need.' Arkwright handed over the documents for her to examine.

'As you can see, it's been rubber-stamped by both our respective governments, with all the "t"s crossed and "i"s dotted,' Hyde continued flippantly.

'It's all here in black and white, Brady. I'm sorry. They've all the authority they require. There's nothing I can do,' said Inspector O'Shaughnessy, looking over at Sergeant Brady who was fuming.

'Bloody Brits, always sticking your nose in and distorting the truth to suit your own ends. You know there's a reason no one takes you or the UK seriously any more.'

'I will take that remark, Sergeant, under advisement, but if you've a problem, take it up with your superiors in Dublin. Now, if you'll excuse us, we have a lot to clean up.'

'Come on, Doc, let's get out of here and let these bureaucratic leeches get on with their cover-up.' They walked out together, pushing past Hyde and his colleague. Sonia handed back the paperwork to Hyde's colleague. She wanted to get out of there as quickly as possible and call Aree.

'Oh, Inspector,' said Hyde as she began walking towards the empty stone arch that was once the door to the friary.

'Yes, Mr Hyde?' she replied, turning back as Hyde's colleague began placing the collected evidence into their own bags.

'Just satisfy my curiosity. What are you doing here? It's for my report, you see. After all, you weren't assigned to this case.' Hyde's voice was tinged with suspicion.

'Nothing sinister, Mr Hyde. I was doing a simple welfare check on my boys, making sure they're doing the best job possible.'

'I see. Well, that'll be all, Inspector. Please remind Sergeant Brady and Doctor Maher, and yourself, that this paperwork also forbids you from talking about this case in any context; otherwise, you may find yourselves in very hot water. Is that quite clear?' She felt his beady eyes scanning her face intensely. She nodded in agreement and left.

Glad to be out from under Hyde's unsettling gaze, Sonia watched as Sergeant Brady and Doctor Maher sped angrily past her in Brady's car, back towards the station. She knew she needed to have a talk with Brady and smooth over his bruised ego from being upstaged by Hyde so unceremoniously. For now, though, he'd have to wait as she had a phone call to make. She sped off towards the R247 and called Aree's number. The phone rang and rang for what seemed like an eternity before he eventually answered.

'Aree, it's me.'

'Sonia, thank God. I was beginning to think something had happened. Did you get a positive ID? Was it the colonel?'

'Yes, it's definitely him and he was murdered, although your Whitehall men are distorting the facts and calling it a suicide. I managed to take some pictures, which I'll send you in a bit, but I warn you; they're not pretty. Our forensics man, Dr Maher, strongly believes the colonel was subjected to torture before he died.'

'Christ, I suspected something had happened to him when he missed his last check-in. I hope he didn't divulge anything. Did he put up much of a fight?'

'He fought to the bitter end. What do you mean, he missed his last check-in? You knew he was here all along?'

'Yes, I did, and I'm sorry I couldn't tell you earlier. I thought it best you didn't know in case those men asked you too many questions.'

'Aree, whatever you're up to, or got yourself into, I'm well out, do you hear me? I've had my fill of chilly breezes and espionage for the year, and as I'm only need-to-know, I'm telling you I don't need to know. Is that clear?'

'I understand, Sonia. I can't thank you enough; and don't worry, I'll make sure you're kept well out of it. Send me those photos when you can, and I promise that when I see you in a few weeks, we're going out somewhere very expensive and work will not be discussed. I'll be in touch. Have a safe journey back.'

CHAPTER SIX

Forty-eight hours later

A mild grey morning ascended over London as the hustle and bustle of thriving city life echoed from every one of its streets. The national economic turmoil over the past year had dampened the spirits of not only Londoners but the entire country. Many were feeling the pinch of austerity combined with tremendous anger towards the financial system over their gross mishandling of the country's finances.

Prime Minister Brooks's government was also on the receiving end of the public's fury and frustrations. They'd given him and his government a real drubbing in the recent local elections for their part in not foreseeing the economic downturn, and also because of a series of scandals, the latest of which involved failed attempts to smear rival political party leader Tom Phoenix, who'd swept up the votes they'd lost, and their defiant announcement to go ahead with their annual extravagant masquerade ball. To the public it felt like a further excuse to waste more public finances and for the elite to get drunk on their money; especially when the government's two-faced party line was 'We're all in this together and we all need to tighten our belts.'

Today's newspapers, filled as they were with scandals and the normal doom and gloom, were also reporting on the Baker Street Five's continuing string of robberies. The infamous thieves had a notorious past and a reputation for having pulled off some daring and elaborate heists before disappearing without a trace. They also had a reputation for theatrics, leaving a Sherlock Holmes silhouette calling card with the number five etched onto the face. It was something that had become a running joke in certain circles; they'd eluded the authorities for so long that perhaps only Sherlock Holmes could unmask their identities and capture them.

Now they were back from a long hiatus and up to their old tricks. Their latest theft had been from the home of disgraced banker Sir Frank Chalmers, who had been an ardent supporter of Brooks's government. In fact, the robbery led the authorities to look into Chalmers, who was later arrested on charges of embezzlement and fraud, with several other charges pending, resulting in the collapse of one of Britain's largest banks.

Despite the excitement of the Baker Street Five's exploits, the papers were also reporting on an event that was taking place at the Imperial War Museum. The event was hosted by the St George's Foundation, a privately funded organisation dedicated to helping armed forces personnel, past and present, and their families enjoy a better quality of life and living standards in the UK. The Pathfinder programme had been the brainchild of their largest foundation contributor, multibillionaire business executive and philanthropist Adam Knight, and had proved to be a great success. The money provided by Adam helped pay for support groups, education programmes, rehabilitation, certain medical procedures and equipment, and arranging suitable housing and schools for their children, as well as helping to find employment in one of his companies or elsewhere after leaving the service. Adam had hoped to keep his participation a secret and remain anonymous, but the other foundation members, a couple of whom served on Knight Technologies' board of directors, insisted on thanking and honouring him in some small way for all he'd contributed and done for the foundation.

The main hall of the Imperial War Museum was buzzing with excitement. The stage had been modestly decorated with digital St George's Foundation campaign trailers along with the Union flag hanging from the central rafter. After a short wait, the foundation's chairman, Kerefese Beckett, a retired British civil servant of South African heritage and noted for his tireless work in improving Anglo-South African relations at the end of apartheid, stepped up to the glass podium to begin the ceremony. He cleared his throat as the junior press delegation salivated like hungry wolves, getting their recorders ready to tape every word and make notes on their information packs.

'Ladies and gentlemen, I'd like to start off by thanking all of you for coming today to our humble reception to show your support for our foundation. Today we honour a very special man, a man whose tireless support, time and considerable funding, both personally and from the profits made by his global defence technology company, Knight Technologies, have made the St George's Foundation a leader in providing services and rehabilitation for our brave servicemen and women, and their families, for as long as they need or want it.'

A wave of applause echoed loudly from the audience as photographers snapped furiously in every direction. Once it had died down, Kerefese continued with his speech.

'This man's generosity hasn't stopped there, though. He's also been instrumental in setting up our first state-of-the-art training and works programme centres, entitled Project Khepri. This latest project, part of our Pathfinder programme, has facilities designed specifically for our servicemen and women who are leaving the armed forces, so they can begin building lives outside of the service with support and encouragement.'

Another wave of applause echoed loudly from the audience through a barrage of flashing cameras and quick-fire questions from the journalists.

'So it gives me great pleasure to present this award as a small token of our appreciation to our hero and friend, Mr Adam Knight,' Kerefese concluded, full of enthusiasm, holding up the crystal award for the audience and press to see.

The audience erupted again, cheering louder than before in a standing ovation as Adam Knight rose from his chair and walked towards the stage, shaking a few hands as he went. Smiling with pride, Kerefese shook Adam's hand firmly and presented him with the award. They exchanged a few pleasantries, and after more photos and rogue questions from the press, the chairman stepped aside to allow Adam to say a few words.

Adam scanned the audience as everyone simmered down and waited for him to speak. Truth be told, every journalist had tried to get an interview with Adam. He was something of an enigma and at the top of his game in the defence technology industry. Only a handful of people knew much about him; he was fiercely protective of his private life and rarely appeared in public. What they did know came from gossip columns and the occasional interview.

'Thank you very much, everyone. I'm deeply honoured to be here today to accept this wonderful award. I fear Kerefese has been far too gracious in his speech by calling me a hero. I'm no hero. That title belongs to the men and women, in and out of uniform, with us here today, those serving across the country and abroad, and those who've been wounded or made the ultimate sacrifice in the defence of our nation to protect the freedoms we all take for granted. They're the heroes,' said Adam with firm conviction.

'I just hope at the very least I've made a small difference to their lives and proved to these wonderful boys and girls that what they do, and have done, does matter, and that their sacrifices and dedication to duty haven't gone unnoticed by this foundation or the public. Thank you very much once again.'

The audience and the foundation members stood in an ovation of applause, moved by Adam's humble acceptance speech. The delegation of junior reporters engulfed the edge of the stage, again firing off questions and trying to get a statement or quote on Adam's thoughts about the government's lack of funding for the armed forces, and about the controversial masquerade ball he was rumoured to be attending. Adam remained silent. He stepped away graciously and faded into the background of the museum. A modest and private man by nature, he hated giving interviews and answering intrusive questions from the press. He was grateful to Kerefese and his friends from the foundation for stepping in and shielding him by answering the barrage of questions the press were now hurling in their direction.

Outside the museum Adam took a deep breath. The cold, sharp air filled his lungs as he rushed back to his Ford GT, taking care not to be seen by any lurking journalists. Once safely locked inside, Adam placed the small award on the passenger seat and let out a sigh of relief that it was over. He flicked a switch on the dashboard, which tinted his car windows to prevent anyone from seeing in, and reached into his glove compartment to take out his hot flask of tea and the morning's newspapers.

It gave him no end of satisfaction to see the amount of press he, his adopted son and his close friends had been getting as the Baker Street Five, and the government's rising unpopularity. The plan he'd devised was working and he was keeping his promise to his old friend. Taking a sip of tea from his flask and perusing the next paper, Adam voice-activated his car's new digital interlink computer, a system of his own design.

'Have there been any messages for me in the last hour, computer?' he asked.

'One new message, Mr Knight,' the robotic voice replied.

'Play the message for me.'

'The message is from your son, Jonathan Carter-Knight, audio only, sir.'

'Hi Dad, call me back when you get this message. Thanks, bye,' Johnny said in his Anglo-American accent. Adam put the paper aside. He was delighted to hear from his adopted son and counted himself very privileged to enjoy a close bond and loving relationship with him.

'Computer, call Johnny's flat, please.'

The video screen bleeped and opened up inside Johnny's flat, or more specifically, his bedroom. Adam could see and hear rustling coming from underneath the duvet and realised Johnny had company. Averting his eyes, Adam decided to interrupt his son's extracurricular activities.

'Good morning, Johnny … Johnny!'

Johnny sat up with a start. He was a handsome young man in his early twenties with blonde hair, light blue eyes and a toned physique that was very much on display. He leapt out of bed taking the duvet and ran over to the video phone whilst also trying to shield his male companion from view.

'Dad, I … just hold on a sec,' Johnny replied, red-faced with embarrassment at being caught in the act, and placed the video phone on hold. Adam, who was still averting his eyes, smiled and shook his head in amusement. He picked up his next paper and began browsing through it while he waited for Johnny to compose himself. Two minutes later the screen lit up again. Johnny had ditched the duvet and was now wearing a pair of grey jogging bottoms and a white T-shirt. His male companion had left the room.

'Hey Dad, sorry about that. I was brushing up on some of my self-defence lessons,' he said, still a little red-faced.

'Yes, I noticed you were putting up quite some resistance. He must be a very good teacher,' replied Adam cheekily.

'I've no complaints,' chuckled Johnny. 'Anyway, thanks for returning my call. I just wanted to say congrats on the award and to invite you and the others to the Atlantic tonight to celebrate. I'll have the champagne on ice.'

'Sounds good to me, but check with the others. What time should we—' Adam stopped mid-sentence, stunned at the front page of the paper he'd just picked up. He wrenched it open at the main article. His eyes fell upon the photo of his old friend Colonel Arthur Monroe below the headline 'Fugitive colonel found dead in Ireland – apparent suicide.'

'Dad, what's wrong?'

'I don't believe it. They got him.' Adam rubbed his forehead in distress.

'What's the matter? You've gone pale.' Johnny's voice cracked with deep concern.

'Johnny, get hold of LJ, Calypso and Cormac, and meet me at Silver Blaze at three o'clock.' Adam put the paper down, oblivious to his son's concerns.

Johnny looked straight at Adam, speechless and with deep apprehension on his face. Adam saw his discomfort at his abrasive request. It was almost the same look that Johnny had given him the day he'd come into his life at his holiday home in Virginia ten years ago. Johnny would have been about fourteen; injured, frightened, and in hiding from the orderlies of the nearby reparative therapy camp he'd escaped from. Utterly repulsed by the existence of these camps, Adam took Johnny under his wing, and in the months that followed a brutal court case, he had Johnny emancipated from his ignorant and abusive father who had left him in that hellhole, adopted him as his own, and had the camp shut down.

'Johnny, I'm fine. I promise I'll explain everything when I see you, okay?' said Adam, managing a small but reassuring smile.

Johnny nodded in acknowledgement and ended the call to carry out Adam's instructions. Once the screen went blank, Adam's smile evaporated as he picked up the paper again. Every part of his being burned with rage, coupled with tremendous guilt that he couldn't save his friend from this awful fate. He didn't believe for a second that the colonel's death was suicide, and chucked the paper violently to one side, hitting the steering wheel of his car hard and making the horn wail. What was he to do now?

There were so many variables to consider. Had the colonel talked under pressure before he died? Did Prime Minister Brooks and his underlings know of his plans? Were they under surveillance? Should his plan be scrapped and all of them disappear? All these questions rushed around Adam's head. He needed information and time to think before making any move on whether to abort or proceed as planned. He pulled out his mobile phone and dialled what was a discontinued phone number and let it bleep three times, then hung up. A minute later, his mobile rang.

'Aree, what the hell happened? When were you going to tell me Arthur was dead? How long has he been dead for?'

'Adam, I know, I'm sorry I didn't tell you but I thought it was best not to until I'd had the chance to do my own discreet digging.'

'He's been dead two days and you didn't think I needed to know? Christ, Aree, I just had a shock from reading about it in the paper. What happened? I don't believe for a second that our good friend took his own life. What have you found out?'

'I've a contact, a friend in Letterkenny, and she confirmed that the colonel was murdered two days ago by persons unknown. She sent me some unpleasant pictures and there's no doubt it's him. I should tell you that there is evidence to suggest he was tortured but somehow managed to escape before being gunned down. He looked quite a mess but by all accounts went out fighting,' Aree replied.

Adam choked at hearing this. He should have been there to protect him. Another layer of guilt drifted onto his already heavy heart. He felt he'd failed his old friend, but deep down he knew the colonel went his own way. He'd mourn him later, but now all that mattered was whether his plans had been discovered and if they needed to be scrapped or put into operation without delay.

'Do you know if he talked?'

'As far as I can make out, they didn't get anything from him. You know what Arthur was like, stubborn to the end; if he'd talked, you and your friends would probably be dead by now.'

'Where's his body? Where have they taken it? He needs to be buried with respect and honour.'

'I'm looking into that now. My friend had the misfortune of meeting two government officials called Hyde and Jones at the crime scene, but I can guarantee they're aliases. They took over the case, cleaned up the scene and put out that false story of the colonel committing suicide. I'll let you know the moment I find out what they've done with his body, and I promise not to keep anything from you from now on.'

'Okay. Thanks, Aree. I'm sorry if I sounded harsh; it's been a long year. Keep me updated. I'll speak to you later.'

Adam hung up and threw his phone onto the passenger seat. He started the engine and sped off into the distance. He needed time to think and reassess.

CHAPTER SEVEN

The worst-kept secret among political and societal circles was that there were deep and growing divisions within the Brooks government. The economic downturn combined with the recent political scandals and drubbing in the local elections had laid bare the fractured relationships between Prime Minister George Brooks, his party and his cabinet. Lines had been drawn, loyalties were being tested and the proverbial knives were out of their sheaths for the PM, but no one was willing to strike and draw first blood. Fear of their leader's infamous temper and the threat of mutually assured destruction to anyone who challenged him were proving to be powerful inhibiters.

Fractious tension hung in the air of the cabinet room like dense incense being burned inside a church. The Prime Minister leant over the conference table, dismayed, as he looked at and listened to his sombre and tired cabinet colleagues arguing among themselves, blaming him and each other for their current misfortunes. How could he have been cursed with such incompetence and stupidity? He was shaking with anger to the point that he felt his hand clench and thunder down on the table, making them all jump.

'I asked you all to help me do one thing – destroy Tom Phoenix's position and credibility at any cost – and this is what I wake up to in this morning's paper,' he said, throwing his copy of *The Times* down on the conference table for them all to see.

'Government Smear Campaign Backfires' read the embarrassing headline. 'Tom Phoenix demands formal apology and the Prime Minister's resignation for his slanderous and false accusations.'

'Are you all completely inept? Can you not follow a simple plan and set of instructions?' Prime Minister Brooks was seething with anger.

'You're out of order, George. It was your plan and we followed it implicitly, despite some of us warning you that this is exactly what would happen,' replied a cabinet minister in protest.

'Yes, and now that this ill-conceived plan of yours has backfired, we're probably going to lose the national election next year because of your damn ego,' said another cabinet member, exasperated.

'Perhaps it's time to think about stepping aside, George, for the good of the party,' said another dissenting voice.

At last, one of the cabinet members finally had the fleeting courage to say what they'd all been thinking for months. The large vein in Brooks's forehead began pulsating maddeningly. He picked up his glass of water from the table and hurled it violently across the room, smashing it against the wall and making some cabinet members recoil.

'You wouldn't dare replace me. None of you have the spines to do it. Remember, I pulled this party back from the brink and gave you your careers. If any of you try to remove me, I'll take you all down. We either all win or we all go down together.

'And as for the arrogant little upstart Tom Phoenix, I will not apologise. This is the cut-throat world of politics; there are no Queensberry rules. If his sensitivities can't handle a little mud-slinging, he should get out of the game.'

A long, drawn-out clap from the junior cabinet ministers, angry at the Prime Minister's attitude, echoed through the cabinet room as he rose to his feet.

'Bravo, George. That display of violent, threatening behaviour will go down well with the public and in the press. You've no choice; you will have to apologise. It was your plan and your fuck-up.'

'Fuck you, Spencer. My plan was perfect. This isn't my failure; it's all of yours. I will not apologise to Phoenix under any circumstances.'

Prime Minister Brooks felt exasperated. Never in his entire political career had he endured this much insubordination, incompetence and lack of nerve from his cabinet colleagues. He'd run out of adjectives to describe his contempt for them all as he fell back into his chair. He began to wonder about the precipice they were now all looking over, as the rest of the cabinet began arguing amongst each other again.

'Enough!' Brooks slammed his hand down on the table again to quieten them. 'The following people will remain behind: Miller, Eric and Richard. The rest of you, get out of my sight. I expect each of you to have come up with a solution to get us out of this mess you've placed us in when we meet back here next week after the masquerade ball.'

A mixture of resentment and anger emanated from those not asked to stay behind as they stormed out of the cabinet room, muttering unintelligibly at each other. Prime Minister Brooks sat up straight and rubbed his hands over his face in frustration. He shunted his chair back towards the fireplace behind him and walked over to the drinks cabinet to pour himself a large pure malt Scotch to steady his nerves. His remaining and most loyal subordinates watched in silence as he placed the rim of the cut crystal glass to his lips and drank until the glass was empty. Brooks savoured every second of that twenty-year-old Scotch as it slipped down his throat like sweet nectar. It was a euphoric feeling as the sides of his mouth curled into a small but satisfying smile that quickly evaporated when he came back to reality.

'You came down on us all pretty hard, George. If you're not careful, the rest of the cabinet and the party may make good on their threats of a vote of no confidence,' said Home Secretary Eric Jackson, breaking the awkward silence as he attempted to relight his cigar.

'Those gutless cowards wouldn't dare, not with what I have on each of them. Besides, with a general election looming next year, a change in leader this late in the game doesn't bring voter confidence; not to mention that Tom Phoenix and the opposition would have a field day,' replied Brooks, pouring himself another Scotch. 'What a bloody fiasco. I can't believe those fools had the audacity to blame me for their shortcomings. Do you think it's my fault, Miller? Have I lost my touch of finesse when it comes to undermining my rivals?'

'Nonsense, Prime Minister, your plan was full of finesse and highly creative. Perhaps the rest of the cabinet didn't quite understand the complexities of such an audacious and intricate plan.

'May I say though, Prime Minister, that I can also see our colleagues' point of view. We didn't have much to play with when it came to smearing Phoenix, and it would be in all our best interests to issue a small private apology to him to take the wind out of the press's furore,' Miller continued, running his hand through his hair and straightening his glasses. The large vein in Brooks's forehead began to pulsate again and his eyes narrowed into a scowl. Foreign Secretary Miller shrunk down into his chair and turned his gaze to the floor like a child who had just been chastised, much to the amusement of Home

Secretary Jackson and Defence Secretary Ashworth, who found his weak manner distasteful.

'Eric, give me an update on where we stand with our Baker Street Five problem. It had better be good news,' Brooks said, turning his fiery gaze and attentions upon his Home Secretary.

Jackson paused for a moment before answering as he watched Brooks take another swig from his glass. How could he give an answer that didn't sound as bad as the news was? He dabbed his face with his handkerchief to wipe away the beads of sweat that had collected on his forehead, took his cigar out of his mouth and cleared his throat.

'George, you know I'm doing my best with those fools in SI7, especially Agents Johnson and Ellis, but they're difficult to work with and proving to be very insubordinate—'

'I don't care about your problems with them, Eric. I want to know what progress you've made in unmasking and catching these bastards.'

'We've some promising leads that Agent Johnson is going to report back to me about this evening that may prove fruitful, but George, you must understand that progress has been slow due to department budget cuts and diverting of other resources to shore up the economy. We've now uncovered the type of drug they're using in their tranquilliser guns to incapacitate our friends, and we are checking out

all the relevant suppliers from whom they could have obtained it.'
Home Secretary Jackson was now babbling.

'Have you nothing else you can tell me? Have you any
recovered fingerprints, DNA, video images, for instance? No crooks,
no matter how smart, are that good to not leave some small trace at the
crime scene.'

'Well, as you know, they leave their notorious calling card at
each crime scene, which we check thoroughly along with everything
else, but so far it's proven negative. But I swear, George, we are close
to catching them. They're bound to make a mistake sooner or later.'

'So what you're saying, Eric, is that in over a year's worth of
investigations you've made little or no progress as to their identities. I
don't want to hear any more bullshit excuses from you. These bastards
are making a mockery of us. You have one more week to pull your
goddamn finger out and bloody well find them, or I'll have your
resignation on my desk next Monday. Do you understand?'

Home Secretary Jackson remained silent, holding in his
resentment at being addressed in such a way. He wiped away some
more sweat that had collected around his fat neck with his
handkerchief, relit his cigar and, folding his arms, sat back with a
seething look on his face.

'I've some very good news for you, George. I've waited until now to be sure, but I'm happy to inform you that my men and I have not only found Colonel Arthur Monroe but have taken care of him for good.'

Defence Secretary Ashworth slid the detailed report he'd been coddling over to Brooks, who perked up at hearing this news. Colonel Monroe had been a major factor in the Prime Minister's sleepless nights and elevated stress levels, but now that was all over. It was as if a huge weight had been lifted and he could breathe again, and he let out a raucous burst of laughter. This was the best news he could have asked for, given the current negativity and incompetence surrounding him.

'Richard, this is excellent news. Did you manage to find out if he'd leaked any information about what he heard that night?' Brooks asked, full of excitement.

'He gave away nothing, Prime Minister, even with my men's methods of persuasion, the stubborn bastard. But if he'd leaked anything to anyone, I assure you he'd have given it up to my man.'

Prime Minister Brooks's face beamed with delight as he continued reading the report.

'Did he die slowly?' asked Home Secretary Jackson.

'He would have done, but he managed to escape from his restraints. Thankfully, he didn't get very far. My man caught up with him and although he received a flesh wound from the colonel, he put two bullets in his chest. Monroe was dead before he hit the ground.'

'And there's no possible fallout that can be traced back to us, right?' Foreign Secretary Miller interjected before anyone else could ask that exact same question.

'None at all. I must confess we did attract some unwarranted attention from the local authorities and villagers, but we were able to clear up any fallout. As far as anyone knows, Colonel Monroe committed suicide, having been exposed under his assumed name, and that is the story that's been reported in all the papers and news outlets today.'

At that moment Brooks's Principal Private Secretary interrupted over the intercom. 'Sorry for the interruption, sir, but your speech adviser is here to discuss next month's NATO summit in Rome.'

'Thank you, Miranda, I'll be right out,' he said over the intercom. 'Gentlemen, I've been pretty harsh on you all today. However, Richard's news has really lightened my mood and I think this is a suitable juncture to part on. I look forward to seeing you all tomorrow at the masquerade ball.'

CHAPTER EIGHT

Adam Knight drove through the charming village of Queen's Castle in Buckinghamshire and down a familiar country lane, pulling into the long driveway of his striking country hideaway which lay about two miles outside the village. He'd aptly named his home Silver Blaze after one of his favourite Sherlock Holmes short stories. Its silvery grey colour and tinted windows shimmered in the afternoon sunlight that had broken through the depressingly grey cloud cover of the morning. Adam had purchased the large house a number of years ago; its seclusion away from London meant he could completely relax and lower his guard. The grounds were surrounded by high weathered stone walls lined with dark green cypress trees interspersed with his self-designed perimeter security system to keep out any unwanted visitors.

He parked up alongside a beautifully restored 1968 MGB Roadster and two slick black Ducati 999R bikes which belonged to his friends LJ, Calypso and Cormac. Stepping out of his car, Adam grabbed the silver briefcase that had been entrusted to him by Colonel Monroe the previous year and entered the house through the large oak double front doors. As he stood in the main hall with the furniture covered in dust sheets, he felt a deep connection and sense of belonging. This place held a lot of happy and precious memories for him which he treasured deep in his heart. He headed towards the lounge. It was spacious and comfortable, with modernist furniture hidden beneath more dust sheets. A large marble fireplace stood as the room's central focal point, and large glass windows, tinted on the outside, dominated one side of the room, allowing it to be illuminated with natural light. Adam's eyes were drawn to a pair of long jean-clad legs in black ankle boots protruding out from his black leather sofa.

'Hello LJ, it's good to see you.'

LJ put the book she'd been reading on the Impressionist masters to one side and turned to face Adam. Her face lit up upon seeing him for the first time in a month. Smart but casual, she looked the picture of sexy athleticism as she jumped up from the sofa and embraced him with the same deep affection they'd had for each other since becoming close friends at university.

'Adam, it's so good to see you,' she said, kissing him on the cheek.

'How have you been, and how's your father?'

'I'm well, thanks. I've just got back from helping my old professor Dr Ali Williams on her archaeological site in Turkey, cataloguing, dating and preserving some newly discovered Hittite artefacts and art treasures. It helped pass the time since we pulled off that last fun job on that banker. Oh, and Daddy's fine, busy doing what ambassadors do. He's always asking after you too … still hoping I'll find a nice husband and settle down.'

'I didn't think you were the type to settle down and get married, LJ,' replied Adam with an amused look on his face.

'Very funny; I'm not, but then again I haven't met a decent man, present company excepted, of course, who doesn't feel threatened by my independence or who can keep up with me.'

Adam laughed at LJ's flirtatious remark. Her hunger for life, adventure and way with words was one of the reasons he admired and respected her so much. He pulled off another dust sheet and set down the briefcase on top of his old writing desk.

'Are the others here yet?' he asked, taking off his overcoat and sitting down on the sofa.

'Johnny's running a little late, but Calypso and Cormac are downstairs blowing off some steam in the training room.' LJ replied, before fixing them both a drink from the cabinet.

Heavy breathing and grunting echoed through the all-purpose training room in the basement as Calypso Forbes and Cormac O'Connell, dressed in full kendo outfits, battled it out with their shinai swords in an intense duel. They disengaged from one another and circled the large mat area of the floor, trying to figure out each other's weak point to exploit and attack.

'Do you give up yet?' said Calypso as she looked through the gauze of her kendo mask at Cormac.

'Not a chance, I've got you exactly where I want you,' Cormac replied, twirling his shinai in his hand as his eyes stared through the gauze of his mask back at her.

They re-engaged one another with swift precision. Cormac swung his shinai towards Calypso in an attempt to disarm her but she blocked him, ducked and swung her sword low, taking out Cormac's leg. He fell hard onto the mat with a thud. Calypso pointed her stick at his chest. He relinquished his weapon and took off his mask, sweeping back his salt and pepper hair off his clammy face and encroaching five o'clock shadow. He stared up at Calypso and raised his hands to concede, if somewhat reluctantly, the duel.

'That was very dirty. You're definitely getting better,' he said, smiling up at her and catching his breath.

Calypso retracted her shinai sword from Cormac's chest and removed her mask. Like Cormac, her face was damp with beads of sweat but also flushed with the pride of success. She stared down at Cormac with those large chocolate-brown eyes Cormac was certain he would lose himself in, and smiled victoriously. She knelt down and straddled Cormac's body, her kendo outfit distorting the true contours of her figure.

'Smooth talker. Even in defeat, that Irish charm always finds a way of disarming me.'

'It's a gift; the only decent thing my father ever gave me.'

The two of them continued to stare fondly into each other's eyes. Cormac removed one of his kote gloves and raised his hand to touch Calypso's cheek and gently push back a ringlet of her short black hair that had fallen out of place. Their growing relationship had been simmering for a number of months, each waiting for and wanting the other to make the first move to take things to the next level.

'Sorry, guys, but Adam's arrived and he'd like you both to come upstairs to the lounge when you're finished,' said LJ, interrupting their moment from one of the view screens.

'Sure thing, LJ. Tell Adam we'll be right up,' Cormac replied, raising his hand in acknowledgement.

Cormac and Calypso smiled at each other as they got up off the mat and made their way out of the training room. Despite their flirtations, mutual attraction and feelings for one another, they decided today wasn't the day to finally say out loud how they felt about each other.

LJ poured another drink for her and Adam and walked back over to the sofa where he was fiddling with the contents of the silver briefcase. She sat down beside him and handed him his drink. 'They'll be up in a moment, but I feel bad – I think I interrupted a private moment between them. They looked a little awkward about me seeing them close together.'

'A budding romance will do that to you when you're not sure how you feel about taking things to the next level and don't want anyone else to know yet,' Adam replied, as he continued going through the briefcase. 'By the way, did Johnny say why he was running late?'

'Oh, something about finishing up his self-defence lesson as it was interrupted earlier,' said LJ.

Adam glanced at his watch, shaking his head with amusement.

'What's so funny?'

'Let's just say Johnny had his hands full earlier. I hope he gets here soon, though. We've a lot to discuss.'

LJ rolled her eyes. Adam knew she didn't need any further explanation as to what her second godson and his libido were up to. She lay back into the sofa, picked up her book and continued reading. After about ten minutes Calypso and Cormac joined them in the lounge, still dressed in their kendo outfits and drinking cold bottles of water.

'Calypso, Cormac, it's good to see you both. How was the workout?'

'Refreshing. I had Cormac beat and bang to rights,' replied Calypso, triumphant in her victory.

'Nonsense; I had you subdued long before that with my pure Irish charm.'

Calypso went to slap Cormac on the arm just as Johnny arrived, dressed casually in jeans, T-shirt and trainers.

'Sorry I'm late, guys. I lost track of the time,' he said, looking a little flustered.

'I've two questions for you, Johnny: what was his name, and how much self-defence was involved?' asked LJ, a mischievous glint in her eyes.

'News gets around fast, Aunt LJ. His name was Nathan and very little self-defence was involved,' Johnny replied, going a little red in the face.

'What happened with Mason? I thought you said you were getting serious?' asked Calypso.

'What is this, the Spanish inquisition? I loved Mason, but I'm not the one who went off and cheated, and cheaters don't get second chances with me,' he replied, his voice tinged with the pain of a bad break-up.

'Alright, guys, that'll do. Let's get down to business,' said Adam, conscious of the time and cutting off the conversation before Johnny could utter a reply.

Adam led the way into the octagon: a reinforced, soundproof, concealed room at the centre of the house. It was dimly lit and sparsely decorated apart from a few antique weapons that adorned the wood-panelled walls. A circular electronic prototype conference table that had been developed by Adam's R&D division for military applications stood in the centre of the room. Adam pulled off the dust sheet, throwing a thin layer of dust into the air, and placed the silver briefcase on the rim of the table as the others took their seats. He was heartened by the loyalty and devotion his son and his friends had always shown him. He looked at the familiar faces around the conference table. He'd asked a lot from them over the past year and they'd followed him without hesitation, despite being fully aware that the stakes they were playing for were high, and that the threat of discovery – and maybe even death – wasn't far away.

'So, Dad, what's made you call this emergency meeting?'

'Yes – when Johnny rang, he said you were anxious,' said LJ, full of curiosity and concern.

'Are we in some sort of trouble?' asked Calypso.

'C'mon, Adam, don't leave us in suspense. What's going on that we don't know?' said Cormac, perplexed by Adam's hastiness at gathering them all here.

Adam remained silent. He took out four copies of the newspaper article about Colonel Monroe which had caused him so much distress and slid a copy over to each of them.

'This is why I've asked you all here this afternoon,' he said, with great unease on his face.

'Christ, I'm so sorry, Dad. He was a good man. Are they positive it's him? Has it been independently verified?' said Johnny.

'He was found dead forty-eight hours ago. Aree, however, didn't confirm anything until I rang him this morning in a flap after seeing the article in the paper. The colonel was subjected to torture before he died – probably on the orders of Defence Secretary Ashworth – and it's that which concerns us all.'

'How do you know that? There's no mention of torture here; it says it was suicide. Did Aree confirm this, and whether the colonel had given anything away about us?' said LJ, clearly alarmed at this news.

'Aree did a little discreet digging for us. He even sent me over the pictures his contact in the Irish Garda took of Arthur's body, which I won't be sharing. Arthur was tortured but he fought to the bitter end. Look, we'll mourn his death later. Right now, time is of the essence.'

'What are you saying, Adam? Are we compromised?' asked Cormac.

'He's saying that if the colonel cracked under pressure, and I'm not saying that he did, he could have told them what he knows; or at least enough to put them on to us. How much did he know, Adam?' Calypso asked.

'Thankfully he knew little. Arthur had made it very clear he didn't want us chasing after him or telling him too much in case of this eventuality. However, we can't afford to be complacent.'

'I don't think the colonel talked. Let's face it; if he'd talked, we'd have all been lifted and stuck in a detention cell; or worse, we'd be dead.' Johnny rose abruptly from his chair. He scrunched up the article and threw it into the wastepaper bin.

'Johnny does have a point there, Adam,' said LJ.

'I agree. If they'd got anything out of Arthur, even with the little he did know we wouldn't be sitting here now, but we'll take full precautions in case those idiots at SI7 or Defence Secretary Ashworth's mob are watching us.'

'So where do we go from here, Adam?' asked Cormac, clearly eager to know what their next steps were going to be.

Adam wondered how they were going to react to the decision he'd made in light of this setback and Arthur's demise. He was confident in his answer and in his plans for the final heist, which he'd spent a year perfecting. Everything was in place, and in his heart it was now or never if he was ever to get his own personal revenge.

'I've decided to move up our timetable. We've had enough rehearsal over the past year. It's time to make our final attack on Brooks and his government, and we're going in tomorrow evening with some contingency amendments I've implemented today.'

'Adam, from the snippets you've told us, this job can't be rushed. We need at least a week of preparation.'

'There's no time left, Cormac. Trust me, we can pull this off, but it has to be tomorrow night in case we're compromised. Otherwise it's never, and I'm not prepared to settle for never,' Adam replied, unperturbed.

'Okay, Adam, let's at least hear your plan in full,' said Calypso, trying to calm the mounting tension.

Adam pulled out four flash drives from the briefcase and slid them one by one across the table. After placing the case on the floor, he stood up and pressed a button on the control panel embedded in the table to activate the five small video screens. LJ, Johnny, Calypso and Cormac picked up their allocated flash drives and inserted them into the USB slots.

'Inside each of your flash drives is the section of the plan you'll be responsible for on the night. Study your objectives with the amendments and then destroy them. LJ and I will be Team One; Calypso, Cormac and Johnny, you're Team Two.'

LJ, Johnny, Calypso and Cormac looked at their assigned tasks and skim-read through the main details of their assignments. The tense atmosphere that had gripped the room began to lighten. It was a highly detailed and well-thought-out plan, but it was reliant on everything running like clockwork, with little leeway for a margin of error. Johnny let out a whistle of delight and excitement.

'This is great work, Dad. Even with the amendments, this is going to be more fun than the job we pulled on that banker, Chalmers.'

Adam applauded Johnny's enthusiasm. He pressed another button on the control panel, which activated the table's holographic projection programme, and inserted a special disc into his master screen. The table produced a detailed holographic projection of the Palace of Westminster.

'Tomorrow evening, despite the wave of public outrage, Prime Minister Brooks's government is hosting the annual masquerade ball inside Westminster Hall,' he said, clicking a button on the remote to enlarge that section of the palace.

'It's the perfect opportunity to gain relatively easy access to the House of Lords and the secret entrance to the undercroft, where, according to my research and reputable sources, the hidden vault is located. Plus, security will be light inside as they'll be focusing their efforts on guarding the perimeter to keep out any rowdy protesters and those going to St James's Park.' He clicked the remote again to show the internal floor plan of the House of Lords and highlighted the area by the golden throne where the entrance to the vault was located.

'Wait a minute. If my history serves me right, the undercroft was sealed off after the gunpowder plot and later destroyed by the fire of 1834. It shouldn't exist any more,' said LJ, looking at the data on her screen.

'You know your history, LJ. The undercroft no longer exists … officially. It doesn't show up on any of the palace's official building schematics, but take my word for it; it's still there, hidden from public view and used to protect certain dirty little secrets including the ill-gotten fortunes of Brooks, his cabinet and various other members of parliament.'

Adam clicked the remote again and the holographic projection disappeared as he retook his seat. He flicked a switch on the control panel, converting the holographic glass screen back to imaging only, and brought up a sequence of photographs of the entrance to the undercroft showing Defence Secretary Ashworth coming out of the secret opening.

'Thanks to our mutual friend Aree, you can see what the entrance looks like.'

Adam zoomed in on Defence Secretary Ashworth's hand where he was holding what appeared to be a gold security pass that he was about to tuck away into the inside of his jacket pocket. 'The only way to gain access to the undercroft and get to the vault is by using that gold security pass. Calypso, we're going to need that special compact copying device of yours.'

'No problem, Adam, it's in my lab downstairs. I'll get it.'

'Oh, and LJ, it'll be part of your job to acquire the original on the night. I'm sure you're more than capable of using your charms to relieve Ashworth of it.'

'Can't I just pickpocket one of the other parliamentarians?' asked LJ, cringing at the thought of what she might have to do to obtain the pass.

'Sadly, no; Ashworth's pass has an all-access clearance grade. Only a few of them have this, and the rest require extra security checks to enter the vault – which we don't have time to get. Plus, from what I've been told, Ashworth is a serial womaniser and the most malleable target to manipulate and take the pass from.'

As the others speculated among themselves, Adam could tell from LJ's expression that she wasn't happy about this part of her assignment, and he hated himself for having to put her through this unseemly act. But there was no other option. Getting that access pass was essential to gaining entry to the vault. He would have a chat with her later but for now he needed to move on with the briefing.

'This is the only picture Aree could get of the vault. Do you think you can crack her open easily, Cormac?'

'That hunk of historic junk looks like it's been there for a hundred years. She'll be like putty in my hands. I've yet to meet a safe who hasn't yielded to me with gentle persuasion.'

CHAPTER NINE

Home Secretary Eric Jackson stared out from the terrace of the riverside bar of the Houses of Parliament, taking in the view of the River Thames and the light evening breeze over a large glass of cognac. After the day he'd had, he needed a pick-me-up to help him through his final engagement. Listening to SI7 Agent Amy Johnson deliver yet another dreary report on the Baker Street Five was bound to raise his blood pressure and infuriate him no end. It was the bitter icing on the proverbial cake to an awful day. He reached inside his jacket pocket and pulled out a crisp Havana hand-rolled cigar and promptly lifted it to his nose to smell the fresh tobacco.

The chimes of Big Ben struck six o'clock and resonated out across Westminster as he lit the cigar and savoured its rich flavour. Jackson looked at his watch to make sure it was accurate and began tapping his fingers on the balcony rail. Where in the hell was Agent Johnson?

From within the terrace crowd, the golden-haired figure of Agent Amy Johnson made her way towards Home Secretary Jackson. She was smartly dressed in a black and white suit with a long, dark overcoat. At her side she carried a small black leather attaché case. Amy knew this meeting was going to be as contentious as the previous ones she'd had with Home Secretary Jackson. It was the part of the week she loathed most and, to her mind, a waste of her time reporting to someone who was more concerned about himself than catching these thieves. Stopping a few feet behind Jackson, Amy cleared her throat to make her presence known.

'What sort of time do you call this, Agent Johnson? When I tell you to be here at a specific time, you be here at that time, not twenty minutes later,' Home Secretary Jackson said, turning around and blowing cigar smoke into her face. He pushed past her and headed towards the nearest available table with his now half-full glass of cognac.

Amy waved the smoke away from her. It was a filthy habit that she despised, and she wondered in this day and age why anyone still did it. She followed Home Secretary Jackson to the table, taking in a long, deep breath and exhaling fast to temper her frustrations. In her mind, Eric Jackson was the worst Home Secretary Britain had ever produced, and only got to his position because of his old school tie connections. He was something SI7 unfortunately had to tolerate and was nothing more than a man of hollow patriotism and bluster; a windbag who needed his overinflated, insecure ego constantly stroked.

Amy settled herself down opposite the Home Secretary, placing her attaché case by her side. Her ocean-blue eyes stared sharp as daggers at him, resentful at the way he'd just spoken to her, but she let it wash over her head. The quicker she got this weekly meeting over and done with, the better for her own well-being and the case as a whole.

'I'll remind you, Jackson, of the complexities of this unique case. My colleague Agent Ellis and I aren't exactly dealing with your average band of thieves.'

'Not good enough. The PM's breathing down my neck about this case. We want rapid results, and all you've come up with over the past year are dead ends and excuses.'

'You want results, Jackson? Then get off my back and let me get on with the investigation. The Baker Street Five are incredibly slick. They plan well and leave nothing to chance. I'll go so far as saying they're the best I've come up against, and the last thing I need right now is you continually harassing me to get quick results so you can run off to the Prime Minister and pacify him for praise.'

'How dare you speak to me like that? You're not speaking to some nobody – I'm the damn Home Secretary!'

'I'll speak to you any way I damn well like, Jackson, when you're costing me time that could be used for the investigation instead of pandering to your fragile ego.'

'Why, you little ... Now, you listen to me—'

'No, you listen, that's why we're here. You listen, I report, and then we part ways until next week,' said Amy defiantly.

Home Secretary Jackson looked ready to explode.

'Fine, give me the damn report. The sooner we're out of each other's sight, the better for all concerned,' he snapped, pulling his cigar out of his mouth and taking another small gulp of his cognac.

'I'm now certain that all the robberies they've carried out over the past year have been nothing more than a sideshow designed to punish the government and their friends. It's as if they've been practising and honing their skills for a very big job that is still to come.'

'Oh really? And pray tell me how you came to that conclusion.'

'A confidential source of Agent Ellis's provided us with certain information that large donations have been made anonymously to numerous military, children and LGBT+ charities, and the amounts donated correspond to the market prices of the valuables stolen.'

'Our financial and cybercrime department is trying to trace the source of these donations, but it's proving difficult. Here's the report on that line of the investigation so far.' Amy reached into her attaché case and handed Jackson her weekly report. He snatched it from her hand and flicked through half-heartedly before chucking it to one side.

'So, what does this tell us, exactly, other than they're getting rid of the valuables as quickly as possible and being labelled modern-day Robin Hoods by the press?'

'It tells us that these elegant crimes are not for financial gain. Their motives are more likely political; a power play, even.'

'A power play to what end, though?'

'We don't know yet. As I said, I'm confident it's in preparation for something big. I'm hoping Agent Ellis's source will provide us with more information, but in the meantime all we can do is wait until they make their next move.'

'Don't you have any idea at all what their next target could be?'

'I'd prefer not to speculate without any evidence to back it up. It tends to distract and muddy the waters.'

Amy knew Home Secretary Jackson was unimpressed with the answers he was getting, but she didn't care. She could only provide him with the facts she had so far, which wasn't much; but then again, this particular case wasn't a straightforward one.

'Do you have any other leads?' asked Jackson, placing his cigar between his stubby fingers.

'We have some other leads pending, but I'm not willing to discuss them with you until we've had confirmation from our sources.'

The Home Secretary stubbed out the remainder of his cigar, exhaling through the side of his mouth, and scowled at Agent Johnson as he gathered his thoughts.

'I'm going to be blunt with you, Agent Johnson, I don't like you. You're insubordinate and disrespectful, and if the PM had listened to me three years ago, SI7 would be on the scrapheap. Your performance and conduct in this case have been abysmal; but then again, what am I to expect from a woman? I'm giving you one more week to crack this case wide open, and if you don't make any such progress, I'll see to it personally that you and Agent Ellis are put on that proverbial scrapheap in disgrace. Do you hear me?'

Home Secretary Jackson downed the rest of his cognac and snapped his fingers at the young waiter who was by the bar to bring him another drink. Amy stood up abruptly, knocking over her chair. She was infuriated. In her ten years of service she'd come up against many obstacles, challenges and opposition from her male counterparts because of her gender, which some of them found threatening, especially in her climb to being considered one of the top agents at SI7.

This was different, though, and Home Secretary Jackson knew exactly which buttons to push to provoke her. She wanted to punch him in the face but that would give him the excuse he'd been looking for. She picked up her attaché case and stormed off, pushing past the waiter who was bringing over Jackson's drink and past the other guests in the bar who'd been watching the heated exchange with inquisitiveness and dismay.

Kevin G. Robinson

CHAPTER TEN

Unlike MI5, MI6 or GCHQ, SI7's headquarters were hidden in plain

sight over St James's Park underground station on Broadway. Every

day, millions of Londoners went about their daily business unaware

that the building above their heads housed the Special Intelligence

Service, Department Seven. Under their motto, transcribed from Latin

as 'Secrecy in Defence of The Realm', SI7 was established at the end

of the Cold War by the then Conservative government, under the

watchful eye of Lord Geoffrey Hush. The service's remit was to deal

with unusual and interesting cases that were considered too secret or

high priority to be handled by the police but didn't warrant the

immediate attention of the other three intelligence services.

The running joke around Whitehall and security service

grapevines in those early days was that SI7 was nothing more than the

other three intelligence service's lackey, nipping at their heels to pick

up the slack. Yet after the attacks on 11 September 2001, those

particular jokes wore very thin, and the other three intelligence

services' resources were diverted to primarily deal with extremist

terrorism.

Agent Amy Johnson strode back to SI7 headquarters in

complete silence. It took about ten minutes from Westminster Palace.

89

She needed to clear her head, but her thoughts kept dwelling on the torturous meeting she'd had with Home Secretary Jackson, and his appalling behaviour, which had left her beyond incensed. She wondered why she put up with so much self-absorbed, testosterone-fuelled arrogance – not just from Jackson, but also from some of her male colleagues in the service who saw her as either something pretty to gawp at around the office or a bitch who was playing in a man's secret world. Despite their put-downs, Amy knew she'd earned her right to serve in SI7. It had been a tough, uphill battle, facing down every prejudice or misconception because she was a woman, since she'd started out as a fresh recruit ten years ago. In the course of those ten years she'd clawed her way up the career ladder to achieve the rank of senior agent in her section with distinction but at great personal sacrifice.

The noise of car horns blaring in the rush-hour traffic broke Amy from her thoughts. She entered St James's Park underground station with haste and used her special security pass to access the hidden lift entrance behind a false wall. She arrived at her floor, walked down the dimly lit corridor and kicked her office door open, then slammed it hard behind her in frustration. The office Amy and her friend and colleague Agent Robbie Ellis shared was simple, consisting of a few bookshelves, two small wooden desks, and a large whiteboard covered with information and tips from sources. Photos of each Baker Street Five crime scene, complete with their infamous calling card, were mounted on a wall map of London, indicating where the gang had struck each time over the past year.

Amy muttered to herself as she dropped her black attaché case and threw her long, dark overcoat onto her desk. She headed straight for the coffee machine in the small kitchen tucked away in the corner. A huge injection of caffeine was what she needed to calm down. Amy was an observant individual, but her current mood made her completely oblivious to the fact that Agent Robbie Ellis was sitting in a large bay window, reading the latest report from the financial and cybercrime department. For a man in his fifties, he didn't look his age, though he was quite a silver fox, always dressed in smart attire and always looking relaxed – surprising for a man who had spent over thirty years in various intelligence service departments, under pressure for Queen and country.

'I take it the meeting went well with Jackson, then?' Robbie said in a sarcastic tone.

'Hasn't anyone ever told you that listening in on someone venting their private thoughts is a sin?' Amy replied, spilling her coffee as she turned to face him.

'If that's the case, I'm in the wrong business and, strictly speaking, I'm way past redemption,' he chuckled. Amy managed a small smile. She always liked the fact that Robbie could lighten the mood and wished she could be as laid-back as him sometimes.

'Have a seat and tell me what happened … no, wait, let me guess: the usual spiel about the PM breathing down his neck followed by numerous put-downs and then threats of firing us – stop me if I'm off base here.' He pushed a seat towards her with his foot.

'Pretty much, only he said it with far more vulgarity. We've got a week to come up with something substantial to find the Baker Street Five or, and I quote, "I will see to it personally that you're both thrown out of the service in disgrace",' said Amy, taking a seat and sipping some of her coffee.

'Moron. In all my years in intelligence, Eric Jackson has got to be the most inept, egotistical and pompous-arsed pen-pusher ever to be given the job of Home Secretary. Does he really think throwing around threats will get us closer to finding these thieves?' Robbie flung the report he'd been reading onto his desk.

Amy stared into the hot black liquid of her coffee before answering him. 'I've given up trying to figure out how that chauvinistic pig's mind works. Anyway, enough about Jackson. How did the financial and cybercrime department get on with those elusive accounts? Did they manage to trace any of them back to our gang?'

'I'd almost finished reading their report when you breezed in, but by the looks of it they were mostly unsuccessful. They did manage to trace some of the accounts to a number of shell companies across the globe.'

'What about the shell companies? Any clues as to who set them up?'

'I put a call down to the ferrets in records to see if they can pull up anything on the companies, but I've no doubt they were sleepers used solely for transferring the money across the globe before it wound up at the numerous and as yet unnamed charities my informant told me about. They won't be used again.'

'It's a shame your informant didn't give have any more info. Might be worth you having another talk with him. I'm not sure he's been entirely forthcoming with us.'

'I'll contact him this evening and ask for a one-on-one meet at one of our usual meeting places.'

'Perhaps I should come with you this time? Having someone who doesn't know him, with an outside perspective, might help us see if he's holding anything back from you.'

'I appreciate that, but I know what Aree's like. He'll only meet with me and no one else; and believe me, he'd know if I wasn't alone. Our agreement is built on trust, and because he's reliable with good info, I have to play it his way or I'd lose him as an informant.'

'Okay, fair enough, he's your source, but I want to know everything once you've spoken to him.'

'Of course, Amy. You know I'd never hide anything from you.'

'Sorry, I don't mean to sound so untrusting.'

Amy got up from her chair and walked over to the other large bay window. Taking another sip of coffee, she stared out into the cold concrete and glass wilderness of the city, frustrated by the lack of progress and evidence they'd obtained. In previous cases her opponents had been formidable and clever, but they always slipped up in the end. The Baker Street Five were different; they left nothing except what they wanted to be found.

'Something's troubling you and don't pretend it isn't, because I know when you're not yourself,' said Robbie, his voice empathetic to her visible frustrations.

'Oh, it's nothing really, Robbie. It's the lack of progress we appear to be making on this case. It's like the Baker Street Five are taunting us when we get a lead, only to have it reach a dead end or wriggle away from us. I'd love to know what they are up to right now. Do you know, Jackson even asked me for an opinion on where they may strike next?'

'What did you tell him?'

'I told him I didn't want to speculate without reasonable cause, which he didn't like one bit.'

'Good. That's exactly what I would've said to the pompous fool too.'

'What do you think? Care to speculate where they might hit next? It's got to be big because they've been quiet since they pulled off their last job on that corrupt banker last month.'

'No, I wouldn't, but personally I'd call their last job poetic justice. Chalmers deserved it for his lies and sheer greed; but, as you say, speculation will get us nowhere. Speaking of Jackson, I hear Control gave you the unpleasant assignment of being his liaison officer for the masquerade ball tomorrow evening.'

'Oh God, I'd forgotten about that. The thought of spending tomorrow night reporting to him after our bust-up this evening is not how I wanted to spend my weekend.' Amy shuddered at the thought of having to be around Home Secretary Jackson for an entire evening.

'Rather you than me, if I'm honest. Make sure you have a drink – you're going to need it to drown out Jackson's incessant nagging.'

'Thanks for the support.'

'Do you fancy going over the road to the pub? We've both had a long day and I think you need one more than I do.'

'Thanks for the offer, Robbie, but I think I'll take a rain check for now. I'm going to stay at the office for a little while longer and go over some of the previous robberies again. Perhaps they left us a clue which we've overlooked.'

Robbie shuffled off the window seat with a sigh and grabbed his coat. 'I'll hold you to that rain check but I'm going to the pub over the road for a couple before heading home, in case you change your mind. Don't work too late.'

CHAPTER ELEVEN

Adam and LJ had opted to remain in the octagon. They'd been sat at the conference table for hours, in deep discussion surrounded by palace blueprints, working out what they were going to do once inside while they waited for Calypso and Cormac to breach the palace's defences from below to take over the security systems. They'd also agreed on the location where LJ was going to take Defence Secretary Ashworth privately to incapacitate him and copy his gold-plated security pass, allowing for enough time to rendezvous with Adam and Cormac in the Lords' chamber.

LJ moved on to Defence Secretary Ashworth's psychological profile workup provided by Aree. The file contained in-depth details which LJ was grateful for. In summary, he was a perverse man who enjoyed many vices as well as a penchant for the finer things in life. In LJ's mind he was a hollow, self-aggrandising, calculated bore. What she really wanted to know about Ashworth was what his tastes were when it came to women, so she could take on those traits and ensnare him. The other burning question of importance was whereabouts on his person he kept that gold security pass.

Looking up from the profile folder, LJ glanced over at Adam, who was in deep concentration as he mixed the fast-acting drug that they would use to incapacitate Defence Secretary Ashworth. In their earlier discussion, Adam had told her he'd acquired this plant-based derivative drug through one of his more unsavoury but trustworthy contacts under an alias, and had it shipped over through a government contact in a diplomatic pouch to avoid customs.

An old grandfather clock that stood against one of the octagonal walls chimed out as the clock struck one forty-five in the morning.

The tech room in the east wing of Silver Blaze more resembled a sterilised laboratory with its computers, glass cabinets, and scientific and technical equipment. To Calypso this felt like a second home, her own personal domain where her creativity could flourish when they needed a device to overcome certain electronic obstacles for a job. Knowing how high the stakes were, Calypso reflected on how lucky she'd been when she and Adam had first met as she worked on adding the finishing touches to the special miniature Knight comms devices so they could liaise in secret at the ball.

Before meeting Adam, Calypso had led a very different life. A computer and technical whizz-kid from a young age and a master hacker by the age of fourteen, Calypso used her skill set to a become a professional data thief, stealing corporate, secret or personal data from companies and individuals, both public and private, to sell to the highest bidder for considerable lump sums to fund her own technological experiments and projects. She considered her work to be near flawless until the night she'd attempted to steal sensitive technical schematics on a new defence super computer from Knight Technologies to sell to a rival tech defence company. The robbery had all gone to plan and it was shaping up to be another easy payday, when all of a sudden the alarms sounded and the vault went into lockdown mode. It had all been a carefully constructed ruse set up by Adam, who'd orchestrated the whole charade to meet and recruit her into his fold.

During that encounter Adam had given Calypso a choice: work for him in his company and use her remarkable skills constructively to benefit others, or be dropped off at the nearest police station with a wealth of evidence linking her to more than a dozen crimes, which she knew would mean a lengthy prison sentence and the threat of every person she'd ever stolen from finding out her identity and trying to kill her. Given the precarious choice Calypso now found herself in, she chose the former, and even though she tried to find a way out for a few months afterwards, in hindsight it was the best choice she'd ever made. It took a few years to build trust between her and

Adam, but eventually their partnership had turned into a close friendship.

Remembering the job in hand, Calypso completed the finishing touches to the Knight comms devices and checked down her list of what she had left to do. Her next task was to assemble the magnetic pulse charges which were to be used on the vault to damage it after they'd taken the contents. After that, she had to configure a tailor-made computer virus that needed to be able to erase – or at the very least, corrupt and damage – the palace's security mainframe beyond repair. Whatever happened tomorrow evening, she was content that she would do her best for Adam and the personal cause they'd been working towards over the past year.

Rubbing her eyes to stem the feeling of tiredness, Calypso reached for her mug of hot chocolate and glanced at her digital clock on the wall. It read two thirty a.m.

Down in the basement next to the training room, Cormac was hard at work doing his due diligence in the equipment room, assembling all the necessary items they would need on the large metal table. He was feeling apprehensive at the job ahead as a heist of this scale, with very little time for preparation, required almost everything in his arsenal of gadgets and tricks.

With everything that was going on, Cormac's thoughts had also turned to the night his luck had run out, when he was caught red-handed in a sting operation with his hand in the safe of a well-respected Irish Minister's home. He knew his apprehensiveness about tomorrow evening must have brought forward these specific memories that been dormant in the back of his mind for so long.

He'd been a decorated and skilled RAF pilot and armourer who'd been through a number of conflicts in his fifteen years of service, some of which had left a lasting and damaging impression on him. After his honourable discharge from the air force and return to Southern Ireland, Cormac had found the transition back to civilian life very difficult. He hadn't been able to get any gainful employment, which exacerbated his dormant PTSD, and as a consequence he'd fallen on hard times, resulting in homelessness, heavy drinking and depression. It got so bad that he became a thief out of a sheer desperation to survive and discovered that he'd quite a talent for it. His former military training and adept knowledge of security systems proved most useful in his thievery. Even the sleight-of-hand tricks he'd learned from his roguish Uncle Seamus as a kid in Limerick City had proved invaluable when it came to picking pockets or locks.

However, that particular night, having been caught and thrown into the nearest Garda police cell had almost broken him, and he was certain he was going to be spending quite a few years in prison. Yet fate was going to reward him with one more chance. His friend Adam, who he had not seen for several years, had somehow found out about his predicament and managed through considerable influence to get the charges dropped after some delicate negotiations. Adam took him back to London and got him the specialist therapy he needed for his PTSD condition, which to this day he was still receiving and was most grateful for, as well as helping him readjust to civilian life. Adam also secured Cormac a job as head of security for Knight Technologies' London office. Cormac felt he'd been given a purpose again, that he mattered to someone, and was thankful every day to Adam for all he had done for him.

Coming out of his thoughts, and with the equipment finally assembled and checked off his list, Cormac sat down at his workbench under the haze of lamplight to begin disassembling, cleaning and reassembling the gang's tranquiliser dart guns. He'd been a little remiss in cleaning them after their last job.

Halfway through the disassembly of the first gun, Cormac glanced at the small copper-encased alarm clock on the bench: it was three fifteen in the morning.

Outside in the garages, Johnny was working on the transportation, giving each of the vehicles a tune-up and a full service. His iPhone was blaring out his favourite playlist mix of songs old and new, which he loved listening to as he worked. Though he loathed his biological father with a passion for the years of hell and abuse he'd put him through, he was grateful in a small way for the mechanical skills he'd taught him when he was young.

Sliding out from underneath the black Range Rover he'd just finished working on, Johnny wiped his greasy hands on an old piece of rag and walked over to his workbench where he'd assembled a large map of Westminster Palace and the surrounding area. On the map, the young amateur mechanic had marked, using pins and coloured string, several routes he and the others could take when they made their escape, including alternatives in case the police or security services cut them off. Johnny also studied the exact position he had to be in to receive the goods from the vault and what strength the current of the Thames would be at that hour of the night, as well as its height. Thankfully, the palace terrace was being shut down as a non-essential area, so security would be light. The only real danger, even though it was going to be a moonless night, came from being spotted in the Thames from a bridge by the police. Overall, Johnny felt calm and collected. The job was going to be challenging, no question, and he knew he had an important role to play, but his belief in Adam was paramount. He was confident they were going to pull this off.

Satisfied once again that he'd memorised all the routes perfectly, Johnny started on the next vehicle, which was going to be used by Calypso and Cormac. He still had a lot to do with his own transportation but it would have to be done last. As he got into position to slip underneath the vintage Alfa Romeo GTV to begin his checks, Adam poked his head round to check on him. They didn't speak as the music was too loud, but he raised his thumb to check everything was okay. Johnny gave the thumbs up back, followed by another hand signal indicating he was making good progress. Adam nodded and smiled in acknowledgement and then disappeared back behind the door. Johnny checked the time on his old, weathered watch: four a.m.

Sunrise broke over Silver Blaze, revealing a foreboding and crisp morning. Inside the lounge, the dying embers of last night's fire finally petered out. Empty pizza boxes and bottles of energy drinks littered the glass coffee table from last night's feast. Adam and the others dozed on the sofas after a long night's work. Adam sat up and let out a large yawn as he felt the roughness of his stubble under his chin. He hadn't been able to sleep well since that night spent listening to the colonel in the Savoy; the recurring nightmares saw to that. He got out of his chair and walked over to open the blinds, allowing sunlight to flood the room. He could hear the sound of birds chirping in the distance as the others began to stir.

'What time is it?' asked Johnny, yawning.

'It's a little after seven,' replied Adam as he stared out at the reddish-blue hew of the skyline.

'Why are we awake? I feel like I only went to sleep twenty minutes ago,' said Calypso.

'I know, and I'm sorry to wake you, but I thought you'd feel more comfortable if you went to your own beds upstairs.'

Adam walked back over to the sofa and picked up his half-full can of energy drink that was now flat. Leaning against the fireplace, he took a swig and swirled the contents around to moisten his dry mouth and throat.

'You know, I'm sure my mammy, God rest her soul, said it was a sin to be up this early before the rooster crowed,' said Cormac.

'Well, if we had a rooster, he would have crowed a lot earlier, but the best I can offer is that the birds are chirping in the distance. Does that count?' said Adam.

'Nope, not even close.' Cormac chuckled.

'Hmm ...what I wouldn't give for a pair of strong hands and a massage right now,' said LJ, stretching out.

'I know a friend of mine who could help smooth out those aches for you, Aunt LJ,' Johnny suggested.

'If it's that friend of yours you've already told me about, I'm not that desperate.'

Adam took another swig and finished the can of energy drink as he watched the others laugh and joke with each other. It was nice to hear that sound resonate through the house again after so much sadness. He couldn't help but beam at the thought of how blessed he truly was to have such good friends and family in his life.

'Guys, I know you're all tired, but I wanted to say thank you for working so hard last night. You're the best, and I'm not sure I will ever be able to repay you for coming on this mad journey with me.'

'Dad, you don't have to thank us; you've done the same for us when we've needed help,' said Johnny, walking up to him and giving him a hug.

'Go on then, off you go, all of you, and get some proper rest before tonight. Make sure you're ready to leave by 1800 hours.' Adam let go of Johnny and patted him gently on the back.

'Aren't you coming up?' asked Johnny, realising Adam wasn't following the rest of them upstairs.

'I'll be up in a few minutes, Johnny. I want to gather my thoughts before I turn in.'

'Don't be too long; we need you at your best this evening,' Johnny replied, closing the door behind him.

The moment Johnny closed the door Adam could feel his stomach turning with notches of nerves, exacerbated by his fear of failure. Tonight was a big gamble; the risks were huge, and if they did fail, the outcome would be extremely grim – not only for him but for the others, who he loved dearly. He reached into his pocket and pulled out the little silver knight chess piece and held it tight to his chest as he walked back over to one of the large windows.

'I promise you all if you're watching and listening up there, as God is my witness, I will not fail any of you,' he said under his breath, looking up into the sky.

CHAPTER TWELVE

The Palace of Westminster shone in all its glory for the Brooks government's tenth annual masquerade ball. A crimson carpet flanked by copper-cased fire torches lined the grand entrance to Westminster Hall, ready to welcome the rich, powerful and famous as they arrived to party the night away in grand style. Stringent security guarded the entire perimeter of the palace and a four-hundred-metre exclusion zone had been cordoned off by multiple Metropolitan Police units.

Opposite, on the college green, selected members of the local and international press, both for and against the ball, had set up to report and debate on the night's events. Outside the exclusion zone, peaceful but noisy protesters had gathered inside St James's Park under close police supervision. *London Evening News*'s political correspondent Sarah Woodhouse was the first reporter inside the park to capture the amazing show of opposition.

'Good evening and welcome to the most controversial and talked about social event of the season as the Brooks government's tenth annual masquerade ball gets underway. Tonight's celebrations are overshadowed this year by the many protesters you see behind me, who are angered at the sheer expense and the Brooks government's defiance to host this event despite the wide economic downturn where many families are struggling to get by.'

The reporter turned to speak to the organiser of the protest.

'Standing next to me leading the charge of this protest is one politician who has recently felt the brunt of a failed smear campaign against him by the government and is appalled by the vast number of his colleagues' lack of respect and failure to listen to the public. Leader of the Phoenix Party, Tom Phoenix.' Cheers could be heard from the protesters behind them.

The cameras homed in on an attractive, tall man in his early forties, a little rough around the edges but elegantly dressed in a bespoke three-piece suit.

'Thank you for speaking with us tonight, Sarah,' replied Tom charismatically, his accent displaying his Norfolk roots.

'So tell us, Mr Phoenix, why are you out here tonight to protest?' asked Sarah as the crowd continued to cheer behind him.

'It's very simple, Sarah. My party and I, not to mention all these wonderful people behind me and across the country, believe this is a gross betrayal of public trust and money. At a time when we are asking the citizens of this great country to tighten their belts, the government and my so-called honourable colleagues should be leading by example and using that money more effectively within our communities, NHS services, housing and infrastructure, or funding rehabilitation projects for our armed forces returning from war – not wasting it on extravagant parties.'

More cheers and applause erupted from behind Tom and Sarah.

'Your fellow protesters seem to agree with you. What do you make of your other parliamentary colleagues and the Prime Minister, who have repeatedly said that all the proceeds from tonight's event will go to various charities and the most vulnerable in our society? Are you saying you don't believe they will make good on their promise?'

'I'm saying that given this government's appalling incompetence and propensity for lying, I wouldn't trust any of them to do the right thing by the people.'

'And what would you say to the people who are watching at home tonight who might not believe you, given the overwhelming negative perception of politicians today?'

'That there are still many of us who do believe in the power of the people's voice and who *will* do the right thing. You are our bosses; we're listening to you and we want to make a difference so that you and your families may prosper. We're not all like the Brooks government and some of my more unscrupulous colleagues,' replied Tom, his voice full of passion and fervour.

Adam and LJ watched Tom Phoenix's impassioned answers on the video screen of their black Range Rover as they waited to clear the last checkpoint. Both of them were dressed in formal black and white evening wear. Adam's attire was simple yet suave: a beautifully tailored black Armani tuxedo over a white cotton shirt with silver cufflinks. LJ's outfit was more multifaceted but just as stunning. Her short black cocktail dress dipped to one side, leaving one of her shoulders exposed. A small white purse was attached to a white belt that hugged her figure, contrasting with her black suede knee-high boots. She also wore a beautiful silver charm bracelet given to her by her father and a plain silver pendant necklace that had been a gift from Adam for her twenty-fifth birthday.

Adam switched off the video screen as they cleared the last checkpoint and drove across Westminster Bridge to the party.

'Sounds like things could get a little heated tonight by the look of that crowd behind Phoenix,' said LJ, summing up the interview.

'So would you if you suspected the government had used your tax money to fund this little soirée this evening,' replied Adam. His voice was a little abrupt, which LJ put down to nerves and intense concentration.

'True, but I guess they'll be having the last laugh after our little escapade tonight, which I know we're going to pull off.' She squeezed his hand reassuringly.

They pulled in to one side and joined the queue of vehicles waiting to be parked by the valets. Both he and LJ placed their small, adapted Knight comms devices in their ears and put on their black Kato masks as they pulled up to the crimson carpet.

'Are you ready?' asked Adam, smiling at her.

LJ nodded as the valets opened the car doors of the Range Rover for them. Cheers erupted from a few supportive and carefully selected fans wanting to catch a glimpse of the rich and famous, accompanied by blue flashes and the clicking of camera shutters from the paparazzi. Adam stepped out of the vehicle, pausing a moment for LJ to join him. She tucked her hand under his arm and together they walked elegantly down the carpet towards the entrance of Westminster Hall.

Westminster Hall was the oldest existing building of the Palace of Westminster, erected in 1097 by William II and later made famous by its beautiful oak hammer beam roof. Dubbed 'the greatest creation of medieval timber architecture', the hall was created for Richard II by the royal carpenter Hugh Herland, and during its long, famous and sometimes infamous history it had been used for several purposes, from judicial court hearings to lying-in-state funerals of

royalty and other important figures. Since then, it had served a more

humble purpose for the odd conference or guided tour.

Clearing the internal security check, Adam handed over his

invitation to the receptionist and proceeded into the hall with LJ. On

scrutinising the invitation Adam had just given her, the receptionist

quickly called over one of the PM's security aides and whispered

something in his ear.

LJ and Adam looked around at the extravagant interior of the

hall which had been divided into three sections and separated by large

ice sculptures on either side. The first and largest section was lined with

tables and chairs decorated in black and white satin for the guests to

enjoy the rich food that had been laid on for them. In the second

section, where some of the five-hundred-plus guests had gathered to

chat, laugh and drink, were two big bar areas serving every alcoholic

beverage imaginable. The final section had been reserved for dancing

to the smooth sounds of the jazz orchestra, who had set up at the top of

the main staircase in St Stephen's Porch, underneath the gaze of the

large stained-glass window created by Sir Ninian Comper.

As they made their way towards the bar through the sea of

masked people, it occurred to Adam how soulless they all looked with

their faces obscured. It reminded him of one of those old macabre movies where the soulless danced and made merriment for their own gratification, unperturbed, caring for nothing and no one. A voice from behind called his name, interrupting his thoughts. He heard it again, this time louder than before, and turned to see where the voice was coming from. The unmistakable figure of Prime Minister George Brooks dressed all in black stood before them, his beady eyes peering out from behind a white lion mask.

'Prime Minister Brooks, how unexpected,' said Adam, feeling his hatred towards Brooks swell up inside.

'So much for masking my identity. How did you know it was me?' replied Brooks, taking his mask away from his face and holding out his other hand to shake Adam's.

Adam hadn't been prepared to meet Prime Minister Brooks at this stage of his plan and he was repulsed by the idea of having to shake hands with a murderer. He felt an overwhelming urge to punch the living daylights out of Brooks for all the pain and heartache he'd caused him, but a squeeze of the hand from LJ, who had felt him tense up, brought his rational side back into focus and he reluctantly shook Brooks's hand.

'We all wear masks, Prime Minister, but some of us are better at hiding who we truly are,' Adam replied, enjoying Brooks' discomfort.

'Quite. One of my aides informed me of your arrival, and I must say it's a feather in my cap to have one of the top leading businessmen, philanthropists and tech pioneers in the world here tonight. So, who is this lovely lady you're with?' asked Brooks, his eyes focusing on LJ and enjoying every inch of her appearance.

'May I introduce my good friend, Lady Joanna Gray, the daughter of our ambassador to Canada, Sir Charles Gray,' said Adam, ignoring Brooks' attempt to flatter him.

'Your Ladyship, it's an honour. My apologies for not recognising you. I had no idea Mr Knight ran in such high social circles,' said Brooks, kissing the back of her hand, much to LJ's annoyance.

'It's quite alright, Prime Minister, and please call me LJ; all my friends do,' she replied, feigning politeness.

'Tell me then, LJ, what do you think of our little charitable soirée so far?'

'It's wonderful, Prime Minister. Don't you think so, Adam?'

'Yes, you've outdone yourself, Prime Minister. Out of curiosity, and between us, could you let me in on a couple things? Which charities are this year's recipients of all the donations? And who's footing the bill for this soirée?'

Prime Minister Brooks's smile and calm demeanour evaporated for a second in a momentary slip. 'I'm neglecting my other guests. Have a pleasant evening, Mr Knight, your Ladyship.' He slithered away, back into the crowd.

LJ looked at Adam with raised eyebrows. He said nothing and they both resumed their course for the bar. Adam ordered a double vodka on the rocks for himself and a glass of Bollinger's specially chilled cuvée champagne for LJ. He took a large gulp to steady his nerves. His watch read nine p.m. – time was ticking by fast. Draining the rest of his drink and placing the ice-laden glass on the counter, Adam signalled to the barman for another double before leaning over to whisper into LJ's ear.

'It's time for us to split up. Go and mingle and see if someone can point you in the right direction of Defence Secretary Ashworth.'

'Okay, I'll see you later. And Adam, no more foolish stunts like you pulled with Brooks while I'm gone. He'll get what's coming to him soon enough.'

'Don't worry, I promise I'll keep myself in check. Good luck.'

LJ gave Adam's arm a little squeeze and disappeared back into the crowd in search of Defence Secretary Ashworth.

The jazz band was playing one of his favourite slow numbers. The barman brought over another drink and he took a sip, savouring it.

As the band were coming to the finale of their current number, Adam heard his name being called again.

'Well, well, Adam Knight. I couldn't believe it when the PM told me you were here this evening.'

Adam turned round to face Home Secretary Jackson puffing heavily on a Cuban cigar.

'Home Secretary Jackson. And what can I do for you?'

'Oh, nothing, I just had to see you with my own eyes. I didn't think a man with your anti-government stances and so-called high morals would be caught dead here.'

'I never pass up on a party and I'm always full of surprises. Being unpredictable has got me to the top of my game, Home Secretary.'

Adam tried to tune out Home Secretary Jackson's long-winded response. He found Jackson utterly repulsive, and his anger and hatred began to swell once more. His fist clenched automatically. You keep talking, Jackson, and I'll make sure you'll be eating that cigar, he thought, as his fist shook by his side.

Just as he thought his anger was going to erupt, his attention was caught by one of the most beautiful women he had ever seen, dressed in a silver satin evening dress and mask. Adam was mesmerised as she came closer towards him and Home Secretary

Jackson, holding two glasses of champagne. He hadn't felt this entranced by a woman since his late wife, Em. Her flowing shoulder-length blonde hair and piercing ocean-blue eyes seemed to have a calming influence on his tortured soul, and his anger had all but subsided by the time she was inches away from them both.

'Where the hell have you been, Johnson? In fact, don't bother answering. At least you brought champagne, proving you're not entirely useless.' Jackson snatched the glass out of her hand.

'Well, Knight, let me introduce Agent Amy Johnson, who's been heading up the Baker Street Five investigation. Poorly, I might add.' Jackson took the cigar from his mouth and drank some champagne.

Adam shot a surprise glance at Amy. He knew about Agent Johnson and the SI7 investigation into his extracurricular activities thanks to Aree keeping him up to date, and like him, he could tell from Agent Johnson's body language that she detested Home Secretary Jackson as much as he did.

'It's a pleasure to meet you, Agent Johnson. You must be a high-flyer in the service to have been chosen for that assignment.'

'It's very nice to meet you too, Mr Knight. I'm just doing my job, but thank you for the compliment.'

'Please, call me Adam. How goes your investigation into these elusive thieves?'

'No point in asking her anything, Knight. When it comes to getting results, Agent Johnson has been found wanting,' said Home Secretary Jackson, butting into the conversation.

'I wasn't asking for your opinion, Jackson. I was asking Agent Johnson because crime has always intrigued me,' said Adam.

'Our investigation is making progress but is ongoing, Mr Knight, and that's all I can say right now,' replied Amy, throwing a critical look at Home Secretary Jackson. A moment later, one of the PM's senior aides rushed over and whispered something in his ear.

'Excuse me: business, I'm afraid. Why don't you keep Mr Knight entertained, Johnson? What you lack in liaison officer skills you make up for in being a woman.' Jackson snorted as he winked at Adam and walked away laughing.

'That venomous tongue of his knows no bounds. He had no right to speak to you that way. Are you alright?' said Adam, with genuine concern in his voice. Amy had frozen, embarrassed by Home Secretary Jackson's chauvinistic remarks.

'I'm fine. I'm used to his pathetic insults.'

Adam thought he saw a tear roll down from under her mask, but before he could be sure, she had disappeared into the crowd. He caught up with her near the dance floor and turned her round to face him. Her eyes were glazed over with tears.

'Agent Johnson … Amy, don't let him get to you. The man's a pig.' Adam wiped her tears softly from her cheeks. Amy took a deep sigh and smiled tentatively.

'I feel so embarrassed for breaking down in front of him. You've no idea what it's like to have to work for and report to a man like that.'

'Don't be, he's not worth your tears, and if anyone should be embarrassed, it's him. Now feel free to say no, but if I'm not being too forward, I was wondering if you'd like to dance with me?'

'Thank you, but I warn you, I'm not much of a dancer.'

'Don't worry, you'll be fine. I'll lead.' Adam gestured towards the centre of the dance floor. As he followed closely behind, LJ's voice buzzed in his ear, making him walk at a slower pace.

'Adam, I've made contact with Defence Secretary Ashworth. Proceeding as planned.'

'Good work, LJ. Calypso and Cormac should be entering the palace any minute now. Text me when you're done.'

Time to enjoy himself, he decided. He went over to the jazz band and made a request. As it started up, Adam took Amy by the hand

and, to the delight of the other guests, they began tearing up the dance floor.

CHAPTER THIRTEEN

Beneath the Palace of Westminster in the abandoned Victorian sewer system, the masked figures of Calypso and Cormac, dressed in black and using night vision goggles, rushed through the dark maze of damp and derelict brick tunnels. The faint smell of sewage still hung in the air like rotten vegetation, making them both heave a little as they followed the schematic on Calypso's phone to their infiltration point.

After what felt like an endless eternity of twists and turns, they arrived at the corroded ladder beneath the old palace courtyard's central drainage grate. Cormac set down his backpack and scooted up the ladder. He took out a small non-light-reflecting mirror from the top pocket of his jacket and pushed it through the grate to get a visual into the floodlit courtyard to make sure no one was about. The courtyard was empty. Cormac placed the mirror back in his pocket and took out his lock picks. He slid his gloved hands through the grate's iron bars and felt around for the heavy-duty, weather-hardened padlock.

Click. That sound brought a satisfying smile to Cormac's face. He'd picked the lock in less than two minutes, which was a new personal best. He removed the padlock and lifted the heavy iron grate just enough to peer out and check once again that the courtyard was clear. He heard a burst of banter and loud conversation, and two armed parliamentary and diplomatic protection officers on their security rounds came into view. They stood a few feet away, casting their shadows over him and the grate. Cormac ducked to avoid being seen, but as he replaced the heavy iron grate, it made a noise. He shot down the ladder and signalled to Calypso to stay out of sight.

The two officers assumed a defensive stance and looked all around, trying to figure out where the noise had come from. They walked towards the grate and shone their torches down into the blackness of the sewer, dislodging some loose stonework that fell to the bottom of the ladder with a splash. Cormac and Calypso had stepped out of the line of sight but were ready with their tranquilliser guns to take them out.

'This place is falling to pieces. It was probably a piece of loose stone that's fallen off and clipped the grate. I'll file a report with building maintenance to come and check it out first thing tomorrow,' said one officer, his voice echoing down into the sewer.

As the voices grew fainter and the shadows moved away, Cormac and Calypso breathed a small sigh of relief. But now they were behind schedule. Cormac picked up his backpack and lifted the grate up again to peer out. He flipped his small night vision lenses up from his mask and watched the two officers go inside a dreary-looking grey cabin on the other side of the courtyard. A temporary staff room, he surmised. Cormac gestured down to Calypso to get ready to move in a few moments. This was one of the trickiest and most nerve-racking parts of the entire operation. It left them completely exposed; they were leaving to chance that they wouldn't be detected on the security cameras, owing to parliament's security system having a state-of-the-art anti-jammer device.

Central Security Control was the central nerve centre for the entire security of the Palace of Westminster. The windowless air-conditioned room was divided into two sections: the lower section contained the kitchen and bathroom facilities, while the upper section was a gantry where three large built-in video screens monitored sections of the palace inside and out for any threats. Directly underneath the gantry were the computer mainframes which stored and logged all the data collected by the cameras. The mainframes were also hooked up to the three computer terminals on the gantry which were continuously monitored by the three security officers on duty.

The buzzer at the front door rang out loudly, interrupting their jovial banter.

'Damn that bloody door buzzer. It's your turn this time. Whoever it is, they better have a good reason for disturbing us,' said one officer as the buzzer went again, a little more forcibly this time.

'Alright, alright, I'm coming,' another officer shouted.

Pressing the release mechanism on the electronic lock, the officer opened the door. Before he could even utter a word to raise the alarm, Cormac shot a tranquilliser dart straight into his chest, knocking him backwards and to the ground, unconscious. The other two officers jumped to their feet and reached for their sidearms and the alarm, but Calypso was too quick for them. She rushed in and fired two tranquilliser darts in quick succession, hitting them both squarely in the back and neck and neutralising them. Cormac shut the door behind them as Calypso, holstering her weapon, darted up onto the gantry to the master computer terminal. She began hacking into the system's mainframe, using her little magic box to take full control of the palace's surveillance and security systems, while Cormac dragged the security guards into the kitchen area and proceeded to tie up and gag them.

'How are you doing, Calypso? Are you inside the mainframe yet?' said Cormac, looking at his watch.

'Stand by, come on, come on … yes, I'm in.' Calypso replied, feeling a sense of extreme pride in her abilities.

'Three minutes and twenty-five seconds; you're slipping, sweetie, but you still never cease to amaze me with your skills.'

'Give me a break! This system had a few layers of encryption and security traps to bypass before it would give me access.'

Cormac smiled at her and placed his finger to his ear. 'Adam, have secured big brother, moving to rendezvous position.'

'Hold on, I'm fixing the cameras. Make sure you all stick to your planned routes if you don't want to be seen.'

'Thanks, Calypso, and remember: keep the door locked and continue to operate our counter measures until we give you the word we're moving out.'

Calypso nodded attentively. 'Be careful, and good luck.'

'I'm Irish, remember? I was born lucky.' Cormac pressed the door release mechanism and slipped out of sight.

CHAPTER FOURTEEN

An inebriated Defence Secretary Richard Ashworth was sat on his chair as he rolled across the dark wooden floor of his office. The chair's path was only lit by firelight as it came to an abrupt halt at the front of his desk with a bump. Out of breath and his glasses askew, Defence Secretary Ashworth slumped on his chair. His eyes were transfixed and hungry with lust as he watched the striking figure of LJ emerge from the darkness and walk seductively across to him. Pulling his chair forward, LJ sat on his lap, wrapping her long legs around the back of the chair and her arms around his neck so he couldn't move. To her eternal disgust she could tell he was aroused but she soldiered on, smiling at him playfully.

'Your Ladyship, you're one of the most dominating and adventurous women I've—'

'Shh,' said LJ, raising her finger to his lips. She flicked her hair to one side and leant in to whisper into his ear.

'Do you know what I would really like right now, Richard?' she said, twirling his undone bow tie around her finger.

Defence Secretary Ashworth couldn't contain himself. He was completely besotted by every inch of her body. He creepily caressed her body with his hands and began kissing her neck. LJ cringed inside with revulsion; this was one of the worst things she'd ever had to do. To spare herself any further humiliation, she grabbed his head and forced it to one side, making him yelp. She could tell by the look in his eyes he enjoyed being dominated.

'I'd like some champagne,' LJ whispered in his ear. She turned on the green and gold banker's lamp on the desk, revealing some of his office's nostalgic furnishings, and getting off his lap, walked over to the drinks cabinet. She pulled out the expensive 1988 bottle of Krug vintage brut champagne which had been chilling in the ice bucket for the past half hour and popped the cork. The champagne fizzed over the rim of the bottle as she set aside two crystal champagne glasses and poured a generous amount of the champagne into each. Out of Ashworth's sight, LJ opened the charm on her bracelet which contained the powerful knockout drug Adam had given her and dropped the liquid concoction into his glass, making the champagne fizz and froth as it dissolved. Carrying both glasses, LJ walked past Ashworth and over to his small sofa. With a gentle twitch of her finger, she enticed him to come and sit down beside her. Defence Secretary Ashworth didn't need persuading.

'To a night of surprises,' said LJ, passing him his drink and raising hers in toast.

'No, here's to you, my enchanting little temptress,' Defence Secretary Ashworth replied, taking a large gulp of champagne. 'Now, my dear, enough games. I think we both know what we want, so allow me to give you a night to remember.'

He moved his hand up her thigh beneath her dress and leant in to kiss her. LJ held her breath and counted to ten, waiting for the drug to take effect. He collapsed onto her chest, his champagne glass dropping onto the floor.

LJ breathed a heavy sigh of relief that the ordeal was over. She drank the rest of her champagne in one large gulp and pushed Defence Secretary Ashworth's unconscious body onto the floor and brushed herself down. She felt physically sick; how any woman could find that slimy, murdering, arrogant son of a bitch attractive was beyond her comprehension. Standing up, she looked down at Ashworth and gave him a firm, satisfying kick in his side with her boot.

'That's for being such a sleaze,' she exclaimed, looking at her phone. She only had a few more minutes if she was to meet Adam at the rendezvous on time.

Regaining her composure, LJ knelt beside Defence Secretary Ashworth and searched his pockets for the gold-plated access card. She knew he had it on his person – he'd been fiddling with the card earlier and bragging about how fortunate she was to be in the presence of such a powerful man. After patting his body down, she eventually found it tucked away inside his jacket pocket. LJ placed her right leg on the sofa and partially unzipped the top of her boot to take out Calypso's small and compact copying device that was strapped to her leg. It looked very much like a ladies' square compact. She placed the card into one slot and the copy card into the other and pressed the button on the device to create an exact duplicate.

Back in Westminster Hall, the party was in full swing. After watching Adam and Agent Amy Johnson tear up the dance floor in considerable style, other guests got up to dance. Adam and Amy had now settled themselves at the bar and were chatting and laughing away like they had known each other for years.

'Well, that's enough about me. Tell me about you, Adam.'

'Oh well, I'm not really that interesting. I wouldn't want to bore you.'

'You aren't a bore. For what it's worth, you're an interesting man; very hard to read. You say a lot without really saying anything,' said Amy.

Adam chuckled to himself at Amy's analysis. He couldn't help but be fascinated by her curiosity and yet totally at ease. Amy was quite disarming in a way that he'd not felt in years, even though they were on opposing sides.

Adam's phone beeped. He looked at the screen and frowned.

'Is there something wrong?'

'My apologies, Amy but would you mind if we continued our chat later? A problem has arisen regarding one of my defence contracts abroad and I've got to make a vital phone call to sort it out,' Adam replied, glancing at his watch.

'Oh, of course; I should go and check on Home Secretary Jackson. No doubt I'll have to do some damage control because he's bound to have offended someone else. I'll see you later, then?'

Adam finished his drink and stood up from his chair.

'I'll come and find you when I'm done, I promise. See you later.' He placed his right hand on her arm and squeezed it gently before disappearing into the crowd.

CHAPTER FIFTEEN

The central lobby was one of the grandest areas in the palace, with its vaulted ceiling, tall windows, ornate statues and intricate mosaics representing the four patron saints of the United Kingdom. To most, it represented a mini time capsule of a time and grandeur that had long since vanished but was kept alive in memory by the glow of the grand chandelier. Adam and LJ breezed into the central lobby and raced down the corridor to the Lords' chamber. They reached the end of the corridor and stopped outside the first set of double doors, which led into the small antechamber. Adam pulled out two pairs of black cotton gloves from inside his jacket and gave one to LJ. After slipping them on, Adam lifted his left leg to expose the underside of his shoe and slid back the hollowed-out heel, taking out the miniature lock picks concealed inside. After a minute spent manipulating the lock's mechanism, it yielded. LJ pushed the doors open and they rushed inside.

Adam made his way over to the set of doors which led into the Lords' main chamber and picked that lock with ease too. They were both amused by the sight that greeted them. At the opposite end of the regal chamber, the masked figure of Cormac sat comfortably on the golden throne, one leg hanging over an armrest, his tranquilliser gun aimed at them both.

'What kept you?' he said, lowering the gun, a roguish grin on his face.

'I'm sorry; if we'd known we were keeping royalty waiting, we'd have been here sooner. It does suit you though, Cormac,' said Adam, smirking.

'All Irishmen are kings, my friend, but it's okay; I'll forgive you this one time for not knowing. How did you get on with Ashworth, LJ? Did he succumb to your charms?'

'Like a moth to a flame, and let me tell you, he was a disgusting pig,' LJ replied, her body shuddering.

'Alright, you two, that'll do. We're running seven minutes behind schedule and we've got forty minutes before Johnny gets into position. LJ, give Cormac the security card.'

LJ reached inside her small white purse, pulled out the copy of Ashworth's card and gave it to Cormac. He slid back the false section on the armrest and slotted the card into the electronic lock. They waited with bated breath for the entrance to open. A small rumbling came from beneath and a section of the floor cascaded downwards to form steps. Adam, LJ and Cormac felt a sense of restrained triumph and relief as they converged on the entrance and peered down at the faint glow shining up from the undercroft.

'Ladies first,' said Adam, gesturing to LJ. She descended into the vault, Cormac following close behind. Adam placed his finger to his ear to talk to Calypso over their secure comms link.

'Calypso, can you hear me?'

'Loud and clear, Adam. It's good to hear your voice.'

'Yours too. We're moving into the vault. Is everything okay where you are?'

'Everything's fine. There's no unusual activity from the security personnel. If I'm honest, it's boring and I wish I was there with you guys to see the vault for myself.'

'Don't worry, you'll be seeing the loot soon enough. Keep monitoring the cameras and the radio traffic and warn us if anyone gets curious.'

'Will do. See you soon.'

Adam caught up with LJ and Cormac at bottom of the staircase. They walked along the narrow wood-panelled passageway and entered a large antechamber. They lowered their black masks, secure in the knowledge there were no cameras in this secret chamber. Highly polished black and white marble covered the walls, ceiling and floor, concealing the reinforced concrete and steel framework. To the right was a large black leather sofa flanked by two imitation plants. To the left was a beautiful hand-carved Georgian oak desk, on top of which lay a large leather-bound book. Above the desk hung an impressive portrait of the infamous Guido 'Guy' Fawkes. However, what drew their eyes was the huge but unknown purple parliament crest in the centre of the black marble floor. Below the crest in gold lettering was a Latin inscription encircled by a border of gold, which directed attention along the main vault corridor to the huge stainless steel vault door.

'Any ideas what the inscription says? My Latin is a little rusty,' Cormac said.

'It roughly translates as "secrecy is the key to wealth and power". It's disgraceful; they should be ashamed of themselves,' said LJ.

'Most of these people have no shame or conscience.' Cormac walked towards the narrow vault corridor.

'It's still disgusting, and what's with the portrait of Guy Fawkes?'

'I'm guessing it's symbolic, a sort of twisted joke. Guy Fawkes tried and failed to blow up parliament to end corruption and install a catholic monarch. They've hung his portrait here so he's forced to watch his failure over and over again,' said Adam.

'Erm, guys, we've got a small problem,' Cormac interrupted.

'What's the matter?' asked Adam.

'See the floor in the vault corridor?'

'Yeah, what about it? Looks perfectly normal to me,' replied LJ, glancing down.

'Aye, but I wouldn't walk on it if I were you. Do you hear that low-pitched humming sound?'

'Yes. What is it?'

'That's the sound of fifty thousand volts running through it. Watch.'

Cormac pulled out a small metal tool from his pocket and threw it down the corridor, onto the floor. The floor sparked and hissed as the electricity pulsated through it.

'Sorry, Adam, they must have installed this recently. It wasn't on the schematics.'

'There's always a surprise. Can you bypass it?' said Adam, frustrated with himself at not having foreseen this security measure.

'No, and I don't have anything in my bag to neutralise it, but there's a computer panel on the wall here. I'm guessing we have to type in a password and it'll deactivate the floor.'

Adam checked his watch again. They really didn't have the time for this but they had no choice. They gathered round the computer panel and Cormac lowered the mini keyboard, triggering the computer's voice-activation protocol.

'Welcome, Defence Secretary Ashworth. Please enter your seven-letter password within one minute or security lockdown protocol will be activated.'

'Damn it. Okay, Cormac, type in what LJ and I say as quickly as possible.'

They began throwing seven-letter words at Cormac drawn from what they could remember of Ashworth's profile. However, each word Cormac typed caused the screen to flash red with the words *Access Denied*. As the small timer in the top right corner reached thirty seconds, beads of sweat began to appear on their faces.

'This is ridiculous; it could be anything,' said Adam, losing patience.

'I've got it: try Charlie,' said LJ, clicking her fingers as the timer hit fifteen seconds.

Cormac typed and pressed enter. The screen flashed green: *Access Granted*. The low-pitched humming sound emanating from the floor abruptly stopped, to all of their relief.

'Who or what the hell is Charlie?' asked Cormac and Adam at the same time.

'Defence Secretary Ashworth loves himself too much. Let's just say he tried to show me his little Charlie earlier, if you get my meaning,' said LJ, gesturing with her little finger.

'That dirty bastard, I've a good mind to—'

LJ kissed Cormac on the cheek. She grabbed his arm and the pair of them rushed down to the large steel vault door. Adam checked his watch again: ten fifty p.m.

'Cormac, I need you to crack her open within five minutes. Time isn't on our side.'

Cormac took off his backpack and dropped it beside him. He set his countdown timer for five minutes and went immediately to work. He closed his eyes and placed his ear to the vault, turning the first combination dial as LJ watched, intrigued by his old-school methods. To pass the time, Adam walked over to the hand-carved Georgian desk and opened up the large leather-bound book. He was curious to see what it contained and started flicking through the pages.

'LJ, would you come here for a minute?' asked Adam. LJ patted Cormac on the back as he tackled the second dial and hurried back up the corridor to Adam.

'What do you think of this?' He stepped aside so she could sift through its pages. As she scanned the written words within, she realised what she was looking at and turned to Adam, mirroring his expression.

'I think we'll take this with us too. It'll come in handy later,' said Adam, unable to wipe the satisfied smile from his face. He picked up the book and they rejoined Cormac, who was working on the last dial with sixty seconds to go. Beads of sweat had formed on his face again as he concentrated.

Click. The last dial dropped into place as his timer beeped out. Breathing a sigh of relief, Cormac turned the steel wheel, retracting the four thick steel bolts that kept the vault door in place.

'Ready, guys?' he said excitedly. They looked at each other in anticipation, then he pulled the heavy steel door open. The three of them stood in awe as they stared into the metallic, sterile room filled with numbered gold-plated security deposit boxes that were now ripe for the taking.

Outside parliament in the moonless night, all was quiet on the murky waters of the River Thames. In between the bridges of Lambeth and Westminster, in the middle of the river sat an unmanned river barge. It had been a security oversight but a useful advantage for Johnny, who'd taken refuge inside it for the last few hours, listening in to the others' progress over his comms device while waiting patiently for his part in the plan to begin. Dressed in his black outfit, gloves and mask, his face covered with camouflage paint, he'd managed to successfully circumvent the external security cordon and row his black dinghy under the cover of darkness up to the barge. Now zero hour was fast approaching. He checked his watch: it had been twenty minutes since Adam and the others had entered the vault.

Johnny stealthily clambered out of the barge and back into his black dinghy. He opened a black case that was resting on the floor and took out a gas-propelled harpoon gun. He connected the harpoon spear to some cable and loaded the spear into the gun. Using the night vision scope, he took aim just above the third-storey window of the tower furthest away from Westminster Bridge and fired. The harpoon gun let out a faint hiss as the spear and line flew through the air and imbedded itself deep in the soft limestone wall with a faint thud. Tying off the other end to his black dinghy, Johnny reloaded and repeated the process, this time firing the second into the palace's limestone base foundation. This second line was to secure him to the building and ensure he didn't drift with the current.

Back inside the vault, many of the safety-deposit boxes had now been emptied and strewn across the floor. Using the large red leather-bound book to his advantage, Adam had taken a special interest in deposit boxes 01 to 04 – they belonged to Prime Minister George Brooks, Foreign Secretary David Miller, Home Secretary Eric Jackson and

Defence Secretary Richard Ashworth. He'd broken them open with pleasure, knowing that the contents inside of each were enough to ruin them all.

'Okay, time's up,' said Adam. 'Cormac, chuck me the mag charge devices, and LJ, don't forget to leave our special calling card.'

Cormac reached inside his backpack and tossed Adam the pouch containing the compact magnetic charges Calypso had prepared. They were experimental explosives that once detonated sent out a controlled but limited range magnetic pulse surge, which not only damaged all electronic devices but also caused severe magnetism in almost any metallic object. Adam had acquired them from a company he'd bought out over a year ago but hadn't had much use for them until now. He got to work setting the charges all around the vault at various intervals on the unopened safety-deposit boxes, to be activated remotely from his master switch later. Cormac and LJ began zipping up all the bags. LJ reached inside Cormac's backpack, pulled out the gang's infamous Sherlock Holmes silhouette calling card and placed the magnetised edges of it on the steel sorting table as Adam finished placing the last charge.

'Okay, let's go. Cormac, tell Calypso to set her computer virus for release in fifteen minutes' time and to meet you outside the Lords' chamber. Once Calypso is with you, head straight for the rendezvous with the bags to meet Johnny. LJ, help Cormac with the bags and tell Johnny to get ready, then wait for me up top.'

'Calypso, are you there?' said Cormac, placing his hand to his ear to talk to her.

'Yes, I'm here. Is everything okay?'

'Yes, everything's ready. Set your virus to corrupt the mainframe files in fifteen minutes and then meet us outside the Lords' chamber as fast as you can.'

LJ and Cormac replaced their masks, lifted the bags onto their shoulders and moved out. Adam finished his checks on the charges and shot out of the vault, using all his strength to close the heavy vault door and leaving it unbolted. He replaced his mask and proceeded out of the undercroft. His mind wandered back to those soulless leeches in Westminster Hall who were oblivious to what was about to take place. He was about to shake their gilded world to its core. He didn't care what happened to him after the fallout; strangely, the only person he was concerned about apart from his loved ones was Agent Amy Johnson. They were on opposite sides, yes, but she'd had a profound effect on him all evening from the moment he'd laid eyes on her. Whether or not he wanted to admit it, something had begun to stir inside him. Could he be developing feelings for her? Was he still capable of falling in love and being able to accept love in return after so much pain and anguish? Those questions would have to wait.

CHAPTER SIXTEEN

'Calypso, what's your ETA?' said Cormac, concerned she hadn't met them at the rendezvous.

'She should be here by now. Something must have happened,' said LJ.

'I don't want to do this but Calypso knows the rules. Cormac, we can't wait any longer. Will you be able to carry the bags yourself?' asked Adam.

'That won't be necessary,' said Calypso, a little breathless.

'Calypso, thank God. What happened?' said Cormac, hugging her with relief.

'I'm sorry I'm late but I had to deal with some security personnel.' She looked over at Adam.

'I'm sorry about my previous comments, Calypso.'

'Don't be; I'd have done the same thing in your place. Go on, get out of here and we'll see you soon.'

'Right. LJ, let's go.'

'See you on the other side, guys.' LJ and Adam rushed out of the antechamber and back towards the party.

Johnny was a little on edge; he felt quite exposed out here in the open. He placed his finger to his ear to find out what was going on. 'Calypso, I'm in position and I'm getting anxious. What's your ETA?' he whispered.

'We'll be with you in forty seconds. Get ready for the transfer,' replied Calypso over the comms link.

Johnny let loose some of his guide cable and floated out until it went taut. He was now completely exposed on all sides. He stared at the window, waiting for them to appear. After what seemed like an age, the window opened and Calypso signalled to him. Cormac was right behind her. They took off their backpacks and took out three zip line clips each, attaching one to each of the bags before securing them to the cable Johnny had shot into the wall earlier, sending them sliding down towards Johnny who caught, detached and placed them on the floor of his small dinghy. The transfer had taken less than five minutes to complete as Calypso sent the last bag down to him.

'That's it, Johnny. Are the bags all secured?'

'Yes, all secured. I'll see you and Cormac at the agreed rendezvous to pick me up in an hour,' Johnny whispered in reply.

He cut through both the cables with his knife, put his oars back in the water, flipped down his night vision goggles and adjusted his position. The current was moving fast and he let it take him as if he were a piece of large driftwood on the water. He knew he wouldn't be safe until he had passed the police security checkpoints.

Adam and LJ had managed to sneak back into the party and were making a beeline for the exit. As they made their way through the sea of drunken, masked guests, Adam remembered his promise to Amy. He grabbed LJ's hand and brought her in close to him.

'Head straight out the main door and get the car ready.'

'Wait, why aren't you coming?' replied LJ, alarmed that Adam was deviating from the plan.

'I'll be along in a moment. I have to take care of one last bit of unfinished business.'

LJ headed to the exit. Adam looked around the hall for Amy. He hadn't been able to shake her out of his mind since leaving her and the party over an hour ago. As he scanned the room, he caught a glimpse of her silvery dress by a table and went straight over to her.

'You know you should never drink alone, Amy.'

'Adam, there you are, I was wondering where you'd got to,' Amy replied, her face lighting up.

'I'm sorry I took so long; however, I'm afraid I have to leave. My business matter couldn't be resolved over the phone.'

'Oh, are you sure you can't stay a bit longer?'

'I'm afraid not, but I'd like to make it up to you. How about dinner, and we can pick up where we left off?'

'Dinner? Well, I'm not too sure when I'll be free next.'

'That's okay, here's my card. My personal number's on the back; call me any time and we'll arrange something if you'd like to. Goodnight, Amy, enjoy the rest of your evening,' Adam replied, tenderly kissing her on the cheek.

He exited the hall and rushed down the red carpet to LJ who was waiting behind the wheel of their Range Rover. He opened the car door and jumped into the passenger seat, slamming the door behind him. LJ pulled out of the parking space and sped off, slapping the steering wheel with pride that they'd got away with it. He looked down at his watch. It was now just after midnight: time to set off the charges. By now Calypso's virus would have been released into the security mainframe and done its job. Adam also hoped that the others had all got clean away and that Amy would be safe in the chaos that was about to ensue. He pressed the button on the remote detonator.

The magnetic charges exploded one after the other inside the vault, ripping the safety-deposit boxes to pieces. The force of the explosions inside the confined area of the vault increased the mag charges' explosive yield so much that a fireball erupted, blowing out the huge vault door and almost ripping it off its hinges as it slammed into the side wall with an ear-piercing crash. The fireball travelled through the undercroft, cracking the marble walls, and engulfed the antechamber. It continued up through the open entrance, spewing fiery debris and black smoke into the House of Lords, shattering and blowing out all the beautiful stained-glass windows and setting the wooden interior ablaze.

Panic erupted inside Westminster Hall as the sound and shock waves from the explosion rippled through the entire palace, causing the electricity to black out. In the hysteria, Prime Minister George Brooks was grabbed by his personal security and escorted out of a side exit with haste as the other guests made a run for the main exit, screaming in terror.

Over in St James's Park, Tom Phoenix and his fellow protesters watched as a breath of flame erupted over the treeline followed by rising black smoke which billowed up into the night sky. The police officers assigned to the park began securing the area to contain the crowd who were now frightened and becoming twitchy. Realising the severity of the situation, Tom rushed over to the makeshift stage, grabbed the microphone and began speaking in an attempt to calm the crowd down and keep them from causing a stampede.

Adam and LJ watched as swarms of emergency and security service vehicles rushed past them towards Westminster Palace in the opposite direction. They carried on in silence to the rendezvous point.

CHAPTER SEVENTEEN

There wasn't a single person from Land's End to John O'Groats who wasn't speculating on last night's explosive events at the government's controversial masquerade ball. What on earth had happened? Smoke and ash permeated the air around the damaged Palace of Westminster which was still in total lockdown with a five-hundred-metre restriction zone in place. All spectators had been evacuated and no member of the public was allowed in or out under any circumstances. Emergency and security service personnel and vehicles were scattered all over the place.

Outside the restriction zone, members of the national and international press were salivating like hungry wolves at the unfolding events. The statement released in the early hours of this morning by the palace's press relations office indicated the cause of the blast was a severe gas explosion. Yet the press thought this brief statement was a feeble explanation carrying very little credibility given the level of security activity, the damage to electronic devices and the lack of any further information. They could smell potential blood in the water, but with little else to go on, and no more updated information from the palace's press relations team or Downing Street forthcoming, the inevitable tide of rampant speculation took hold. Everything, no matter how reasonable or downright crazy, was being discussed and debated, from the ghost of Guy Fawkes taking his revenge to far right and left anarchists or terrorist groups trying to upend the establishment and terrorise the country; or even it being an innocuous gas explosion as first reported.

Agent Amy Johnson stood outside one of the entrances to the palace, holding a flask of strong black coffee. Having suffered only minor abrasions and bruises, and a mild concussion from the chaos that had ensued after the explosion, Amy had been kept in overnight at St Thomas's Hospital for observation, much to her irritation. While being checked over, she took it upon herself to write up her witness statement while it was still fresh in her head, and then spent the next few uncomfortable hours under observation before being discharged and picked up by the car that Robbie had sent for her to take her home. Amy had other ideas. She pulled rank and made the SI7 driver wait for her while she went up to her apartment to change and freshen up, before taking her to the Palace of Westminster.

Amy entered the palace and headed towards the House of Lords. Though she felt fine, her face showed clear signs of stress and fatigue. In the back of her mind she knew her experience from last night had left her a little shaken. Nevertheless, her personal feelings and traumas would have to wait for the reluctant conversation with the

SI7 shrink she knew she was going to have to have at some point. Right now, the overriding feeling currently welling up inside her was anger. Anger at herself for having had too much of a good time last night and not being more alert, and anger at the preliminary reports Robbie had updated her with. There was no doubt that the Baker Street Five had carried out this attack on parliament, and she had two burning questions on her mind. How had the Baker Street Five managed to slip into one of the world's most secure buildings undetected, right under their noses, and get clean away? And why had they suddenly changed their MO? This was the first time in over a year's worth of investigations that they'd changed how they operated from covert to overt with a literal bang. Amy knew this had to be significant in some way.

As she stepped over the threshold into the Lords' chamber, she was met with a sorry sight. The entire chamber had almost been completely burned out and was water damaged from the firemen fighting to extinguish the blaze which had consumed most of the old opulent furnishings and furniture. The smell of burnt wood, charred leather from the once burgundy red benches, and smouldering heaps of ash, debris and twisted metal hung in the hazy, sunlit air. Stone, mortar and glass cracked underneath her feet. The chamber was a hive of activity with authorised personnel surveying the damage and collecting potential evidence. But despite all this activity, Amy was still trying to process the devastation. Her eyes were drawn to the now vacant limestone window frames where stained-glass windows depicting religion, chivalry and law once proudly stood. Now they'd been completely blown out. Even a substantial section of the public gallery had also collapsed.

At the opposite end of the chamber, by the toppled sovereign's gold throne and canopy, Agent Robbie Ellis was hunched over a table with one of his MI5 counterparts: a man called Calder who Amy regarded as an interfering nuisance. Two team leaders from the fire brigade and the police were also with them, examining evidence collected by the forensic teams. Next to the examination table lay the now exposed, smouldering secret entrance to the undercroft chamber. Even Amy was taken aback when Robbie reported its discovery to her. Now, seeing it for the first time with her own eyes, it reminded her of a rotting wound that had finally burst.

As she approached, Amy could see Robbie was engrossed in deep conversation with them as they pored over the evidence bags. She'd always admired how thorough and meticulous Robbie was when he was going over the evidence. Looking up for a moment from his examinations, Robbie did a double take.

'Amy, what are you doing here? I told you go home and rest. I can handle things here for the time being,' said Robbie, embracing her.

'Thanks, but I'm fine. You know I wouldn't sleep or relax at home, and I'd rather be here being useful in trying to deal with this mess.' Amy gestured to the destruction that surrounded them.

'I know, but—'

'What the hell is Calder doing here? Is Thames House trying to muscle in on our investigation or just make us look like we don't know what we're doing?' Amy's voice was peppered with animosity and suspicion.

'Relax. Calder is just an observer and liaison for Thames House; they've no say over our investigation. Control had to concede some ground given the explosion and it potentially being an act of terrorism. This does kind of fall under MI5's remit.'

'Fine, but keep him away from me. The last thing I need right now is another idiot in Home Secretary Jackson's mould hounding me with stupid questions. And before you ask, I haven't heard from him, which is unusual.'

'Ah, I've news on that front. Control has managed to get Jackson and the others off our backs for a while. He put in a strongly worded complaint, and given the gravity of what's going on here, the PM agreed to keep everyone at bay for now.'

'That's one blessing. Anyway, enough about them. Bring me up to speed. Where do we stand and how much do the press know?'

'The press know nothing beyond the statement issued to them this morning; that a severe gas leak sparked and caused a massive explosion. I asked our gurus in the media department to monitor all social media platforms, and they've reported that speculation is rife. The press smell blood in the water.'

'Well, give them credit; they're not stupid, and they're bang on the money that this isn't a simple gas explosion. We'd best get the palace public relations team to issue another statement to keep the wolves at bay a little longer.'

'I'll get onto that once I've finished briefing you.'

'Thanks, Robbie. You'd better give me the rundown on everything since your last report but make it the abridged version. You can fill me in on every detail later back at the office.'

'Well, thanks to the fire brigade's brave efforts, they've managed to contain the fire and stopped it spreading, saving any potential evidence for us to find and collect. We've structural engineers on site making sure the shock wave from the explosion hasn't compromised the rest of the palace's structure. Four of our forensic teams are also on site, one in here as this chamber seems to have been our elusive friend's main objective, and the others dotted about the palace and grounds at various points thanks to witness accounts from the security personnel who encountered our friends before they were incapacitated by them.'

'Were there any fatalities?'

'No, they've all got headaches and will feel a bit groggy for a while, but other than that they'll recover, which fits with our friends' MO of incapacitating and not killing their targets.'

'Do we know how the hell they got into the palace and bypassed all the security protocols?'

'As I said, we have the forensic teams working on it, but it looks like they may have gained entry from the old disused Victorian sewer system; and as for bypassing the security protocols, it appears they managed to take over the Central Security Control room as the guards were all found incapacitated in the kitchen. The CSC is a complete mess inside.'

'Christ almighty, no wonder they felt comfortable wandering about, without fear. Is there any chance of recovering any security footage?'

'I don't know yet. According to our tech guys, the security systems have been badly damaged by some sort of virus, set off, no doubt, by our friends, as well as the explosion. They really weren't taking any chances. The internal chips and circuitry of the servers and the data saved on them might be beyond repair, but we won't know until our tech guys have been over every inch of them.'

'Great. Do we at least know how they escaped?' said Amy.

'It's possible that they went back the way they came, but they may have also escaped by boat. There's evidence to suggest such a scenario. I've got one of our forensic teams checking it out. They'll give me their report later this afternoon.'

'A river escape? That's pretty ballsy of them given the extensive perimeter security we had in place,' said Amy, kicking a piece of rubble to the side.

'Given the chaos that ensued, I think we could cut them a little slack. I know you're pissed off. So am I, but let's put any recriminations aside for now.'

'You're damn right I'm pissed off, but I'm sorry for snapping at you. I didn't mean to,' Amy replied with a deep sigh of vexation.

'It's okay. Are you sure you want to continue?'

'Yes, I'm sure.'

'Good, because you're not going to like the next part of our discussion, or the tour.' Robbie wrapped his arm around her shoulder and ushered her closer towards the exposed and smouldering secret entrance to the undercroft.

'What have you found down there, Robbie?'

'You'd better have a look for yourself, but I'll say this: we're standing on what's left of the proverbial Pandora's box. Follow me down, and watch your step.'

Amy took another gulp of coffee from her flask before placing it on the table. She acknowledged Calder and the others who were still gathered round the table of evidence, before following Robbie down into what was left of the secret undercroft chamber.

CHAPTER EIGHTEEN

Amy reached the bottom of the staircase and followed Robbie through the narrow, blackened, wood-panelled corridor. Treading carefully, they stepped over the puddles in the chamber foyer. A miasma of lingering smoke, made visible by the portable forensic lights, filled the dense air in the chamber which was still warm despite the fire having been extinguished. The chamber roof was being held up by structural supports supplied by the fire brigade in case of any collapse. Amy couldn't believe what she was seeing as she looked around and searched the chamber. Kicking aside some debris and rubble, she caught sight of the huge purple parliament crest imprinted on the now cracked black marble floor. She knelt down to translate the motto:

'"Secrecy is the key to wealth and power." Huh? Someone has a twisted sense of humour.'

'That's not the half of it; wait until you see inside the vault itself.' Robbie walked past, ushering her to follow.

Amy followed him down the vault corridor, past the damaged vault door which was now embedded in the marble and steel wall. As they entered the damaged vault room itself, they were met with the sight of twisted metal and shrapnel from the broken and displaced safety-deposit boxes. Amy picked up one of the damaged pieces of metal to examine but it flew out of her hand and stuck to the wall.

'What the hell was that?' she asked, taken aback.

'Give us five minutes, guys,' Robbie said to the forensic personnel, who took their leave from the vault.

'Apologies, Amy, I should've warned you about that. It appears whatever explosives they used left some highly magnetised residue behind, which also could explain why the electronic devices went out last night as well. Our experts are analysing traces of the explosives and they should get back to us later this afternoon with their findings. What do you think, then?'

'Well, they've outdone themselves this time, that's for sure. What do we know so far about this underground vault room?' Amy was awestruck. It was quite surreal to see it all.

'According to every official building schematic the ferrets at HQ could find, this undercroft should no longer exist as it was supposedly destroyed in the fire of eighteen thirty-four; but here it is, and I think we can both guess what our so-called noble and common friends were storing down here from the strewn debris and damaged safety-deposit boxes,' replied Robbie, kicking one of the empty boxes aside.

'What are our so-called noble and common friends saying?'

'Nothing. They know damn well what's down here, but they're all keeping quiet. Too afraid of the impending fallout, I imagine.'

'No surprise; you can smell the stench of corruption a mile away. But nevertheless, we will continue to do our jobs professionally and we will not withhold any evidence that comes to light. I don't care if it's damaging to them. Is that understood, Robbie?'

'Of course, and I agree, which is why I've asked that any and all potential evidence from these boxes is to be stored separately and catalogued for the CPS to review after we're finished with them.'

'Did our elusive friends leave their usual calling card?'

Robbie stepped over to the buckled stainless steel sorting table and picked up the evidence bag containing the magnetised and charred trademark of the Baker Street Five, and handed it over to Amy.

'Yes, they left us their usual parting gift but with something written on the back this time. A pretty hefty ransom demand, don't you think?'

Amy skim-read the back of their infamous trademark card. The typed laminated message was still legible and hadn't been too burnt by the fire.

'Something's troubling me, Robbie. Why change their MO now when they've been using stealth tactics over the past year to steal from their targets? It makes no sense for them to use explosives and up their ante from thieves to terrorists.'

'Look, I don't believe they're terrorists. Part of me wants to say they've become even bolder, but the other part thinks there's a bigger game afoot here than we realise. I think they wanted us to find this place and that everything over the past year is connected somehow. We just need to fit the pieces together.'

Amy had always admired how Robbie could make her feel better through his optimism. In the six years they'd been partners at SI7 they'd shared many strange and exciting adventures, which had garnered a mutual sense of loyalty and trust between them.

'Okay, I've seen enough for now. Let's go back up top.' She glanced around the vault room once more. 'Did the security officers offer any descriptions of our elusive friends?'

'No, all they could provisionally tell me was that they were dressed all in black and their faces were covered by masks. One officer from the CSC did say that before he passed out completely, he thought he heard the two Baker Street Five members talking about their two accomplices at the ball, but he couldn't remember if they mentioned any names,' replied Robbie.

At that moment an SI7 messenger came rushing into the chamber and handed Amy a handwritten note. It was from Ten Downing Street, requesting her presence at once.

'Robbie, I have to leave. But here's what I want you to do. Keep pressing the security personnel for details, especially the one who overheard two of our elusive friends talking about their accomplices at the party. Clearly two guests from last night are involved, which explains a lot. I want you to coordinate with our other departments and go through the guest list, making all the usual checks. Also, don't forget to ensure the palace press office issues another statement; maybe give them a few pointers. Then, I want you to bag and tag as much evidence as you can and bring it all straight back to SI7 headquarters.'

'Okay, but that may take a good while, considering the size of the guest list.'

'That's okay; I'll hopefully be back in a couple of hours to give you a hand.'

'Fine, but where are you off to now?'

'I've been summoned to Downing Street; so much for that guarantee. I guess it's time to face the jackals, who are no doubt anxious to know how much we've uncovered. I'll see you later.'

CHAPTER NINETEEN

Outside Ten Downing Street, a large contingent of journalists from various news outlets had gathered under the watchful eyes of an increased security presence. They'd all been searched, hemmed in like sheep behind security barriers, told to wait patiently, and informed that the Prime Minister would be making a brief statement in due course. Despite their best efforts to probe their usually reliable sources for information, the press couldn't get a single comment or statement from anyone in an official or unofficial capacity. It was as if everyone in the Westminster establishment had developed a severe case of deliberate mutism. What were they all hiding and what didn't they want us to know? were the burning questions on all their minds.

A Jaguar XJ carrying Home Secretary Eric Jackson sped through the gates of Downing Street and pulled up outside Number Ten. Stepping out of the vehicle, Home Secretary Jackson, puffing heavily on his trademark cigar, was met by a barrage of camera flashes and an endless stream of quick-fire questions from the throng of journalists.

'Home Secretary, Home Secretary, do you have any comment on last night's events?'

'Can you tell us why there has been such a veil of silence from the government?'

'What are you hiding from us and the public if this is just a simple gas explosion?'

'Was this a terrorist attack on the British Parliament?'

'I've no comment or statement to make at this time,' said Home Secretary Jackson, waving to the press as if everything was normal. He ignored their questions and scrambled into Number Ten to escape their scrutinising gazes.

As the door of Number Ten closed behind him, Jackson took out his pocket square and wiped the beads of sweat running down his face. He would never admit this to anyone but he was afraid, and he knew that if they didn't get a handle on this fiasco soon, they'd all be serving some quality time at Her Majesty's pleasure. The atmosphere inside Number Ten was a mixture of controlled chaos and confusion as staff dashed about in every direction like headless chickens, paperwork clasped in their hands, pages of which were coming loose and spilling out onto the floor. Number Ten's switchboard was ringing off the hook, the staff unsure of what to say to the callers other than 'No comment at this time' or 'We'll get back to you'.

Home Secretary Jackson made his way through the chaos from the grand hallway down the corridor to the cabinet room, pushing the junior staff aside if they got in his way. He heard raised and panicked voices resonating from within. Straightening himself up and slicking back what was left of his waning hairline to look presentable, he took a deep breath and entered. His colleagues were bickering among themselves but fell silent the moment they saw him. All eyes were on him as they waited with bated breath to hear the news he'd gathered from his discreet enquiries. Prime Minister Brooks stood up. His thin, bony face was contorted with an expression of tempered anger and frustration.

'Well, Eric? Stop standing there looking like a gormless idiot. What did you find out? And how much did those bastards take us for?'

'Everything, George. My contacts tell me over half the safety-deposit boxes were looted, and both the vault and the undercroft have been pretty much destroyed. Of course, I may have acquired more detailed information had you allowed me to lean on that bitch Agent Johnson instead of—'

'Oh, will you shut up about Agent Johnson? Whatever your problem is with her, you'd better bury it right now, because if she's worked out what our little secret chamber is for, she'll bury us with it – I am in no doubt of that. Besides, I've requested her presence here,' said Brooks, cutting off Home Secretary Jackson's rant.

'Are you fucking serious, George? Why the hell have you asked her here? You don't invite the fox into the hen house if you know she can smell blood.'

'Do not question my judgement. I warn you, Eric, you'd better sit down now and shut up before we both say something we regret later. Now!'

Home Secretary Jackson took his seat without another word, but he was positively seething inside. How dare Brooks speak to him like that? How dare he invite that unreliable bitch here? He might as well have put the rope around their necks and activated the trap door.

Prime Minister Brooks leant heavily on the table, head in hands, while the rest of the cabinet resumed their infighting. Talk of resignations and ruin began to surface, breaking out into another heated debate of recrimination.

'Quiet, all of you.' Brooks's gruff voice cut through the monotonous infighting. He began circling round the table like a vulture searching for his pound of flesh.

'Instead of bickering amongst each other like a bunch of snivelling cowards, how about you help me work out what I'm going to say to that rabble outside? They expect and want answers, and we'd better have something good to give them so they can swallow it as the truth.'

'I agree, Prime Minister. It's imperative we control the narrative before the narrative runs away and writes itself,' said Foreign Secretary Miller, his high-pitched voice anxious with foreboding.

'Thank you for that startlingly stupid answer, Miller. What do you suggest we do, then? Seeing as you seem so keen to share your thoughts …'

'We stick to the story about the gas explosion. Nothing's been reported to say otherwise, and why give the press more ammunition or speculation than they already have?'

'You're a naïve fool, Miller,' interjected Home Secretary Jackson. 'How dense do you think the press are? They can already smell blood and they know something's up. With this level of exposure they will find out, mark my words, so if you're going to speak, at least have something credible and useful to say.'

'Don't you talk to me like that, you self-absorbed narcissist. This mess is your doing, and if your agents at SI7 were better—'

Brooks slammed his hand down on the table to shut them both up, making Foreign Secretary Miller and the other cabinet members jump. He continued circling around the cabinet table as if he were a headmaster in charge of a dysfunctional group of ill-disciplined students.

'Does anyone else have anything useful to contribute, or are you all just going to sit there in silence like a bunch of whipped dogs?' Brooks's voice was filled with contempt. The rest of the cabinet remained silent. 'Right then, let me give you something a little less vexing to handle. This is a question I've been asking myself since last night.'

'And what is that, George?' asked one of the other cabinet ministers.

'How did the Baker Street Five find out about and gain access to our little secret? Because in my mind, there's only one possible explanation.'

'What are you saying, George?'

'There's a Judas among us. Someone sitting around this table or from one of the other parties must have told them about the vault and given them their access card to infiltrate the undercroft and steal from us all.'

'This is outrageous, George. How dare you even think that one of us would be—'

'There's only one way to prove it. All of you, hand over your security passes right now.'

Exasperated, the rest of the cabinet dug into their wallets and bags for their passes. Defence Secretary Richard Ashworth, who'd been found unconscious during the security evacuation sweep of the palace, was completely unaware of the unwitting role he'd played in the Baker Street Five's plan. He'd remained silent throughout the ongoing spectacle, sitting in a corner of the room nursing a severe hangover and bruised ribs with no memory of what had happened to him. Though he was feeling awful, he managed to fish out what he thought was his pass and held it out in front of him.

Prime Minister Brooks went around to each of them, taking their passes. They might have all appeared to have their passes on them, but that didn't mean that someone might be holding a fake to throw him off the scent. Somebody must have talked and somebody must have helped them – but how, and, more importantly, who?

'Eric, what about the other parties and their members who had safety-deposit boxes in the vault?' asked Prime Minister Brooks.

'I spoke with the other leaders earlier on your behalf and they're adamant that none of their members has betrayed us, George,' replied Home Secretary Jackson, stubbing out his cigar.

'And you believe them?'

'Yes, I'm sure. Their members are too feeble and too intimidated by you to have orchestrated something on this scale, much less hire the Baker Street Five.'

'Well, I don't believe them, and you're going to go back to Clarke and Donaldson and force them to gather up their members' security passes and meet at the usual place, so we can test them all out and make sure they're telling the truth.'

'They won't like that, George.'

'I don't care what they like. And while you're at it, I've decided you're going to draw up a DA notice to issue to the press to protect us and anyone potentially damaged by any fallout.'

'George, that won't wash. We'd be admitting to lying to the British public about what really happened last night; not to mention the press will have a field day citing the Freedom of Information—'

'Fuck the Freedom of Information Act, Eric. National security comes first. Just get the bloody notice prepared and ready to be distributed to all major departments and news outlets.'

'I'm afraid you're too late for that, Prime Minister,' said a calm and collected voice. All the cabinet members turned their heads in the direction of the doorway to see who the voice belonged to.

'Sorry, but the door was open and I couldn't help but hear your conversation,' Agent Amy Johnson continued.

'Agent Johnson, at last. What do you mean, it's too late?'

'I suggest you turn on the news and see for yourself, Prime Minister,' she replied.

Brooks switched the TV screen on the back wall to BBC News 24.

'Sources have now confirmed that the explosion which occurred last night at Westminster Palace, inside the House of Lords' chamber during the government's annual and controversial masquerade ball, was not caused by a simple gas explosion but was, in fact, an explosive device used by the infamous Baker Street Five. Further reports have also confirmed the explosives were used to bring to light a secret underground vault said to have contained the illicit fortunes and scandalous secrets of high-ranking government and parliamentary officials.'

Everyone around the cabinet table was speechless, except Agent Amy Johnson who had a look of utter contempt on her face. The cabinet's worst nightmare had been realised. They continued to listen, unable to take their eyes off the screen.

'In related news, *The Times* newspaper has confirmed they have received damning evidence from the Baker Street Five concerning Foreign Secretary David Miller. Photographs stolen by them from the vault last night, which have been independently verified as genuine, suggest that the Foreign Secretary has been partaking in bondage with a certain Miss—'

'Oh my God, I'm ruined,' said Foreign Secretary Miller, falling off his chair.

Smash! Prime Minister Brooks violently threw a water carafe from the cabinet table at the television, shattering the screen into pieces. The fallout from this was potentially career-ending for them all, but he wasn't going without a fight.

CHAPTER TWENTY

A wall of tiredness crept up over Agent Robbie Ellis as he sat at his desk, surrounded by a mountain of evidence bags, witness statements and preliminary reports that didn't seem to decrease despite his best efforts. It had been a very long and stressful day, and he didn't even want to look at the other piles of evidence bags still to be logged.

Robbie looked up at the wall clock and checked his own watch. It was after seven. Where the hell had Amy got to? He stared at his computer screen, frustrated by her continued absence. It had been hours since they'd last spoken to one another. Given the bombshells the Baker Street Five had dropped throughout the afternoon – the first of many revelations, no doubt – he assumed that the Downing Street clowns would be too self-absorbed with their own fears or hiding themselves away to detain Amy for this long. Rubbing his hand over his eyes, Robbie stood up from his chair to stretch. His entire body ached from having been stationary for so long. He even felt hungry for the first time in hours, but his stomach would have to wait a little longer. Right now, he needed a pick-me-up to keep himself awake.

He poured himself some strong coffee and went back to his desk, sat down and reached into his bottom drawer, pulling out a tattered hardback copy of an old John le Carré novel entitled *The*

Perfect Spy. It was one of his favourite stories from the master espionage writer, but the inside of the book had been hollowed out to conceal a silver hip flask containing some very fine cognac. Robbie poured a little into his coffee, stirring it in with the end of his pen. He took a sip and savoured the taste. It was just what he needed. Over thirty years in intelligence, despite the more modern and stricter regulations about drinking on the job, had taught him to always keep some on hand for medicinal purposes when working on a very complex and stressful case.

It was time to switch things up. He decided to go through the Westminster Hall footage that the tech department had salvaged from what was left of the CSC mainframes. Robbie was intrigued by the witness statement from one of the palace security officers about potential accomplices or members of the Baker Street Five being at the ball. If he scrutinised the salvaged footage for long enough he might find something of interest, and maybe Amy would be back by then.

An hour and a half later, and for a third and final time, Robbie replayed the footage from the hall. His eyes had become strained and he decided that after this last viewing he was going to call it a night. Reviewing the footage on repeat like this felt like looking for a needle in a haystack, but he was confident that he may have found something of potential interest, even if it was only circumstantial. The door to their office creaked open. Robbie looked up and saw Amy leaning against the door, looking flustered and tired. Clearly she'd been put through the ringer by them all.

'Evening, Robbie. I'm so sorry I've been away all day and left you to cope with everything on your own, but after the afternoon I've had I needed some time,' said Amy, her voice hoarse and sounding strained.

'I can't say I've enjoyed being left to cope with all this but I understand why. I was starting to get worried they were going to detain you indefinitely. Where have you been? Come on, sit down. I'll fix you a drink and you can tell me what's been going on.'

Amy took off her overcoat and sat down next to Robbie who was rifling through his bottom drawer again for his flask of cognac. 'Here, drink some of this, it'll help.'

'Thanks, but I don't think I should, not on duty; and in any case, I don't fancy the regulations being read to me if Control catches us.'

'One, our shift ended half an hour ago, and two, I happen to know Control keeps a bottle of Scotch in a file marked "Eyes Only" on top of his filing cabinets. Besides, this is purely medicinal and you look like you need it.' Robbie held out the flask. Amy took a large swig and handed it back.

'That's better. Now, tell me what happened in that nest of vipers.'

'In all honesty, I've never seen anything like it, Robbie. There was so much recrimination and venomous vitriol being thrown around that table, I think everyone had a bite taken out of them. There wasn't one shred of decency or real remorse between them, not even when our elusive friends dropped that bombshell about Miller's extramarital affair or the others that followed. All they cared about was self-preservation above all else.

'Then, as I was on my way out after a drawn-out, heated discussion with them, Home Secretary Jackson pulled me into a side room and wanted to know about the ransom demand the Baker Street Five had left. He'd found out about it through one of his little spies and demanded why I hadn't shared it with the cabinet. I then spent the next three hours arguing it out with him to no avail. We parted on less than amicable terms and I've no doubt he's told Prime Minister Brooks by now.'

Robbie took a last swig from the hip flask. 'I've been catching the news reports this afternoon. I didn't think that little weasel Miller had it in him to have an affair, let alone bondage. As for Jackson, forget him. It's an inconvenience that he knows about the ransom demand, but he's an insufferable arsehole and we're going to ignore him; all of them, for that matter. Our job is to catch the Baker Street Five, not play nursemaid to those chinless morons. They made their choices, Amy, and they can face the consequences of their actions. We should have a word with Control in the morning about having a Chinese wall put between our investigation and the government, given the mounting evidence we have and the revelations that have come to light so far.'

'I agree. Let's do that in the morning first thing and get the ball rolling.'

'Good. So where did you go after your fallout with Jackson?'

'I decided to go back to the palace; you know, get a feel for the place and how our elusive friends managed to pull it off. It's helped me focus and get some perspective, but I lost track of the time. Anyway, enough about that. How have you been getting on? I can see you've been hard at work.'

'We hit a wall with all but one of the eyewitnesses, I'm afraid, and most of the security footage was irretrievable. Our tech guys found traces of a highly intricate virus in the CSC mainframes which, combined with the magnetic pulse charges that were set off, contributed to their destruction. However, despite these setbacks, the tech guys were able to recover some of the footage from Westminster Hall, which I've been going over for the last hour and a half. Before I get to that, though, do you remember the security officer who said he overheard two of the Baker Street Five talking about their accomplices or other members who were at the ball?'

'Yes. His witness account sounded very promising. Have you been able to corroborate anything he said?'

'I think so but—'

'You found something?' said Amy, excited at this new development.

'It's circumstantial at best, but who's this guy you spent some of the evening talking to?' Robbie isolated and enlarged the image from the security footage on his screen.

'His name is Adam Knight.'

'The philanthropist and CEO of Knight Technologies?'

'Yes, we met by chance last night – believe it or not, through Jackson. He was quite a hard man to read. Between us, I found him enigmatic and charming, and he made the evening pass more pleasantly than I was expecting; until the explosion, of course. Are you telling me he's a person of interest?' Amy replied with unease in her voice.

'It's possible. You see, I've been over this footage several times and as far as I can tell, only three people are unaccounted for during the time period we estimate the robbery to have been carried out: Adam Knight; Defence Secretary Ashworth, who we found unconscious in his office during the evacuation security sweeps; and the woman you can see here, who I've identified as Lady Joanna Gray. She happens to be the daughter of our ambassador to Canada and she appears to have been Knight's plus one last night. Did you know he'd come with a plus one?'

Amy paused for a moment. She didn't know if it was jealousy or anger, but whatever the ill feelings were, they were making her blood boil. She already felt guilty and foolish for having had too much of a good time and not being alert, but to discover the man she'd spent a portion of the evening with, and who she found intriguing, was now a chief suspect was beyond the pale.

'No, he didn't mention he'd come with anyone else and I didn't see this Lady Joanna Gray all evening. Anyway, how can you tell they were the only three people to leave the hall? It was crowded and we were all wearing masks,' she replied, trying to hide her anger.

'Precisely, and thanks to palace security measures, every guest at the party had to provide a detailed description of what they would be wearing on the night, including their unique masks, which meant we could use the masks to identify everyone on-screen.'

'That's brilliant, Robbie, but how do you know that some of the guests didn't change their outfit at the last minute?'

'Because they had to notify palace security of any changes twenty-four hours beforehand, otherwise they wouldn't get in.

Thankfully, I also found out that all the guests' pictures were secretly taken on arrival and their names checked off with a time stamp. Palace security paranoia at its finest, but their over efficiency was ours to take advantage of. Did Mr Knight say anything to you before he left?'

'He received a message during our conversation and mentioned that he needed to make an important phone call regarding a defence contract that had gone off track. Did you find him on any other footage outside the hall, making that phone call?'

'No, but as I said earlier, the rest of the palace footage was too corrupted to retrieve. I did question witnesses from the hall to see if they had seen him or the other two leave, but it didn't lead anywhere. The phone call he allegedly made should be easy enough to check out, but let me put it this way: the only time he reappears again on-screen in the hall is when he's walking towards the exit with Lady Joanna Gray, just before changing course to talk to you at the bar and, I assume, say goodnight, before leaving prior to the explosion.'

As Robbie continued to report his findings, she heard his voice fade in and out. Although she would never admit it, her mind was reeling. Had Adam played her like a fiddle? She knew Robbie was right when he said this was all circumstantial, yet what he'd found was compelling, regardless of how shaky a foundation they had built it on.

'Amy … Amy?' Robbie waved his hand in front of her eyes to bring her back to reality.

'Sorry, Robbie, I was lost in thought.' She hoped he hadn't seen any bitterness on her face.

'I said there's more. Forensics came back with a hit on the explosives they used. They're called magnetic pulse charges. Very nasty devices, by all accounts. Anyway, I did a little digging in Companies House's records, and the company that designed and owned the patent on these devices, Ares Incorporated, was bought out and taken over by Knight Technologies a year ago.'

Robbie brought up the file on his computer screen for Amy to have a look at. She reached over for the mouse and began skim-reading the important contents of the file on the background and purchase of Ares Incorporated by Knight Technologies. To Robbie's credit, it confirmed most of what he'd said. It warranted further investigation, but how best to approach it? This was the icing on the cake to a terrible day. She wanted so much to pick something up and hurl it against the wall, but what would that solve? No, she needed time to reassess everything and put it into perspective before making their next move.

'Okay, Robbie, you've given me a lot to think about. Why don't you head home? You've done more than enough for today. I'm going to stay here for a while and go through some more evidence.

Plus, I need some time to gather my thoughts.'

'Are you sure? I can stay if you need me to.'

'No, I'll be fine. Thanks for everything and for the drink. See

you tomorrow.'

CHAPTER TWENTY-ONE

The ambient night lamps of Hyde Park sprang into life as darkness fell across the capital. Adam Knight, dressed in casual evening wear, cycled fast through the grounds. He'd left the others and the secure confines of the safe house above the Atlantic Club flush with reserved pride from the previous night's success and the first wave of information bombshells he and the others had dropped this afternoon that had the entire country talking. Though Adam was looking a little worn due to lack of sleep thanks to his recurring nightmares, he was running on adrenaline and caffeine. Despite his fatigue, Adam was on his way to keep a very important appointment at the confessional of St John's Church, where he was meeting up with his most important contact and source in Whitehall. The location for the meeting with Aree was an unusual if innocuous choice on Adam's part, but it served its purpose as a primary information exchange drop and also as a means of giving Aree new instructions for the next phases of his plan without arousing too much attention.

Adam checked his watch. He had fifteen minutes to get to St John's, otherwise Aree would walk away and leave a marker as to when they could next meet. Adam vaulted out of the park's western gate driveway, ignoring the vehicles whose drivers were honking their horns at him for his recklessness. He followed Brook Street all the way round, flew over the roundabout, up and past Gloucester Square, on to Southwick Place and finally Hyde Park Crescent, where he cycled across into the grounds of the old Victorian church. Having locked his bike up against a railing, Adam walked at a swift but steady pace up the stone steps to the church doors. He looked up at the faded grandeur of its exterior walls and couldn't help but reflect on how it symbolised the state of a country that was now in flux. It had changed so much since this church's construction, and yet, it was stuck in the past where its establishment and institutions were still clutching onto the last shreds of an identity that had declined and was no longer relevant. He hoped this would change if he succeeded in his plans.

Entering the church, Adam was greeted by the sight of an evening mass being performed and attended by a small group of its devoted congregation. A heavy, perfumed aroma of incense saturated the air. Adam wasn't a religious man by any means, but he paid his respects and moved as quietly as possible, so as not to disturb the service, towards the small confessional box in one corner of the church. He entered one of the small compartments.

'Tell me, my son: is it better to be a saint or a sinner?' said a calm, clear voice on the other side of the confessional window.

'It is better to be both, for no one is all good or all evil,' he replied.

'Good evening, Adam. It's good to see you, even if you are a minute late.'

'Thank you, Aree, and yes, I realise I'm a minute late. You don't have to infer the protocol to me; I wrote it, remember? In any case, it couldn't be helped, and you did decide to wait.' Aree's affinity for timekeeping irritated him.

'You make a fair point. My humble congratulations to you all on a job well done so far. The colonel would be very pleased and proud.'

'Thanks, I'll pass along your compliments. So tell me, what's the chatter been like in the halls of power? Did you manage to clean up any compromising evidence we may have left at the palace in our haste? What about the security footage?'

'Whitehall is all a quiver with chatter over this. They're all scared, owing to the amount of people that could be implicated. I have it on good authority that Prime Minister Brooks and his cabinet were blowing a gasket in this afternoon's emergency cabinet meeting. As for any incriminating evidence, don't worry about it; your mag charges and virus destroyed most of the security footage. I'm running interference through all the usual channels and have taken care of anything that could lead directly to you.'

The church organ began to play as members of the congregation stood up to sing the last hymn of the mass, interrupting Adam and Aree's conversation for a moment. Its angelic sound echoed loudly around the church.

'Good. As always, Aree, you're the best. Now, have you managed to put Agent Johnson onto me yet? It's time to start reeling her in and have her dancing to our timeline.'

'Yes, the seeds of suspicion have been planted and I expect you will be hearing from her tomorrow or the day after. I still don't see why we needed to pull her in. It's a very risky strategy, and I warn you – she isn't to be underestimated at any cost.'

'I'm well aware of Agent Johnson's talents, now more than ever. I can handle it, and besides, we need her; she forms a necessary part of the next phase of the plan. We need her to be the unassuming, independent and irreproachable witness if the plan is to succeed.'

'Okay, well I trust your judgement as long as you know where the line is, Adam, that's all.'

'What do you mean?'

'That footage I was talking about shows you and Agent Johnson very taken with one another, if you get my drift. Is there anything I need to worry about?'

'No, and you don't have to worry; I know where the line is and nothing is going to get in the way of me, us, achieving our end goal.'

Adam checked his watch. Time was getting on and they could hear the vicar giving his final sermon. 'We need to wrap this up, Aree. The mass will be over in the next few minutes. Did you get me everything on Tom Phoenix and his party that I asked for?'

'Yes, everything you requested, including all the usual trimmings,' Aree replied, sliding the grid of the confessional that separated the two boxes ajar and passing the mini hard drive through the small hatch.

'Are there any skeletons I should be aware of that could hamper his or his party's abilities?'

'As far as I can tell, he and his party seem to be pretty clean apart from a few questionable antics of underhandedness and skulduggery; nothing really to worry about. When do you plan to make contact with him?'

'Later this evening once I've had a read of what's on this drive. Phoenix is another integral cog to our plan's success and from my preliminary studies, he and his party seem to be the best candidates to leave the country to once the real fallout begins.'

'Very well, I'll be ready. Do you have anything for me?'

Adam reached into his pocket and pulled out a mini flash drive and passed it through the tiny hatch into Aree's hand, 'Here are your instructions for the next phases of the plan. Make sure you destroy that drive once you've read and memorised your objectives. The next time we meet will be at Chequers. Don't be late and have a good night. Oh, and Aree ...'

'Yes, Adam?'

'In case I forget to say it later, thank you for everything you've done. We couldn't have come this far without you.'

'It's not over yet, but I appreciate the sentiment. See you again soon.'

Adam heard Aree get up and leave his side of the confessional and waited a few moments before leaving himself so as not to arouse any suspicion. On opening the door, he observed that the church service was over and the congregation was making its way out. Adam pocketed the flash drive, stepped out of the confessional and casually slipped in amongst the small crowd.

CHAPTER TWENTY-TWO

Dóchas House, on the corner of Caxton and Palmer Street, was the political party headquarters of the Phoenix Party. The beautiful old Victorian building had over the years played host to several historically important political and social events which saw upheaval and change for the better both in the UK and abroad. It was for this reason that the Phoenix Party had chosen to set up their HQ here, hoping to emulate its history of progress and change. However, to their detractors and critics this was nothing more than idealistic nonsense from a naïve political party who didn't understand how Westminster worked.

Outside, beneath the amber haze of the street lamps, a small group of restless journalists under the watchful eye of extra security guards had gathered near the steps of Dóchas House in the hope that they might get a statement from the Phoenix Party press office or, better still, from Tom Phoenix himself. Though Tom Phoenix and his party hadn't been mentioned yet, there was rampant speculation among the press about whether they too had any skeletons lurking in the closet waiting to be exposed, given that they prided themselves on being the most transparent and open party in the country. The press could well imagine all the party press secretaries foaming at the mouth, begging their party leaders to let them issue a statement to control the narrative and stop an increasingly disillusioned and growingly frustrated public from taking to the streets in mass demonstrations or potential rioting.

Looking out from his small office window at the top of the building, Tom Phoenix stared down at the group of journalists waiting like hungry wolves to see whether he or his press relations team would go out and talk to them. He'd been expecting a gathering all afternoon since the Baker Street Five's explosive revelations, but now that they'd finally showed up, he was wrangling with the pros and cons of making a statement. He'd never been this uncertain before in his political decisions, but this time it was different. One wrong move or misinterpreted comment could have dire consequences for him and the party, though he was confident they had nothing to do with the secret vault or anything to fear about skeletons in the closet being dragged out into the daylight. Part of being a Phoenix Party member was being subjected to a thorough independent series of screening tests to prevent any unsavoury individuals from joining.

What to do? What did he make of the Baker Street Five, the central figures in this rapidly unfolding scandal? What was their angle and motive, and where was it all going to end? His conscience was in two minds. Although he disagreed with their criminal activities, he couldn't quite bring himself to condemn them fully. In his own way, he kind of admired them for their cunning and daring to pull off such an audacious crime right under Prime Minister Brooks and the establishment's noses.

It was a little before ten p.m. and Tom wanted to catch the late evening news headlines that were bound to be reporting up a frenzy of speculation and opinion. He picked up his remote and turned on the small TV that sat in the corner of his spartan office.

'Good evening, and welcome to this special report live from outside Ten Downing Street. In a few minutes we will be going live to our colleagues around the country, as well as here in the city, to gauge the reactions and opinions from today's damning revelations that have shaken Westminster to its very core. But first, a rundown of what we know so far,' said the news broadcaster, his lilting Welsh accent only heightening the severity of the scandalous situation.

'Last night, during the government's annual but controversial masquerade ball, an explosion ripped through the Palace of Westminster, causing severe damage and mass panic in what was first reported as a suspected gas leak according to a statement issued in the early hours of this morning. However, this afternoon the criminal gang known as the Baker Street Five, who have been making headlines with a string of high-profile robberies from government officials, ripped apart this false statement by claiming responsibility for the explosion and subsequent robbery of a secret vault beneath the House of Lords.

The vault is alleged to have held secret, scandalous material and the personal fortunes of many high-ranking members of parliament. The claim by the Baker Street Five was further strengthened and supported when they delivered material including compromising photographs of Foreign Secretary David Miller to various newspapers and media outlets. Though the Foreign Secretary hasn't yet offered his resignation, several high-profile names from Prime Minister Brooks's government and other parties have already resigned.

'One thing is clear, though; with the Baker Street Five threatening to release more scandalous material in the coming days, how long can the government, or any political party, afford to remain silent before mounting public anger causes London and the rest of the UK to descend into chaos and anarchy?'

Tom switched off the TV. He'd heard enough and couldn't disagree with the broadcaster's assessment. The country was on a knife-edge, and this paralysis from the political establishment was only further exacerbating the public's frustrations and anger. With everything else the nation was enduring, the last thing it needed was anarchy on the streets.

A firm knock on the office door interrupted his thoughts.

'Come in.'

The door opened and Khalil Shah, Tom's most trusted deputy and friend, walked into the office having returned from his own private evening prayers. A well-travelled and educated man in his mid-fifties, Khalil was a spiritual and progressive individual who shared Tom's vision for change and was passionate about making a real difference to lives of the people in Britain. He sprouted a neatly trimmed grey beard and was dressed smartly in a navy-blue suit. A fine white topi prayer cap adorned the top of his head, which he wore as a mark of respect to the prophet Muhammad and to his personal faith.

'Good evening, Tom.'

'Good evening, Khalil. How were your evening prayers?'

'Reflective, instructional and calming as always; especially in this current situation we find ourselves in.'

'Yes, it's unbelievable. This Baker Street Five gang have certainly upended the balance of power and may have given us a chance for the rebirth in politics this country very much needs, even though I disagree with their methods. Did you discuss me talking to the press with the other members?'

'I did, and they've been talking to our grass-root activists and party members, and we all agree you should. But they will support you whatever you decide.'

'Good. And what do you think, Khalil?'

'We should definitely capitalise on this; you said yourself that the Baker Street Five have kicked the door down, so let's walk through and shake things up further by being the first party to talk to the press. Allow them access to our records and try to answer some of their questions. Being open and honest can only benefit us in the long term. However, if you're going to talk to the press, you need to change into that spare suit I know you keep lying around in that cupboard. You can't speak to them dressed like that.'

'As always, your opinion is important to me, and thank you for your clothing suggestions. We'd better get the press assembled inside and—'

Tom's private phone rang. 'Hello?' he answered cautiously. Only a trusted few in his inner circle had this number, and he knew none of them would be calling at this hour.

'Mr Phoenix?' replied a deep, calm voice.

'Yes, who am I speaking to?' said Tom, unable to place the voice at the other end of the line.

'My name isn't important, and please don't try to trace this call. I'm bouncing it around so many satellites you'll only end up tying yourself in knots and wasting both of our precious time.'

'I see. Well, what do I call you, then?'

'A concerned citizen. All you have to do is listen to what I have to say; that's all I ask. I'm the head of the Baker Street Five. I take it you've been enjoying our little information dump this afternoon?'

Tom sat up straight. 'That was quite a performance you pulled off,' he replied, motioning to Khalil to pick up the extension.

'Thank you for the compliment. I'll come straight to the point, Mr Phoenix, as I'm on something of a timetable. I've a proposition to put to you regarding our current Prime Minister.'

'Look, I want Prime Minister Brooks and his cronies out of office as much as the next person, but I will not negotiate with criminals to achieve it.'

'Oh, come on, Mr Phoenix. We both know you're not averse to bending the rules with a little underhandedness and skulduggery. I've read your file and various other members' files too within your party. Nevertheless, your integrity does you credit, and that is part of the reason why I chose you. You're different and I respect that you want to win fairly at the ballot box, but in this instance it would be in your best interest to listen. I've all the evidence you will ever need to bring down Brooks's government and the whole rotten political house of cards, if you want it.'

Tom's eyes widened. How the hell did this person get hold of these files? What game was he playing? More importantly, what was in it for his new mystery friend? He paused for a moment, looking to his old friend for guidance. Khalil gestured at him to take the man up on his offer as it was too great an opportunity to pass up.

'Alright, what will I have to do to obtain this potential evidence, and what do you want in return? A pardon?'

'No, and that's the beauty of it, Mr Phoenix. Neither I nor my friends want or need anything in return from you or anyone else. All you have to do, as your friend Khalil suggested five minutes ago, is hold that press briefing condemning Prime Minister Brooks and his government, and I'll handle the rest.'

'You son of a bitch. You bugged my office?' Tom stood up abruptly, searching around his desk for a hidden microphone.

'Spare me your outrage, Mr Phoenix. I just robbed one of the world's most secure buildings and brought to light one of the biggest political scandals in recent memory. Do you really think that bugging your phone is beyond me? Think of it this way: I'm giving you an opportunity to take the keys to Number Ten and the kingdom, and I suggest you take it.'

Tom was annoyed but curious as to how one of the Baker Street Five got into his office without being detected, but his outrage would have to be sidestepped for now. He looked to Khalil for further guidance.

'Okay, I'll play it your way for now.'

'Good. Once you hold that press briefing, that will indicate to me that you're serious and we have a binding agreement. I'll be in touch.'

'Wait, how do I know—'

The phone line went dead. Tom and Khalil put their phones down in disbelief at what they'd been promised by their new Baker Street Five friend. Why them? Why their party? Tom walked over to the window to look down at the press once more. What to do? Could he trust this man? Was he legitimate or was he a crank? Had he damaged the party by agreeing to this? What if it all went wrong? Questions bounced around in his head like ping-pong balls.

'Tom … Tom, what are your instructions?' Khalil snapped him out of his thoughts.

'What do you want me to do, Khalil? It's a huge risk to us and the party if it all goes wrong. How can we be sure he wasn't a crank or a member of the press pulling a fast one?'

'He didn't strike me as the sort, and this is an opportunity we can't afford to pass up. As you always say: dare nothing, achieve nothing. I guess we'll find out if our trust will be rewarded.'

'Okay, Khalil, assemble the press in the main hall for that briefing, and get a special security team up here to do a sweep and locate and remove all listening devices from my office and the

building. I dislike being spied upon.'

CHAPTER TWENTY-THREE

The quarter bells of Elizabeth Tower echoed out across the capital, announcing it was eleven fifteen p.m., as Home Secretary Eric Jackson ascended the tower's spiral staircase up to the clock chamber. He'd managed to avoid the media frenzy after the Baker Street Five's damning revelations and had been hiding out at his club in Pall Mall after a very tense and difficult afternoon. Even his latest scathing confrontation with Agent Amy Johnson had sent his stress levels through the roof.

It was in his club's dining room, summing up his limited options regarding his political future and trying to enjoy a large sirloin steak accompanied by a bottle of 2005 St-Émilion Château Bellevue-Mondotte to settle his nerves, that he received a cryptic message from Prime Minister Brooks. The tone of the message was abrupt but with a hint of desperation, asking him to come to the clock tower tonight: something he found curious but at the same time impertinent, and he was tempted to ignore it. He was still furious with Brooks for the animosity between them and for undermining his authority over Agent Johnson, emboldening her to be even more insolent than usual. Yet, in amongst all those mixed feelings he was fearful that if he ignored the message, he'd be accused of disloyalty; and the one thing Jackson prided himself on above all else was loyalty.

Sweating and short of breath as he reached the top after his long climb, the muscles in his legs aching, Jackson reached the old wood and iron door to the clock chamber and was greeted by Peter Berry, one of Prime Minister Brooks's most trusted aides and bodyguards. Wiping the sweat away from his face with his handkerchief, Jackson could hear raised voices coming from behind the door. He reached out for the door handle to find out what all the commotion was about when Peter stepped in front and blocked him from entering.

'I'm sorry, Home Secretary, but you can't go in. I've my orders to keep you here for a few moments while the Prime Minister finishes with Foreign Secretary Miller.'

'Now you listen to me, Peter, I'm not some grass-roots party member or junior minister you can intimidate. I'm the bloody Home Secretary, and I'm not accustomed to being summoned in this manner, nor do I have the patience to be kept waiting. Get out of my way.' He tried to catch his breath, angered by being treated with such disrespect.

'With respect, Jackson, I couldn't care less if you're the Home Secretary or the President of the United States. I have my orders and I am authorised to use excessive force to keep you here if necessary.'

Home Secretary Jackson's fist made contact with Peter's face, splitting his lip open and catching him completely by surprise. He fell to the ground, unconscious. 'You'd better learn some respect, you jumped-up little shit, or it'll be more than my fist next time,' he said, stepping over him.

Wiping the specks of blood from his hand, Jackson opened the door and entered the clock chamber. He was met by the sorry sight of Foreign Secretary Miller, looking dishevelled and blatantly drunk, in tears and on his knees, clutching Brooks's legs. The unmistakable sound of the mechanical clock gears twisting and turning hummed continuously above their heads. John Cook, Prime Minister Brooks's second most trusted aide and bodyguard, stopped him from going any further, putting his finger to his mouth to make sure he kept silent while the whole sorry spectacle came to its conclusion in front of them.

'George I'm begging you, I've been a devoted and loyal party member and friend for over twenty years. Show me what my loyalty and devotion have purchased. If they found out about my affair and the undercroft vault, then they'll find out about what we did last year to those soldiers; and I'm telling you now, George, I can't go to prison. I'm a weak man. I wouldn't last a day.' Foreign Secretary Miller sobbed uncontrollably.

Prime Minister Brooks picked Miller up off the floor and slapped him across the face. 'Pull yourself together, David, for God's sake. Everything is going to be fine, I promise. None are more loyal than you have been, my friend, and I always reward those who stick by me. The press aren't going to find out any more than they already have, especially about that. Now, you've been through a lot today. I'll have Peter and John take you home so you can rest; and don't worry, you're under my personal protection.'

He signalled to John to take Miller off his hands and then his gaze rested upon Home Secretary Jackson. Peter had finally regained his senses and rushed into the room, blood trickling from the corner of his mouth.

'I'm very sorry, sir. I tried to stop Jackson from barging in, but—'

'That's Home Secretary Jackson to you, Peter, you blithering idiot, and never mind about that now. Help John take Foreign Secretary Miller home and ensure that no one disturbs him, and for God's sake get some ice for that bust lip before you come back to get me,' Brooks replied, indifferent to Peter's excuses.

Peter scowled at Jackson, who was enjoying the dressing-down. He wiped away the congealed blood that had accumulated at the side of his mouth, before hurrying over to take one of the Foreign

Secretary's arms. Miller was now mumbling incoherent sentences, and they carried him out of the clock chamber, closing the door behind them with a bang.

The quarter bells rang out again; it was now eleven thirty p.m.

Home Secretary Jackson covered his ears, wincing at how much louder the bells echoed inside this chamber of stone, glass and metalwork. Prime Minister Brooks didn't flinch or wince in the slightest; instead, he embraced the dulcet tones as he casually walked over to one of the giant glass faces, opened a small window and stared out at the city glowing with such majesty under the overcast night sky. Silence quickly fell once again inside the chamber. Jackson took his hands away from his ears and looked at Brooks, hoping he would now tell him why he'd summoned him here, of all places. His patience was being tested to the limit; he couldn't stand awkward silences, or his time being wasted.

'How did you manage to slip past the security cordon when the tower is currently off limits?' Jackson said, unable to take the uncomfortable silence any longer.

'The same way you did. I didn't slip by, as you put it. I'm the Prime Minister and you're the Home Secretary – no one refuses us entry.'

'Why have you summoned me here, George? I've nothing more to say to you after you undermined my authority in front of Agent Johnson.'

'Don't be so bloody foolish. You know damn well she has us over a barrel with what she and her partner may have discovered about us from the vault. I calculated it was better to keep her on side for the time being.' Brooks seemed irritated by Jackson's insolence.

'You still haven't answered my question.'

'You know, of all the places in this magnificent palace, this is my favourite; a constant reminder that while we may hold the keys to the kingdom, our time in office and in these opulent surroundings is fleeting. And yet, as I stare out at this city, I know out there somewhere those degenerates are staring right back, biding their time to sew our destruction sooner than any of the electorate ever could.'

'It's not like you to be sentimental, George, and nor does it suit you. That's more Miller's department, and judging by the state of him, it proves to me beyond all doubt that sentiment is for the weak.'

'I maybe sentimental on the rarest of occasions, Eric, but don't think for one second that implies I'm weak or have suddenly developed a conscience. As for Miller, part of me feels sorry that he had to be one of the first of us to be taken down. Despite his shortcomings, loyalty like his is a rare quality in people these days. However, I can't say that it'll weigh too much on my conscience when I throw him and the others to the wolves so that the plebs and the media can have their pound of flesh.' The PM moved away from the window towards a small table with a bottle of whisky and two glasses.

'A fifty-year-old Glenfarclas, distilled for the Queen's coronation and a particular favourite of yours, I believe. Care to join me?' He beckoned Jackson over to join him as he poured a generous amount of the expensive single malt into each glass.

'To survival, at any cost,' Brooks said with fervour. The two men clinked their glasses together and drank, each of them savouring the single malt's exquisitely sharp and woody flavour.

'Another one, Eric?' Brooks asked, holding up the bottle. Jackson nodded, handing over his glass, and was poured another generous measure.

'Now, Eric, the reason I've brought you here away from prying eyes and ears is this: I need to know what the mood of the party and the remaining cabinet members is concerning both me and this serious situation which involves a wide range of us across both Houses.'

'Well, to be frank, George, I've heard whispers that they want you – us – out. They feel you're taking the party in the wrong direction, given this unprecedented scandal now engulfing us and your refusal to pay the ransom which the Baker Street Five have demanded. There's talk of a complete front bench overhaul to appease the public demand for blood. Heads are going to roll,' Jackson replied with a grimace.

Brooks downed the rest of his drink and threw his glass at the giant mechanism that controlled the hands of the clock. The glass shattered, small pieces flying in all directions.

'Cowards, traitors ... how dare they presume they can do that to me, us. Well, if they think they can get rid of me, they're very much mistaken. I built this party up after years of infighting and stagnation, and if they want me out, I'll be sure to take as many of them with me as possible,' the Prime Minister replied, seething, as the quarter bells rang out again, announcing that it was now eleven forty-five.

Jackson winced again at the intensity of the bells as they drowned out most of Prime Minister Brooks' angry, impassioned and vitriolic rant.

'So, the public are baying for our blood. When aren't they? This thing with the Baker Street Five is a small blip that they'll get over – you know why?'

'No, George, I don't.'

'Because the truth is, the public don't really give a shit about what we do as long as we appear to be doing something for them and their pathetic lives. You and I both know there's no other credible alternative in government. Christ, Clarke and his bloody opposition couldn't run a committee, let alone a government; Donaldson's a waste of space; and as for Phoenix, he's an idealistic, naïve and liberal moron who thinks putting the public interests and needs first is the way to good governance.'

'Fine words, George, as always. But what happens if this scandal does prove to be our undoing? What will we do then? Because I'm telling you, I have very little faith in Agent Johnson or her little minion Agent Ellis to come up with anything that will quell the media or the public.'

'Then you'd better make sure she does.'

'And if she doesn't? Then what are we going to do except kiss goodbye to all of this and watch the public and the media be judge, jury and executioner? Please tell me that hasn't escaped your mind.'

Prime Minister Brooks's face was turning a dark shade of crimson. The large vein on his forehead pulsated violently. But then, as if by flicking a switch, he regained his composure.

'Of course, you're right, Eric. I don't think it will get to that point. But if by some small chance it doesn't go our way, we'll find a way to fix Agents Johnson and Ellis as well as those Baker Street Five cretins. I also have an escape plan for us. You and I are similar; we're survivors. Both of us have clawed our way to the top from the bottom, and we need to look out for one another.'

'Get to your point, George.'

'My point, Eric, is I've made sure that funds will be available for us to go wherever we wish and live very comfortably, should the need arise, in countries with no extradition treaties with the UK. My plans are only for two, however, but think of the possibilities we'd have.'

'What about Richard? Have you made the same offer to him?'

'Richard can make his own plans; this one is for me and you only.'

'It's a good offer, George, May I have some time to consider it?'

'Of course. Let me know in a few days, but let's keep this between us. If you accept, I'll send you the details, and if things do go wrong, be ready to move at a moment's notice and I'll get us both out.'

It was five minutes to midnight when Prime Minister Brooks looked at the shadows of the clock's hands through the glass facia. 'Christ, is that the time? I think we'd better leave here and wait for Peter and John on the ground level before Big Ben deafens us both. For whom the bell tolls, hey Eric?' he said, picking up the bottle of Glenfarclas as he walked towards the door.

'Yes indeed, George, but whom will it toll for in the end?'

Home Secretary Jackson muttered under his breath as he followed him

out of the clock chamber.

Kevin G. Robinson

CHAPTER TWENTY-FOUR

A glimmering architectural jewel of London's skyline, Crown Plaza
Tower was owned and operated by Castle Acquisitions, a subsidiary of
Knight Technologies. To the outside world, the tower was created as a
self-sustaining entity for small tech start-up companies in the fields of
science, technology and engineering to research and develop their ideas
and inventions with Knight Technologies' support and financial
backing. Moreover, it was a wider platform for these small start-ups to
flourish and share their ideas with a wider audience to create a more
sustainable, cleaner and greener future.

At the top of the tower was one of the hottest and most
exclusive clubs in London, the Atlantic Club. Set up by Adam's son
Johnny as his very own independent entrepreneurial business, it catered
for Knight Technologies employees and the tech start-ups as well as his
dad's clients. Johnny had tried to encompass a perfect blend of Anglo-
American culture in his interior design to represent both his home and
adopted nations. The club also gave an almost unobstructed three-
hundred-and-sixty-degree view of the London skyline, one of its many
alluring charms.

It was a little after one in the morning and the club was in full
swing with people enjoying themselves and the view, dancing to the

latest hits under the ambient lighting. Johnny looked sharp in his evening attire as he made his routine checks around the club, making sure his guests were enjoying themselves and that no one was causing any trouble. Contented that everything was as it should be, Johnny slipped behind the bar in the centre of the club and headed for the secret private lift in his small office. Though registered on every building schematic and document as a building with thirty-five floors, Crown Plaza Tower actually had thirty-six. He slotted in his key card, typed in his five-digit pin and placed his hand on the biometric panel. The lift doors closed and he ascended to the concealed floor above which had been converted into a safe house where he and the rest of the Baker Street Five had been holed up since the robbery.

Johnny couldn't help but be in good spirits as he contemplated the magnitude of what it was like to be a part of perhaps one of the most audacious crimes of the twenty-first century. The irony was that there weren't any real victims as the assets they'd stolen from the undercroft vault were all undeclared and illegal in the eyes of the very law that was now trying to hunt them down. It had brought the entire political system near enough to a halt, the public waiting with bated breath to see what new scandals and secrets would be released. That last thought focused Johnny's attention. Planning and carrying out the heist was child's play but implementing the rest of his dad's plan with the others would now be the most dangerous and challenging task of all. He was confident they would accomplish this, though; he shared the same desire as Adam and the others for revenge, and it was the only way they would be able to move on with their lives.

The lift doors opened onto a comfortable, sleek and contemporary open-plan apartment. Johnny's eyes lit up at the sight of his godmother LJ, Calypso and Cormac, who were busy sitting at the table with gloved hands getting the next information dump ready to be sent out to the media as per Adam's instructions. They had to choose wisely what they wanted to release; it needed to be enough to be a thorn in the side of the establishment but also to continue to feed growing public resentment and anger, which was already simmering, until the absolute right moment when they would push them over the edge.

'Hey guys, how's everything going?' asked Johnny.

'All good, thanks. Thank God for that ledger; it's been a great help. We're nearly finished with the next information dump. There's so much material to go through, though. How is everything going downstairs?' Cormac replied.

'Yeah, it's all good. It's another full house tonight.'

'Any good-looking guys down there who have taken your eye?' LJ couldn't contain her curiosity.

Johnny went a little red in the face with embarrassment. Despite exuding a confident exterior when it came to being asked about his love life, he was always uncomfortable being asked this question. A hang-up, perhaps, after everything he'd been through in the US conversion camp, which he'd never been able to fully overcome.

'A few, but Aunt LJ, you know I hate talking about my love life.'

'I know, but I'm your godmother and I love you, and I want you to find someone who makes you happy.'

'I appreciate that and when I do, I'll let you know. Anyway, changing the subject, is Dad back yet from his rendezvous with Aree?'

'Yes, he got back hours ago but didn't say anything. He just walked out onto the balcony, lost in his thoughts as usual, holding what looked like a mini hard drive and his laptop,' said Calypso, finishing up her pile of documents and placing them into the box beside her.

Car traffic and London nightlife drifted up from the streets below as Adam Knight paced the length of the small, hidden balcony. It had been a very long night. He leant against the steel rail, trying to stem the tiredness he felt creeping over him as he reflected on his conversations with Tom Phoenix and Aree, and the information Aree had provided. All of it had been fruitful, but there was still so much to do and play for before all the pieces were in place. A bird flew past, bringing him out of his reflections with a start. Adam picked up his laptop and the hard drive from the small table and slid the glass partition door aside. Johnny, LJ, Cormac and Calypso were all sitting on the sofas, talking amongst themselves.

'Evening, everyone. Apologies for not talking to you all earlier, but I had a lot on my mind and I needed sometime to myself to think,' said Adam, interrupting their light conversation.

'No problem, Adam, we understand the next phases of the plan are the trickiest and most important part. We all need some alone time every now and then,' said LJ, her voice full of optimism. 'Did everything go well with Aree and Phoenix?'

'Yes, the meeting with Aree went very well despite his usual eccentricities. I've given him the last set of instructions for the final phases of the plan and he will follow them to the letter. He also said to congratulate you all on a job well done so far. As for Tom Phoenix, he was a little harder to gauge but I think I tweaked his interest.'

'Do you think he will keep to your terms?' asked Cormac.

'Well, he gave the press conference that I asked him to do and he followed my instructions to the letter, so I'm going to say yes, he's on board.'

'I saw the headlines. He made quite a stir and now the other parties are trying desperately to get in on the action. It won't do them much good,' said Johnny.

'Speaking of headlines, I hope we will be making some of our own in tomorrow's news. Have you sorted through the stuff from the deposit boxes yet?' asked Adam.

'Yes, it took us a good while, but as Cormac said earlier, thank God we took that ledger with us; it proved a big help because there was so much stuff. Still, we've managed to sort the majority of it into two piles and set aside the papers we think will continue to build on the public's simmering anger and outrage.'

'That's great, LJ. Johnny, you're still okay to drop off the packages tomorrow to the various news outlets?'

'No problem, Dad. I'll take all the precautions necessary, like last time.'

'Good. Make sure you vary your route and drop off each parcel in staggered intervals. Oh, and Calypso, how did we make out on the money side?'

'Cormac and I estimate six figures. It's a tidy sum given the limited time you had in the vault. All our selected charities will be very pleased about receiving another large, anonymous donation.'

'That's great, guys, it really is. And how long do you think you need to digitise all the papers we're not sending out, Cormac?'

'I think if the four of us worked around the clock we could probably have everything digitised and the originals ready to move in about forty-eight hours, give or take.'

'What are you going to do with the rest of the material we've held back, Adam?' asked LJ.

'Don't worry, I've something planned for it all; you'll see. In the meantime, I want you, Calypso and Cormac to pack up everything and head out to Silver Blaze tonight. Johnny, I want you to go down to the garage and change the plates on the vehicles, and then follow on to Silver Blaze tomorrow once you've closed up the club and delivered the packages.'

'What are you going to be doing then, Dad?'

'I've some important business to take care of at the office for our latest R&D project, ready for tomorrow's meeting and demonstration with the MOD. Despite this cause taking up a large amount of my time, I'm still the CEO of a major defence technology company, you know.' The mood successfully lightened, Adam headed towards the lift. 'If you need me, I'll be there all night and tomorrow.'

'Say, Dad, one last thing before you go, just to satisfy my – our – curiosity; who was that beautiful blonde girl you were dancing with last night? Calypso said you looked pretty taken with her, from what she could see on the cameras.'

Adam hesitated. He knew they weren't going to like his answer. However, like he'd told Aree earlier this evening, he was confident he knew what he was doing and that despite his conflicted feelings, which he wasn't really processing, it wouldn't be a problem.

'If you must know, Johnny, it was Amy Johnson, the SI7 agent who's been after us for the past year.'

'Dad, are you crazy? What if—'

'I've already been through this with Aree. It's not up for discussion. I know what I'm doing. I can handle Amy ... Agent Johnson, I mean. She's part of the plan. My interest in her is nothing more than professional and platonic. Anyway, I have to go now. See you all later.'

Johnny and the others began packing up the contents from the vault, deep in contemplation about what Adam had told them.

'I don't know about you guys, but I saw a look in Dad's eyes. He likes her. And what's this about her being part of the plan? I wish Dad would tell us everything,' said Johnny, frustration echoing in his voice.

'Look, he tells us what we need to know at the right time. Your dad has always been a private person and he plays his cards close to his chest. You know that, Johnny. He knows what he's doing because he's dedicated to this cause; and when it comes down to it, the cause always comes first.' Cormac was firm but calm.

'Cormac's right, Johnny. Adam wouldn't jeopardise it when we're so close to our endgame,' added Calypso reassuringly.

'Fair enough. It's not that I object to him dating at all; in fact, I've been trying to encourage him to go out on dates. It's just Dad has a blind spot when it comes to women and romance, like I do when it comes to men.'

'Alright, you guys, that's enough,' said LJ, cutting off the discussion. 'I agree with what you're saying, Johnny. Adam does look pretty taken with her. Calypso, you said that Agent Johnson was pretty taken with Adam too last night, right?'

'Yes, she was, and if they weren't on opposite sides, they'd make a very cute couple.'

'Exactly. So, I say let's just keep a careful eye on the situation for the time being and only act if it becomes necessary.'

CHAPTER TWENTY-FIVE

Sunlight pierced through the open blinds of Adam's soundproof bedroom. He was in a state of restlessness and disturbed sleep. The nightmare he feared every time he closed his eyes and entered his dreams had once again taken hold. He'd hoped that after their successful heist at the palace, it would have subsided. But it hadn't. Adam could see and hear gunfire, people screaming, and the bloodied and mutilated corpses of Unit Six, but now there was a new addition to this nightmare. His old friend Colonel Monroe, his hands covered in his own blood, was reaching out to touch Adam's face, screaming, 'Adam, you're failing us.' He froze in horror as the apparitions and voices grew louder and louder.

Adam shot upright from his nightmare in a panic and a cold sweat. His breathing was heavy and he felt disorientated but after a few minutes he composed himself. He lay back down, despondent, but his ordeal wasn't over. He was still in his nightmare and now someone was lying next to him under the sheets, which had turned crimson with blood and smelled of death. Adam recoiled and threw back the sheet. To his horror, he saw the mutilated body of Jamie, the lieutenant who'd been in command of Unit Six. Jamie's dead, vacant eyes opened and met

Adam's, and he grabbed at one of Adam's arms with one of his burnt hands.

'Don't fail me,' he said in a haunting tone.

Adam found himself on the bedroom floor. He bolted up onto his feet, shaking in terror. Breathing heavily once again, he stared across at the empty bed and twisted bed sheets. Jamie had disappeared, and this time he knew he was awake. He dropped to his knees and let out a deep sigh of distress. He was close to tears. How much more of this nightly torture could he take? His nightmares were taking their toll on him, both physically and psychologically. Despite his best efforts to ignore these haunting manifestations, they were getting stronger and more powerful. Since that terrible night of revelations a year ago, it was as if he was wondering around aimless and alone in that dark place he'd fallen into. Adam had concluded that absolution would only come once he'd completed what he'd set out to do. He picked himself up off the floor and headed straight for the shower. Naked, he stepped under the gushing hot water and enjoyed the sensation as it fell like a waterfall onto his body, massaging and opening up all of his pores to wash away the ills of the night.

Twenty minutes later, having showered, brushed up, and put the haunting images of his nightmare to the back of his mind, Adam slipped on a pair of grey jogging bottoms and headed for the kitchen.

He flipped a switch at the top of the staircase which deactivated the smart glass film tint to allow natural light to flood in as he descended the floating steel steps. In daylight, with its contemporary artwork and furnishings Adam's office resembled a bachelor pad. Next to the staircase was an immense picture window and to the left of that was a small library containing numerous books, including Adam's prized collection of first edition Sherlock Holmes novels and short stories. In the centre, in a lowered box section of the floor, was Adam's personal video conference suite encompassed by images of the Knight Technologies chess piece logo emblazoned with blue light around the edges.

Fixing himself a light breakfast of toast with marmalade, and Greek yoghurt with berries, Adam was oblivious that someone else was in his office. As he filled up the kettle for his tea, a voice came out of nowhere.

'Good morning, Adam.'

Adam dropped the kettle in the sink. Though the voice sounded familiar, he was surprised that this individual, whoever they were, had not only managed to bypass his security but had also slipped into his office without being detected. He spun round and was secretly delighted to see Agent Amy Johnson sitting behind his desk. She had the same disarming effect on him as she'd done at the party, and had

Adam not become aware of the growing silence, he was sure he would have drowned in her beautiful ocean-blue eyes as she waited for him to reply.

'Amy, this is a surprise. How did you get in here?'

'Well, we SI7 Agents have our secret ways, Adam.'

Was it his imagination, or was she casting an appraising eye over his bare chest? 'I see, and have you given everything the once-over?'

'Pardon?'

Adam allowed himself a small smile. 'I take it you've had a good look around the place?'

'Oh yes, a little. I was curious to know more about you and what you do. I hope you don't mind?'

'Not at all. Would you care to join me in some tea or breakfast?' Adam asked, putting the kettle on while he observed Amy looking at the small silver-framed photograph on his desk.

'Thank you, just the tea, white and no sugar, please.' She picked up the frame. 'Are these your sons?'

'Yes, my late wife Em and I were blessed with our eldest and then I was blessed again when I adopted my youngest, fourteen years after her death.'

'I'm sorry to hear that. I didn't realise you'd been married.'

'It's alright. It was a long time ago and Em always said she didn't want me wallowing after she passed.'

'She sounds like a wise woman. You must be very proud of your sons. I see one of them is in the armed forces, too.'

'She was, and yes, I'm very proud of them both. My eldest never wanted to do anything other than serve his country and keep it safe. In fact, we've something of an ongoing chess game that we haven't got round to finishing yet,' said Adam, pointing at the dusty chess set that sat on the right-hand side of his desk. Amy went to pick up one of the pieces, much to Adam's agitation.

'Oh, Amy, if you don't mind. I haven't touched that chess board since my son went on deployment and I haven't yet got round to placing all his moves on the board from his last email.'

The kettle whistled loudly as it came to the boil.

'My apologies. Who's winning, by the way?'

'My son. We used to play every night when he was little, and over the years he's become very good. Anyway, what can I do for you, Amy? I get the feeling this isn't a social visit.' Leaving his breakfast on the side, he walked over to her with two cups in his hands.

Amy got up and took her tea. Their hands brushed against one another for a brief moment. Taking up his seat, Adam picked up the photograph and placed it inside a drawer.

Amy took out her notebook and pen. 'You're right, it isn't a social call. I need to ask you some questions regarding the other night's explosive events. It's just a routine procedure to eliminate you from our enquiries, you understand.'

'Of course. By all means, ask your questions.'

'Could you start by telling me your movements at the party?'

'As I recall, I arrived with my good friend LJ between half eight and nine p.m. We mingled for a while and then separated, which is when I had the pleasure of meeting you. We danced, we chatted, and then I got that unfortunate message and had to leave you and make a call to see if I could resolve the issue. After that, I came back inside having been unable to resolve the problem, met up with LJ and told her to get the car ready. I found you again to say goodnight and left just before midnight.'

'I see; and you've known your friend LJ for how long?'

'Oh, a long time. We met at university; she saved me from a bunch of guys who disliked someone of my class being given a scholarship. We've been great friends ever since. Her father, Sir Charles Gray, is our current ambassador to Canada – did you know?'

'Yes, I did. LJ sounds like she can handle herself pretty well in a fight.'

'Yes, she certainly can. It's one of her many talents.'

'Do you know where we could find her? I'd like to ask her some questions but she seems to have fallen off the grid.'

'LJ is something of a free spirit. She often falls off the grid for a while. I've no idea where she might have gone since I last saw her.'

'I see. Well, I guess I'll keep making enquiries. Anyway, going back to when you were making your phone call, did anyone else see you outside Westminster Hall who could vouch for your whereabouts?'

'Not that I recall. I was distracted. I don't really take much notice of my surroundings when I'm engrossed in sorting out business problems.'

Amy paused for a moment to take a sip of her tea and write some more notes in shorthand.

'Now, about this phone call you made; who was it to, and could I speak to them to verify what you've told me?'

'Ah, I'm afraid I can't tell you anything about that phone call, Amy, not without special authority, which you'll have to get as it was part of a major security project overseas.'

Adam's voice cracked. He knew his deliberate response had come across as evasive and a little defensive, and looking at Amy as she continued writing in her notebook, he was sure it hadn't escaped her attention. With any luck she would assume he was using a loophole in the classified technology directive or trying to hide something from her, which would compel her to investigate him further. Either way, he needed to continue to reel her in so that she'd dance to his tune and play her unwitting part in his plans later on.

'Adam, would you mind looking at these component fragments of debris and telling me what they are?' Amy produced some photos from her coat pocket and placed them on Adam's desk.

He set his tea aside and examined the photos, which contained several blown-up images. 'Well, my best guess is that they look like pieces from magnetic pulse charges, a nasty prototype weapon from a company I took over a year ago; but I'm telling you, that can't be possible. I personally had that project mothballed, and all the working prototypes were destroyed because of their instability. I've all the relevant legal documents signed and witnessed to prove it, if you'd like copies.'

'Yes, that would be most helpful.'

'Good, send a messenger over for them over this afternoon.'

Adam looked up at the clock: eleven fifteen a.m. 'I'm afraid that's all the time I can spare you right now as I have a very important meeting in forty-five minutes with my advisers and a practical presentation to prepare for, but I'm more than willing to continue this conversation over dinner later, if you're free? My offer from the other night still stands.'

'Some other time, perhaps, but do me a favour, Adam and don't leave town. I've a feeling my colleague and I will need to speak to you again very soon. Thanks for the tea,' replied Amy, placing her notebook and the photographs back into her coat pocket.

'You're most welcome. Oh, and Amy, don't worry, I've no intention of going anywhere for the time being.'

Amy ignored Adam's last words as she closed the door behind her. Adam reflected on their conversation, feeling very pleased with himself. But he would have to be careful. There was something about Amy that made him feel he'd found an equal to spar with on every level. More importantly – and against his better instincts – as Johnny and the others had expressed last night, perhaps his growing feelings for her ran deeper than he was willing to admit. The mutual attraction between them was strong and charged with chemistry. The only problem was they were on opposing sides. He hoped that would change when this was over.

Kevin G. Robinson

CHAPTER TWENTY-SIX

In a small urban area of Pimlico, in one of its charming little squares, was a parade of shops selling curiosities and trinkets. Forty-Two Pimlico Square housed an innocuous rare bookshop called Thoth's, run by an elderly gentleman of German descent in his early seventies, Herr Johannes Schriftsteller. To most people who lived or visited the square, Herr Schriftsteller was a respectable, friendly seller and purveyor of rare books. What they didn't know was that he'd been a deep cover double agent for MI6 behind the iron curtain during the Cold War, before escaping from East Berlin to Britain a few months before the wall fell and settling into civilian life.

Herr Schriftsteller had run his little bookshop for almost twenty years, and despite its dusty, bland interior and faded exterior, it always seemed to do a fair bit of business. However, and unbeknownst to the other shopkeepers on the square, Forty-Two Pimlico Square had a secret. Deep beneath the shop, in a secret sub-basement, was a large concrete room which housed all of SI7's records and archive material. Herr Schriftsteller had been approached by the service to build the secret sub-basement under his shop in the late nineties and to be its loyal curator, record and gatekeeper – an opportunity he jumped at, as it was a quiet but exciting desk job after years of undercover work.

Inside the SI7 archive, the classified documents and material were contained within six large free-standing and secure deadbolt computer mainframes, super-cooled by liquid nitrogen from six small tanks. At the far end, opposite the lift, was a small, dimly lit room made of reinforced frosted glass that was kept at room temperature and housed the main computer mainframe search engine. Provided a person had permission and clearance, they would be able to find and even cross-reference with other archived material from Scotland Yard, Special Branch and GCHQ, to name but a few.

Agent Amy Johnson arrived at Forty-Two Pimlico Square a little after one p.m. The conversation she'd had with Adam had been gnawing away at the back of her mind ever since she'd left him. Her instincts told her something didn't add up. She was sure Adam was their man, but where was the concrete evidence to prove it? She didn't have any. And what were these feelings she had for him? She had to admit she found Adam very attractive and intriguing, even more so after this morning. She hoped she was right and that the attraction was mutual. For the moment she tried her best to put it to the back of her mind and focus on what it was she'd come to Forty-Two Pimlico Square for.

'Good Afternoon, Herr Schriftsteller.' Amy smiled and held out her hand.

'Ah, Fraulein Johnson, it is good to see you back again so soon. What can I do for you today? Is there something you're looking for in particular?' Herr Schriftsteller took her hand.

'It's good to be back. A client of mine is looking for a rare copy of Geoffrey Chaucer's *Canterbury Tales* if you happen to have one?'

'Come, I may have a copy in the back; but first, you know my rules. If you please, leave any belongings, electronic devices or recording equipment in the lockers provided.' He gestured to the lockers by the counter. Amy placed her belongings and electronic devices in one of the lockers and followed Herr Schriftsteller into the back of the shop, making light conversation. Once out of sight and earshot of the other browsers, they dropped the act.

'Fraulein Johnson, do you have your permissions to access the archive?'

'Here you are. It should all be present and correct.'

'Good. May I have your identification card? And please sign the register.'

'Certainly, here you go,' said Amy, handing over her SI7 credentials as she signed the register with her initials and number. 'I may be some time. I hope that's alright.'

'Take as long as you need. I will be here if you need anything. Oh, and one last thing; you have today's password, yes?'

'Yes, I do, thank you.'

'Good. Then I shall leave you. I hope you find what you're looking for.'

On that note, Herr Schriftsteller turned on his heels and sauntered back into the shop. Amy walked over to a large antique bookcase and tilted one of the dusty old books to the right, causing the bookcase to swing open and reveal a hidden lift. She stepped inside. On the control panel, she typed in the day's random phrase password: a line from the works of William Blake. The lift doors closed and she descended into the archive.

Under the light of a small desk lamp and the hum of a black and white converted television set from the nineteen eighties which broadcasted the news in the background every hour, Amy searched through the reams of archive material about Adam Knight. Several newspaper reports had appeared regarding his philanthropic work with various military, children and pro-LGBT+ charities, which fitted in with the modus operandi of the Baker Street Five but was still at best circumstantial. There were also extensive profiling reports and checks on Adam and his defence technology company, all of which proved to be insightful but not especially relevant. What drove such a highly respected and successful man to commit such crimes? Was it for the thrill? Was it boredom? Or was it something that she couldn't for the life of her see yet? She also found it odd that while there was limited information on his friends, colleagues and acquaintances, there was next to nothing on Adam's family, his past or his personal life. What was he really like beneath all that armour and guarded exterior?

From her personal experience over the past thirty-six hours, Adam had been a mix of charm, playfulness but also defensiveness. There was something awry, even foreboding, about him that her instincts couldn't ignore. Who are you, Adam? What makes you tick? Even Adam's flimsy alibi for the evening was ambiguous and far from watertight. People she'd spoken to remembered having conversations with him but not the exact time or place; and, of course, he'd spent some of the evening with her, which further confounded the situation.

Frustrated by the lack of any progression or personal insights into Adam, Amy pushed the keyboard away. She was feeling sharp pangs of hunger – she hadn't eaten since this morning – but she couldn't leave, not until she had something to show for her afternoon's toil. Stifling a yawn, she went back to the main search engine and typed in a request to access all intelligence organisation archives again for anything to do with Adam Knight that required high-grade security clearance. To her surprise, the computer brought forward several files from the SIS ghost drive under the umbrella code name of Operation Guardian Angel. The file had only been added to the archive a month ago and was labelled NTBR – Never To Be Released. Amy tried to recall where she'd heard that code name before but the entire case, along with her conflicted feelings for Adam, weighed heavily on her mind. Unable to shift this haze, Amy double-clicked on the file in the hope it would give her some of the answers she'd been looking for. Perhaps even a greater insight into Adam? Her enthusiasm was short-lived as the file flashed up in bold letters: *Unauthorised Access Detected. Access Denied. Triple A Authorisation Clearance Required.*

'Damn it.' Amy smacked her hand hard on the desk. Feeling defeated, she sat back on her chair and sighed as another newsflash update began.

'Good evening, this is your hourly newsflash. Our top story continues to be the fallout from yesterday's shocking revelations in Westminster. This afternoon, the Baker Street Five released more damning and scandalous material to various media outlets, bringing into question the reputations of many parliamentarians. In the main line of fire on day two of this sensational unfolding story are Justice Secretary Lord Jeremy Hall and Home Secretary Eric Jackson. The leaked documents suggest they've been taking bribes to grant the early release of violent prisoners. Lord Hall and Home Secretary Jackson issued a joint statement a few moments ago, strongly denying the allegations.

'In related news, Tom Phoenix and his party remain the only political party to have allowed the media complete access to their records and cooperated fully, following an unexpected press conference late last night in which Mr Phoenix stated it was of paramount importance that every politician and political party needed to be open and transparent with the media and the British public—' The TV set went dead. Amy turned her head and flinched at the sight of Robbie standing to the side of her, looking most displeased.

'Robbie, why do you always feel the need to sneak up on me like that?'

'It's a force of habit. Would you care to tell me what the hell you were thinking of, visiting Adam Knight like that and without even a heads-up to me this morning?' he snapped.

'Look, I know what I did might seem rash but—'

'The surveillance boys clocked you going in to see him this morning when I specifically told you not to until we had something more concrete. The boys also said you were in there for some time, so I'm going to assume you spoke with him?' said Robbie as he threw down some photos showing Amy entering Knight Technologies.

'Yes. We had an amicable conversation over tea, as a matter of fact,' replied Amy.

'How very civilised. Were there scones, jam and clotted cream as well?'

'Alright, alright, I know you're pissed off with me for leaving you out of the loop. It won't happen again. But if you get off your high horse for one goddamn minute, I'll explain.'

'Okay, but it had better be good, and you can also explain this to Control and Jackson who've been on my back all afternoon, wondering where you've been.'

'Forget about Jackson. Haven't you seen the news? He's as good as toast. You know as well as I do that he has a serious conflict of interest, and that Control will have no option but to use his executive power to remove him from our investigation and transfer oversight to the Joint Intelligence Committee.'

'I guess that's one bit of good news to come out of this. So, what did you find out? Please tell me you didn't search his office. I know you know better.'

'In answer to your first question, not much. He was playful and charming but defensive, although he tried to mask it, and he was evasive towards the end. He identified the mag charge components and said that as far as he was concerned, they'd all been destroyed. He claimed to have the relevant papers to prove it.'

'Did you check it out?'

'Yes, I got one of the SI7 couriers to go and collect them this afternoon. He brought over the copies of the destruction paperwork. It all appears in order, signed and sealed, but I can't help but feel they're a smokescreen. How did you get on with his phone records?'

'No success yet. I'm having trouble getting a warrant and permission to bypass the classified technology directive for access, but I'll keep on it. Going back to you, please tell me you didn't search his office, did you?'

'I may have had a quick look around his office just to get a feel for the man ...'

'Oh, that's great. So what you're telling me is that we have nothing more than circumstantial evidence and that you searched his office without a warrant. You do realise you infringed upon his privacy and had he caught you, there would've been hell to pay? Not to mention that any potential evidence you may have found would've been inadmissible, right?'

Robbie began pacing the floor back and forth, looking disappointed and perturbed. Amy stood up from her chair and grabbed

Robbie's arm, spinning him round to face her. She placed her hands on his shoulders, meeting his eyes with conviction.

'Let me finish. He asked if I'd looked around. I said I had, and he brushed it off like it didn't bother him and offered me tea. Do you not find that odd behaviour?'

'Well, that is odd behaviour but not an admission of guilt. I'll grant you, it's an unusual human reaction from a suspect who's just found out you've been snooping through his personal belongings. He's a very cool customer indeed.'

'Listen, Robbie, you put the finger on him and singled him out above all the other guests. Why?'

'I don't know, I guess my instincts told me something was amiss about him.'

'Exactly, Robbie. There's something off about Adam Knight. He's hiding something. I saw it in his eyes, which is why I've been down here all afternoon in the archive, trying to gain better intelligence and insight into him.'

'I know you have. Herr Schriftsteller was getting worried that you would never come back up again, which is why he called me. You know he's a stickler for procedure. Anyway, did you find out anything else about Adam Knight?'

'I'm afraid not. Our archive and most of the others contain standard or irrelevant information. Hell, there's not even anything about his family or his personal past. It's almost as if the information was intentionally omitted.'

'So we're back to square one, then, but with a circumstantial suspect? This case is really beginning to get under my skin at the number of circles it's thrown us around in.'

'No. I did find one potential lead. It was buried deep in one of the SIS's ghost archives with the highest security grade possible, codenamed Operation Guardian Angel. For the life of me I know I've heard of it before, but I can't remember where.'

'Guardian Angel ... Guardian Angel ... Oh Christ, you must mean that fiasco in Afghanistan last year when those special ops soldiers were massacred in an unsanctioned and illegal mission, trying to save a potential pro-west tribal leader.'

'That's it, now I remember. The commanding officer, Colonel Arthur Monroe, was said to have exceeded his authority and gone off the deep end, or something to that effect. He was blamed for the entire thing. But didn't he recently turn up dead?'

'Yes, in a small fishing village in County Donegal, Ireland; in very suspicious circumstances, I might add.'

'We need to get into this file, Robbie. I know we won't get clearance, so I'm going to need you to put your impeccable skills as a hacker to good use. How long do you think it will take you to hack through security?' said Amy, pointing to the computer screen that was still flashing the *Access Denied* message.

'Difficult to say. A file with this high a security grade will have at least a level twelve encryption, not to mention numerous traps and firewalls ... possibly seventy-two hours, maybe less.'

'I know you'll do your best, Robbie, but I don't like it. I mean, what's the connection between all of them and the tragic events of last year? And how does it tie in with what the Baker Street Five have been doing this past year and the establishment, especially Prime Minister Brooks and his government?'

'Let us pray some if not all of the answers can be found in this file,' Robbie replied. 'Alright, if I'm going to do this, I want you to do something for me and it's not negotiable.'

'What's that?'

'Go home, get some dinner, even sleep for a while to recharge your batteries. When I'm hacking into something secret, I work better alone.'

'Okay, I'll go, but I won't be in the office until late morning or early afternoon tomorrow.'

'Oh, and why's that?'

'Before I left Adam's office, I managed to sneak a peek at his diary and there was an entry dated tomorrow that roused my curiosity. I'm going to check it out and take some photos of the meeting he's having. Best take the surveillance boys off him until I get back.'

'Amy, I don't think that's a ... What's suspicious about it?'

'I need you to trust me, please, Robbie. It's taking place in War Memorial Park Cemetery. What better location could there be if you don't want anyone to overhear what you're discussing?' she said as she gathered up her belongings from the desk.

'Amy, I have to ask you this,' said Robbie in a stern tone of voice as she opened the glass door to leave.

'What?'

'I couldn't help but notice on the CCTV footage of the hall that you and Adam Knight looked quite taken with each other, and by your reaction yesterday. Are there any deeper personal issues I need to be concerned about?'

'No, there isn't. My personal feelings don't matter. I intend to see this investigation through with the utmost professionalism, wherever it may lead. You've nothing to worry about,' Amy replied as she left, irritated by the impertinent but fair question.

Once inside the privacy of the lift, she reflected on her last comment to Robbie as the cold steel box and hum of the lift mechanism brought her up to ground level. She didn't like lying to him; deep down she knew she was conflicted. Would she be able to separate her personal feelings from her duty?

CHAPTER TWENTY-SEVEN

A cold, crisp morning brought with it a cloak of white mist which hovered like a spectre that had exhaled its breath among the polished granite headstones of War Memorial Park Cemetery. It was a solemn, tranquil place of remembrance where the dead of Her Majesty's armed forces were laid to rest after a lifetime of service or for having made the ultimate sacrifice in their duties defending the UK from threats both foreign and domestic.

Agent Amy Johnson drove through the open wrought-iron gate at the entrance to the cemetery and into the small visitor car park. The white chalk gravel crackled under the tyres of her dark blue Volkswagen Golf GT. In the distance, at the centre of the cemetery, Amy could see the one-hundred-foot obelisk of remembrance. Its tall structure protruded out of the mist and dominated the skyline as if it were a spear that had pierced through the earth, angling its way up towards the heavens. Surrounding the obelisk was the large reflective pool of contemplation, flanked by four bowed statues of angels who protected and stood guard over the dead. Amy knew Adam was – or would be – having his obscure and curious meeting somewhere in this isolated place. The entry in Adam's diary hadn't been as forthcoming on detail in terms of who he was meeting or the number people involved, just the time, place and topic of discussion: something called the Janus Protocol.

The clock on her dashboard read six forty-five a.m. Another fifteen minutes before Adam and whoever he was meeting arrived. She pulled out her flask of hot coffee from her glove compartment, her first dose of caffeine to get her through the day; she hadn't managed to get a lot of sleep last night. So many questions were whirling around in her head that her mind simply wouldn't switch off. Amy wondered what she was about to witness. Would it be something beneficial and of note to the case or a complete red herring? With the way this case was turning out, nothing was what it seemed.

She finished her coffee, placed the flask back inside the glove compartment and pulled out her SI7-equipment-issued camera with its special lenses. Once it was assembled, she gave it the once-over to make sure it was all in working order. The car clock now read seven a.m. In the distance she could see movement down by the obelisk. Peering through the lens of the camera and adjusting the focus, Amy observed Adam coming into view with a group of people, in what appeared to be a heated discussion. She recognised Kerefese Beckett, the chairman of the St Georges Foundation trust. What was he doing here? Could the Janus Protocol be for the foundation? From her time spent in the SI7 archive yesterday, Amy knew that Kerefese Beckett and Adam were well acquainted with one another due to Adam's financial contributions and philanthropic work for the foundation. As for the other individuals, Amy speculated but she had no idea who they were; perhaps other members of the foundation, or even the Baker Street Five? Regardless, they were persons of interest for their association with Adam, and she snapped away, taking close-up photos of each of them as well as wide-angle group shots. In hindsight, Amy wished she hadn't asked Robbie to pull the surveillance team off Adam – they had the special equipment to overhear what was being said. Whatever the Janus Protocol was, Adam's friends didn't seem pleased by what he was saying.

After about half an hour the conversation appeared to mellow, judging by the group's body language and interaction. Amy deduced that the meeting must be coming to a close. Her entire body tensed up as she watched Adam pass a fat manila envelope to Beckett. She could just make out the red lettering on the front: *Private and Confidential: Janus Protocol Implementation in the Event of my Death or Absence.* She snapped several shots of the envelope as Adam handed it to over. What are you up to, Adam? Getting ready to run or die trying? Maybe she was a lot closer to exposing Adam and the Baker Street Five than she'd previously thought.

The group said their farewells. With the meeting over, Amy noted they all looked sombre but indebted in their facial expressions and body language as they all hugged and kissed Adam goodbye. There was a look and a feeling of finality to their farewells, almost as if they didn't expect to see him again, as they parted ways. Adam remained at the pool of contemplation and looked deep in thought. Amy knew she had to get closer, but first she needed to send Robbie the photos. Keeping one eye on Adam, she undid the back of the camera and took out the SD card. She placed it into the slot on the car dashboard and fished out her phone.

'Robbie, it's me. I'm sending some pictures over. Could you please pass them along to the ferrets in research and ask them to find out who these people are and what their connection is to Adam Knight?'

'Sure, I'll get right on it. You saw something of interest then, did you?'

'Maybe, but we'll know more once we get the workups and information back from the ferrets. Also, I need you personally to look into something called the Janus Protocol for Knight Technologies. Adam handed an envelope over with those words on it. I think we might be closer to catching Adam and the Baker Street Five than we thought, but he may be getting ready to make a run for it,' said Amy, stepping out of her car and trying to keep her eyes on Adam in the distance. 'Let's put a stop on his passport, just in case. I'm going to follow him to see if I can gather any more intel to help us further. Speak to you later.'

Amy rang off. She looked through her camera lens once more and observed that Adam was now walking away down one of the pathways. She got out of her car and went into a light jog to catch up to Adam. She reached the obelisk and pool of contemplation within a few minutes and turned into the windy, tree-lined path Adam had taken, but he was nowhere to be seen. He couldn't have gone that far, surely. Amy clasped the small sidearm in her pocket she'd brought with her as a precaution, as she continued down the path.

'Hello, Amy,' said Adam, calling out from behind her in a calm, collected voice. Amy swivelled round on her heel and saw him sitting on a stone bench partly obscured by foliage.

'You won't need that gun of yours. I'm unarmed and I don't plan on being violent, so I'd appreciate it if you'd take your hand out of your pocket. It'll make us both less nervous,' he continued. Amy remained silent as she walked back a few steps to get a better view of him, taking her hand out of her pocket only after she was certain he wasn't going to be a threat.

'That's much better. I suspected you might be lurking nearby this morning. You're tenacious, I'll give you that. Do you make a habit of rifling through and reading other people's diaries without a warrant?'

'Not normally, but when you hold meetings in suspicious places, you're bound to attract attention; speaking of which, would you care to tell me who those people were and what the Janus Protocol is? You wouldn't be planning on running out on me when we have unfinished business, now, would you?'

'Ah, you saw that. I guessed you might have done. It was nothing to do with whatever business, as you call it, is left between us. And why would I run? I haven't done anything wrong.'

'You've a good poker face, Adam, but let's drop the pretence. I trust my instincts and I think you know why I'm here.'

'Let's assume I don't for a moment. What exactly are you accusing me of, Amy? You see, I've rather a lot on my mind at the moment and I dislike playing guessing games.'

'All I want to know is why you did it. Why have you been on this crusade for the past year? Something terrible must have happened to make you commit these crimes. I know it's not for money, so it must be personal or political, or both.'

Adam smirked as he got up from the bench. Amy took a step back and placed her hand up to her pocket once more. Adam raised his hands to reassure her he meant her no harm.

'Let me see if I understand you correctly. You suspect or are accusing me of having a personal vendetta and being part of the Baker Street Five, who've executed several near perfect robberies over the past year, culminating in the parliament job against the establishment. And all for some unknown reason? Well, that is some imagination you have.'

'It's not my imagination if it's true, and that sounds to me like an admission of guilt on your part.'

'I'm admitting nothing because I haven't done anything, and last time I checked, you needed hard evidence to back up these accusations of yours. Do you have hard evidence against me?' said Adam, staring straight at her, his face remaining neutral as she remained silent. He took a few steps closer. She didn't move a muscle as they stood almost face to face.

'I didn't think so, Amy. Otherwise, I'm certain we wouldn't be having this polite conversation. Or maybe you do, and what's really stopping you is that you felt something for me, like I did for you, that night at the party, which prevents you from taking action.' Adam turned to walk back down the path.

Amy grabbed his arm and gripped it firmly. She struck Adam hard across the face. 'How dare you? I might not have anything concrete yet, but I will stop you from throwing this country into anarchy. Sooner or later you'll make a mistake, and I'll be there to get you and put a stop to whatever this madness and vendetta of yours is.' She released his arm and stormed off down the path.

Adam soothed his cheek and let out a deep sigh. Amy had disappeared out of sight. He knew he'd touched a raw nerve by trying to use her feelings as a weapon against her, which was a shitty thing to do. However, no matter his feelings, Amy needed to be taken care of as she was getting too close, too soon. He pulled out his burner phone and dialled Aree's emergency number.

'Aree, it's me. Thanks for the heads-up about Amy but we have a problem. Tell the others I'm advancing our timetable and bringing the final phase of our plan forward to tomorrow. Amy has got further ahead than I wanted her to be, though she has no hard proof yet. We need to do something about her tonight.

'Adam, I warned you this would—'

'I don't need a lecture, Aree. Just do what I ask and meet me at the usual place in an hour so we can discuss it further.'

Adam rang off and exhaled deeply. Amy had left him no choice. Nothing was going to get in his way now.

CHAPTER TWENTY-EIGHT

On the rooftop of the Chaturanga Banking Group tower, the fifth tallest building in London and the closest to Knight Technologies, Agent Amy Johnson and Agent Robbie Ellis, dressed all in black, were setting up the special equipment they'd requisitioned from SI7's K Division. Their aim was simple: to zip line across to the rooftop of Knight Technologies and break into the executive office of Adam Knight.

Since her last encounter with Adam, Amy had had a seething bee in her bonnet. The photographs she'd taken of Adam's meeting and the other people involved had all led back to that Guardian Angel file, which only added to her frustration. Robbie had done his best to get out of her what had passed between them, but Amy refused to open up. She knew if she told Robbie the truth, he would have no choice but to report her to Control and she'd be taken off the case.

'Is everything ready, Robbie?' said Amy, peering across at Knight Technologies' rooftop with her night vision binoculars.

'Yes, we're almost ready to go, but are you sure you want to do this? This is reckless behaviour and a direct violation of SI7 protocols, not to mention several laws.'

'To hell with protocol and the law for the moment. We're doing this because your informant Aree gave us this tip-off this afternoon, and I want that irrefutable evidence that's hidden somewhere in Adam's office.'

'You know what, Amy? I'm prepared to tolerate a lot from you but stop treating me like I'm the enemy, okay? Whatever happened between you and Knight this morning, snap out of it. In the next few minutes we're going to be committing several crimes and I need to know you've got my back.'

Amy took the binoculars away from her eyes and turned to face Robbie who was now making the last checks on the equipment. For the first time today, she realised how cold she'd been towards him since she'd got back to headquarters.

'I know you're not the enemy, Robbie, and you can trust me to have your back.' She placed her hand on Robbie's shoulder.

'Alright then, let's get on with it. We haven't got all night,' he replied, moving the equipment into place. He took aim and fired the air-compressed harpoon cable towards Knight Technologies. It whizzed through the air and hit the target area, the steel piton embedding itself deep into the concrete wall of the roof's emergency fire exit. Amy picked up her small backpack, got into position and attached herself to the cable.

'I'll see you over there in a few minutes,' said Robbie.

Taking a deep breath, she counted to three and pushed herself off the ledge.

The nightwatchman of Security Team One made his routine patrol around the executive floor of Knight Technologies. Having been made redundant due to defence cuts and left out in the cold by the government, he felt blessed to have been offered work here thanks to Mr Knight's scheme of hiring former military personnel for security, headed up by his division chief Cormac O'Connell. He slotted his key card into the electronic lock, disabling the security systems, and entered Mr Knight's office. Low ambient lighting lit the room as he scanned the office, making sure all was in order.

'McCabe to O'Connell, come in, please.'

'Go ahead, McCabe.'

'The executive floor is clear and secured, sir. No sign of any disturbances.'

'Thank you, McCabe. Check the floors below one more time and then go on your break. You can report back to me in an hour.'

'Aye, will do sir, over and out.'

Up on the roof, Robbie had zip lined his way across to join Amy and was hard at work on his small computer, overriding the building's external security protocols to open up the large smart glass skylight window. It took him a few minutes but the last of the security protocols finally gave way and the window opened. Amy dipped into her rucksack, took out a black climbing rope and secured one end to the steel safety rail at the edge of the building. She unfurled it and dropped the rest by the side of the open skylight. Wearing special infrared goggles, Robbie peered into the office. It was wired up to the hilt with state-of-the-art security systems such as a laser grid, motion detectors and pressure pads. It was the kind of challenge a seasoned hacker like Robbie loved to crack when given the opportunity.

'Internal security systems and backups all disabled, Amy.'

'Well done, Robbie. Let's get in there and make a thorough search of the place,' replied Amy, grabbing the rope and letting it fall into the sunken floor below. She positioned herself over the opening and slid down into the office, with Robbie following close behind. At last they were in. Amy hoped above all else that the information Aree had provided would prove to be the breakthrough they needed.

'Good work again with the security, Robbie. Remind me exactly where you learned how to do all that?'

'When you've broken into as many security complexes as I have over the years, it becomes second nature – but if I told you where

I learned it all, I'd have to kill you.' said Robbie jokingly. 'Where shall we start searching?'

'Wherever you like. Let's hope this so-called evidence irrefutably ties Adam to all the robberies over the past year and explains the connection he and those other eight people have to Operation Guardian Angel – and, with any luck, Adam's motive for doing all this against the government.'

'Aree hasn't let us down so far, but if this turns out to be a red herring, we're going to have to rely on my hacking programme and that file.'

'How much longer before we have complete access to the file?'

'The hacking programme should be through the last firewall by tomorrow afternoon. We'll have complete, undetectable access then.'

'Good. Right, let's get started. If I know Adam like I think I do, any evidence that may be here will be cleverly hidden in plain sight.'

They set to work, searching through every cupboard and drawer, behind every painting and photograph, knocking on walls and floors for fake panels. They searched upstairs in Adam's bedroom, the kitchen and around the library area. But much to their exasperation, after an hour of rigorous searching they still hadn't found one shred of the evidence that Aree claimed would be here.

Robbie gave up. He walked over to the picture window where Amy was still searching. 'Amy, stop. You're not going to find anything.'

'No, there has to be something here; there has to be.'

'Look, Aree must have been wrong. He's fallible like the rest of us and makes an occasional mistake. We've searched everywhere and have found nothing. I suggest we leave before we're found out.'

'No, Aree can't be wrong. The evidence has to be here in a small file or flash drive in a—'

Amy stopped dead. She looked over Robbie's shoulder at the bookcase containing Adam's first edition Sherlock Holmes novels. She'd searched there earlier, but now something caught her eye that she hadn't noticed before, even on her previous visit to Adam's office. It was a rather worn-looking book at the centre of the bookcase, which didn't look like it belonged amongst the other pristine first edition copies that Adam had taken great care of. Amy rushed over to the bookcase and looked closer at the title.

'Robbie, come here!' she said, her heart pumping with growing excitement.

'What have you found?'

'I can't believe I didn't notice this earlier. Look at this book. It's called *The Vital Message*, but that's not a Sherlock Holmes story, and it's far grubbier than the rest. Now why would Adam have another Conan Doyle book on this shelf that has nothing to do with his literary hero, Holmes?'

'Hmm … I guess he wouldn't. Open it up and let's see what inside.'

Amy opened the front cover of the grubby-looking book. Her eyes widened as she and Robbie observed that the interior pages had been hollowed out and replaced with an electronic switch. Amy pressed firmly down on the small switch which deactivated the concealed lock behind the bookcase with a loud click. A few seconds later, the bookcase containing Adam's first edition Holmes stories split in half, the two sections concealing themselves behind the adjoining bookcases, revealing a hidden safe.

'You were right when you said it was hidden in plain sight. Remind me to thank Aree later.'

'Let's see if I've learned a thing or two from you about safe-cracking.'

Amy placed her ear against the small door of the safe and began fiddling with the dials, listening to the cylinders drop into the right place. It took her a little while but eventually she cracked the combination. She opened the safe door with great anticipation; at last, some tangible and concrete evidence to arrest Adam with. But all she saw inside was a Baker Street Five logo with a small Sherlock Holmes quote written underneath. Her heart sank.

Robbie peered over Amy's shoulder to look at the laminated logo.

'What does it say?'

'"You see, but you do not observe; the distinction is clear."'

An alarm began wailing as the security lockdown protocols for Adam's office came crashing down around them. Sheets of reinforced metal plating screamed across the windows, doors and skylight, cutting off all escape routes. The main lighting went dead, leaving them and the office completely bathed in the glare from the blue lighting that outlined the large Knight Technologies logo on the back wall. Amy and Robbie scrambled around the office, trying to find something to pry the metal sheet back from the doors, without success. A whistling sound echoed all around the room in which they were now imprisoned.

Amy fought for breath. 'What's going on?' she said, clutching her throat and coughing.

'It's gas. I … can't … breathe.' Robbie gasped for air but the gas was too powerful. He collapsed over Adam's desk with a crash, knocking various papers and objects onto the floor with him. Amy could do nothing but watch with blurred vision as she collapsed onto the floor, helpless. She tried with all her might to crawl towards Robbie but it was futile. Reaching out her hand, she called out Robbie's name in a faint whisper before succumbing to the gas. Her blurred vision turned into darkness and the alarms became nothing more than a distant echo in her ears.

CHAPTER TWENTY-NINE

Agent Amy Johnson woke from her unconscious state. She raised her head up slowly and peered out of the window. It was still dark outside. She felt dazed and dehydrated from the effects of the gas that had knocked her and Robbie out. As her eyes and mind refocused, Amy realised she was bound tightly to a chair in the middle of Adam's office, which had reverted back to normal. How had they tripped the alarm? A panicked thought then flashed across Amy's mind: where was Robbie? She looked around but he was nowhere in sight. Using all the strength she could muster, she tried loosening her restraints to break free, but it was no good.

The locks on the main doors of Adam's office caught Amy's attention as they retracted. Her nerves faltered but she was determined not to show it in front of Adam or whoever was coming in, and she struggled vigorously to get out of her restraints.

'Hey, Agent Johnson, stop that and stay calm. No one is going to hurt you,' said Johnny, rushing over to her with a glass of iced water in his hand.

'Forgive me if I don't believe that,' Amy replied, turning her head to see her captor. 'Wait, I've seen your face before. You're—'

'I'm Johnny Carter-Knight, Adam's son. Here, drink some of this water.' He held the glass of ice-cold water to her lips.

'Thanks for the offer, Johnny, but you can shove it.'

'I'm not going to poison you, Agent Johnson – may I call you Amy? Besides, the iced water will help counter the side effects of the dehydration you're experiencing from the gas.'

Amy paused for a moment. She was thirsty, and as she was in no position to go anywhere, she relented and took a couple of large gulps of water. Johnny removed the glass from her lips and placed it down by her side. He walked over to Adam's desk, pulled out a chair and wheeled it back over. He sat down opposite her.

'What's going on? Why am I tied up? Don't you know it's a crime to hold a member of Her Majesty's Government hostage? And where is my colleague Agent Ellis? What have you done with him?'

'Let's not talk about crimes, Amy; after all, you're the one who broke in here tonight, and, I'll bet, without any official authorisation. Your colleague Agent Ellis is fine. We took him home unharmed, but he'll wake up, like you, with a bit of a headache and dehydration. As for you, well, my dad wants to have a private and frank chat with you – though for the life of me, I can't understand why. He seems to have a very soft spot for you.'

'Does he now? Well, I hope as part of our little chat he'll be voicing a full-blown confession. You do realise, Johnny, that Adam clearly isn't in a stable state of mind, and whatever he and the rest of you are planning will tear this country apart?'

'He hasn't lost his mind, Amy. He's thinking very clearly, and you're going to realise that soon enough.'

'Listen, why not make things easier on yourself and tell me everything you know? I could put in a good word for you if you untie me and tell me what he's planning and how I can stop him.'

'I admire what you're doing, truly, but Adam is the best father I could have ever wished for. He's a good man and I'd die before I'd ever betray him.'

'Good men don't commit multiple crimes and go out of their way to destroy other men, even if they are guilty and deserve it. This isn't the Wild West, Johnny. Let the system and proper authorities hand down justice in accordance with the law.'

'They do when people like you can't see that those men control the law and the system and use it as their own personal playground to lie, manipulate, steal, destroy and murder for their own selfish gains. You don't understand. But as you Brits are so fond of good old-fashioned fair play, you will soon enough.'

'That'll do, Johnny. I can handle it from here, son,' said Adam, standing inside the doorway of his office.

Amy and Johnny both looked towards him. Johnny nodded and got up from his chair, and without saying another word, walked past Adam and left the office. Adam closed the door behind him, his eyes not leaving Amy's intense gaze as they sized each other up.

'You'll have to forgive Johnny's abrasiveness, Amy. He's a good kid. He's just very loyal and protective towards me. Now, I must also apologise for restraining you, but it was the only way to ensure you wouldn't slap me again or try to escape before we had our little discussion.'

'This morning was a mistake. But tell me, before we begin to satisfy my curiosity, how did you know we'd be here tonight?'

'Surely that's obvious? I knew you would be here tonight because I arranged it that way. You see, your reliable contact Aree is really my reliable contact, and very useful he's been too over this past year.'

'You bastard,' she cried out, trying to break free from her restraints once again. Was Adam telling the truth? Had Aree been betraying her and Robbie for the past year? If so, how did they not see his treachery?

'I realise this is hard for you to accept, but he was always part of my plan – and on that subject, let's get down to business, shall we?'

'I'm all ears to what you have to say, but it's a shame you dragged your son into this; you know he'll be going to prison with you. And I dread to think what your other son will think of you when all this comes out,' said Amy as Adam walked over and sat down in the vacant chair opposite her.

'You know, Amy, for a woman as intelligent and brilliant as you, you're quite blind at times; hence my message in the safe. You see me as the villain but you only know half of the story. So, allow me to fill you in on a few facts.' He pulled out a DVD from his jacket pocket and held it out for her to see.

Johnny made his way down a narrow corridor to join Cormac in the executive board room. Cormac sat at the long table, shuffling a deck of cards to play a game of solitaire whilst enjoying a large mug of hot chocolate.

'How's sleeping beauty doing?'

'She's awake and pissed off, but Dad's with her now. By the way, congrats on those experimental hidden motion cameras; they worked better than I thought they would. I didn't think you'd tested them out fully on that separate power system?'

'I have McCabe to thank for that. When he checked Adam's office out earlier this evening, the cameras sprang to life and followed his every move. All the testing I needed. Which reminds me; I must make sure he receives a small bonus this month.'

'I'm sure McCabe will appreciate that,' said Johnny, looking at his watch. 'All we can do now is wait it out and hope. I think I'll call Aunt LJ and Calypso and tell them what's happening.' Johnny took out his mobile phone and walked to the other end of the boardroom. Cormac sat back and took another sip of his hot chocolate. He looked at the large digital clock on the wall – 0200 hours – before reshuffling and dealing out the cards.

Two hours passed and Cormac was halfway through his third game of solitaire, but his concentration was being stretched to the limit by Johnny's restless nature and impatience. He kept pacing up and down the length and breadth of the boardroom, and Cormac could tell he was getting frustrated and angry.

'You'll wear your bloody soles out if you don't stand still for a moment,' he said, giving up on his game and throwing down the rest of his cards on the table.

'What's taking so long? He's been in his office with her for two hours.'

'Adam knows what he's doing, Johnny. Just relax and remain focused. Jesus, you're beginning to put me on edge with all your pacing.'

'We should all be on edge. I thought we agreed to keep an eye on Dad so that all of this wouldn't have been necessary.'

'Look, we all trust your dad, right? Regardless of whatever feelings he may or may not have for Agent Johnson, he never does anything without thinking it through first.'

The DVD came to an abrupt end. Amy was as white as a sheet, stunned, sickened and saddened by what Adam had just shown her. 'My God, so that's it. For all your theatrics and denials, it's revenge, pure and simple; you're getting back at Prime Minister Brooks and his cronies for what they did to those poor soldiers and your friend Colonel Monroe. And the other parliamentarians were what, collateral damage? Adam, what they've done is sick and unforgivable, but—'

'But nothing,' said Adam angrily. 'Politicians like Brooks and his ilk care for nothing and no one but themselves. They destroy lives through their greed, corruption and political power games. And as for the ones that do care, their voices never get heard where it matters; but that is a problem for Tom Phoenix to sort out. Call it what you like, Amy, but I intend to make sure Brooks and his cronies pay for what they've done. The others? Well, they had it coming. Besides, it's about time Westminster had a purge; plus, I've got the aggrieved public on my side and exactly where I want them.'

'Wait a minute … Phoenix? Tom Phoenix? He's working for you too?'

'Not exactly. He doesn't know who I am or what my other intentions are, but after today he and his party will be the only practical choice the public will be able to stomach in government, thanks to my subtle direction. After all, he and his party were the only ones who've been completely open with them and the press.'

'But there's still one thing I don't get. What's in it for you personally? Your willingness to sacrifice everything must have a personal cause and I know it runs deeper than avenging your friend. I've seen it flicker in your eyes. Tell me why.'

Adam quickly turned his head away from Amy and cleared his throat. After a brief pause, he opened the bottom drawer of his desk and took out a rectangular silver box.

'I knew my mask wouldn't fool you forever, Amy. You're a remarkable woman and you're right, I do have a cause, and it's worth a thousand lifetimes in prison; but I'll simply say you already know the answer to your question because you held it in your hand.'

'Adam, please, it's not too late. You don't have to do this,' Amy pleaded, trying to break through his armoured exterior and appeal to his better judgement.

'It's already too late. Amidst the chaos of today, when you read that Guardian Angel file – and I know you will – you'll understand my personal motives and why I have to finish this.'

Adam opened the lid of the silver box and reached inside, pulling out a tranquilliser gun. He took aim and fired before Amy had the chance to utter any pleas. The tranquilliser dart hit Amy straight in the chest and she slumped in her chair, unconscious, and everything went dark once again.

CHAPTER THIRTY

On the streets of London and throughout the country, angry protesters from every walk of life clashed violently with the authorities, outraged and disgusted by their elected officials' corrupt and treacherous actions, exposed by the Baker Street Five over the past few days. The latest revelation was the final tipping point. Prime Minister Brooks and his government had as good as murdered those soldiers from Unit Six, along with innocent Afghan civilians. Chants of 'The Establishment Must Go' could be heard in unison across the land. Buildings were smashed, looted and set ablaze, the flames licking through shattered windows. Molotov cocktails and rocks were thrown at the police and into cars. In response, the Metropolitan Police's TSG units countered by launching tear gas and rubber bullets into the crowds, as they struggled to regain any sense of order.

Agent Amy Johnson was lying on top of her desk in a semi-conscious state. She could hear the news channel broadcasting in the background.

'Our top story continues to be the ongoing and unprecedented rioting and violence in London and other parts of the country, following the Baker Street Five's latest and most damning scandalous act against Prime Minister Brooks's government. Evidence delivered by them anonymously to various media outlets this morning indicates that key members of the Brooks government, including the now former Prime Minister himself, conspired with the well-known and now deceased Islamist insurgent commander Mahmud Al-Kabir in a monstrous deal that saw the UK gain a territorial advantage in a brutal region of Afghanistan, giving Prime Minister Brooks a stronger standing with American and NATO allies. Al-Kabir's price was paid for with British taxpayer money, given to him and his followers as compensation for the loss of his territory and opium fields, alongside permission to massacre the special forces team Unit Six in revenge for them having killed his brother. The compelling and damning evidence also suggests that Prime Minister Brooks and his cabinet accomplices set up Unit Six's commanding officer Colonel Arthur Monroe to take the fall, whose death …'

The broadcast faded into the background as Amy woke fully from her unconscious state, jolting upright, disorientated but aware that she was in her office at SI7. She wondered how the hell Adam had got her back inside SI7 but there wasn't any time to dwell on it. She needed to get to the situation room and report. The conversation with Adam last night had had a profound and chilling effect on her. She needed to know what was in that Guardian Angel file, and she needed to find Robbie and stop Adam before he could inflict any further damage.

Dragging herself off the top of her desk, Amy could hear wailing sirens and the sound of chaos outside resonating through the large windows in her office. She looked at her watch and was stunned to discover that she'd been unconscious for over ten hours. The news broadcast suddenly caught her attention again and she dashed over to the television to listen to the tail end of the report.

'There is no denying that the unveiling of these and other damning revelations, combined with the level of corruption exhibited by our elected political elite, has brought an unprecedented historical shame and chaos to the UK from which it may never recover.'

The reporter's summation of the situation cut Amy deeply. Her worst fears had been realised. Adam had unmasked one of the most damaging scandals of recent times – deliberately sending soldiers to their deaths – knowing full well that this latest exposé would be the one to tip the public's anger and outrage over the edge. She rushed out of her office and hurried towards SI7's main situation room.

The situation room was in a state of frenzy. Robbie and the other SI7 operatives were rushing frantically around, coordinating with the Phoenix Party, intelligence services, Special Branch and various police forces via phone and satellite links to try to restore order. Robbie had been put in charge of the coordination efforts for SI7 and was talking on a secure line with Police Commissioner Celia Charnwood-

May whilst monitoring the deteriorating situation on the large viewing screens.

'I don't care how you do it, Commissioner. Regroup if you have to. Hold them back until I can sort out reinforcements from the armed forces,' said Robbie, his voice tinged with frustration, as Amy burst through the double doors of the situation room.

'Amy, thank God, you're awake at last' said Robbie, slamming the phone down and rushing over to her.

'Thank God you're alright too, Robbie. What did Adam do with you after everything went dark?'

'Nothing, he clearly didn't want me. I woke up in my apartment, dehydrated and nursing a small headache. When I called into the office to report what had happened, they told me they'd found you unconscious on the steps of the underground station below. I had the boys bring you to our office to recover. You must have got a stronger dose of the gas than me to have been out for that long.'

'I didn't. Adam tranquillised me after we had a long chat. Listen to me very carefully, Robbie. Adam has planned this all along. The robberies, exposing these damaging scandals, using us as pawns in his game … it's all linked. Even your contact Aree has been working for Adam this whole time and leading us on.'

'I know about Aree; it didn't take me long to figure out how and why Adam was lying in wait for us. Aree tipped him off. We'll deal with him later. Did Adam give you any indication of what he plans to do next?'

'No, but I've a fair idea. Before we get into that, though, I need to know the status of the situation on the ground.'

'In brief, it's anarchy. They're protesting and rioting in large numbers in London as well as other parts of the country. We've managed to secure the main hospitals, all the prisons, and major airports and ports as a precaution. Prime Minister Brooks is rumoured to be close to cracking, or perhaps already has. His government collapsed this afternoon and he is hiding away inside Number Ten, surrounded by a large security wall. The Phoenix Party, thank God, have stepped into the fold and agreed to be the acting government for the time being, so we at least have a chain of command. To top it off, the military aren't being as cooperative as they could be, given the recent revelations and the scandal with Defence Secretary Ashworth.'

'We need to keep an eye on Tom Phoenix and his party; he's another pawn in Adam's plans and is working unknowingly for him as well.'

'Tom Phoenix is working for Adam too? Amy, this is unprecedented. We've got to report this to Control and get new instructions.'

'No, we can't trust anyone above us. Not even Control right now. Who knows how many people Adam has participating in his plan, wittingly or unwittingly? In any case, we need Tom Phoenix as acting PM to help us restore order. Send some more agents we trust and can spare over to him, and tell them to report on everything he does.'

Robbie picked up the phone, 'This is Agent Ellis. I need you to send over a couple more agents to surveil Acting Prime Minister Phoenix and report back on his movements.' As he put the phone down, Amy grabbed his arm and pulled him inside one of the small offices and shut the door.

'Now, tell me what's happened to Defence Secretary Ashworth.'

'He's catatonic in St Thomas's Hospital under heavy guard. While you were unconscious, Adam and his friends also released evidence that Defence Secretary Ashworth had been using defence budget funds to finance his debauched sexual and gambling appetites. Apparently, he'd been redirecting funds meant for equipment procurement for our frontline troops abroad to accounts in the Turks and Caicos Islands under an assumed alias and was aided by that disgraced banker Chalmers.'

'Jesus Christ,' gasped Amy, sitting down in disbelief.

'An angry mob overwhelmed his protection detail and beat him senseless as he tried to flee. They then burned his residency to the ground before we were able to intervene and pull him and his detail out for their own safety.'

'We need to pull all the high-ranking ministers and political names, including Prime Minister Brooks, and have them detained here or at one of our safe houses.'

'You can't be serious, Amy. There's no way the PaDP will be able to get through to us in this chaos, especially not with ministers in the back of their vehicles. My God, you might as well pin a target on all their backs.'

'We'll use our own men and women to do it. Look, Adam was seething with such hatred last night. I know he's going to try to make a play for Prime Minister Brooks, and when he does, I'm certain he's going to kill him.'

'That's insane, he won't get anywhere near Brooks. He's in Downing Street, surrounded by a ring of close protection.'

'Rationality and reason have left Adam's mind, Robbie. You didn't see the hate, the rage nor the cunning and determination in his eyes last night. If I'm sure of anything, it's that he'll have planned everything down to the last detail to find a way to get to him.'

A loud knock rattled the office door.

A junior SI7 agent entered and whispered something into Robbie's ear that Amy couldn't make out. The whispering continued for a couple of minutes before the junior agent rushed away and Robbie closed the door again with a solemn look on his face. Amy sensed that something had gone awry.

'What's the matter, Robbie?'

'Another report from the police commissioner. The Metropolitan Police are struggling to maintain order around the area of Downing Street. Too many people are causing trouble and the commissioner is worried that they may break through their defence barricade.'

'If they break through that barricade, it will give Adam his opportunity and there'll be hell to pay. How long can the police hold out for?'

'I don't know. I'm hoping the military will see sense and aid the police to shore up their defence perimeters, particularly around Downing Street.'

Amy placed her head in her hands and closed her eyes to think. Her mind was racing from all the information she'd learned over the past twenty-four hours. She stood up, her thoughts echoing in her head as she grabbed a pen and paper from the desk and scribbled something down in a hurry.

'Are Major Corcoran and his unit here, Robbie?'

'Yes, we're going to deploy him and his men once the military are on board. Why?'

'Well, he and his men aren't going with them now. Get him in here.'

Robbie seemed perplexed by this course of action but did as Amy asked. Several minutes later, he returned to the office with Major Corcoran in tow. He looked suitably imposing in his uniform.

'Major Corcoran, it's good to see you.'

'Agent Johnson, what can I do for you?'

'Major, I know that as a man in uniform, your feelings must be pretty sour towards the Westminster establishment right now. But this is an emergency. Priority one: I need you and your men to go out and arrest everyone on this list on charges of corruption, conspiracy to murder and treason, and bring them back here or to one of our safe houses – by force if necessary,' said Amy, passing over the list for him to see.

'It'll be my pleasure for me and my staff to round them all up,' Major Corcoran replied, his face lighting up at the numerous names on the list. He darted out of the small office with speed, slamming the door behind him, to carry out his orders.

'You and I, Robbie, are going to deal with Adam and his friends. Do we have any intel on where they may be at this moment?'

'No. We raided Knight Technologies and the other holdings that we know of a few hours ago, but there was no sign of Adam or any of the other Baker Street Five. We also discovered that those people you saw with Adam in War Memorial Park, including Kerefese Beckett, are all founding members of the St George's Foundation and are also part of his company's board of directors, believe it or not. They informed us that Adam had not only handed control of his company to them and the other board members but had already transferred some considerable personal assets abroad.'

'This just keeps getting better and better. So I was right; he was getting ready to run, or worse, which makes him even more unpredictable and dangerous. We need to find him now, Robbie.'

'Don't worry. We're holding the St George's members for further questioning as they are tied to the Guardian Angel file as well, and Adam can't leave the country through official channels; I made sure of that.'

'Good, we'll talk to them later. Right now, where do we stand with the Guardian Angel file? Adam seemed to allude to everything becoming clear once I read that file.'

'My hacking programme broke through the last firewall this afternoon. I'll get it up for you now.'

Amy's eyes widened with anticipation. Now she'd finally understand Adam's motives and what he meant when he said that she'd held the answer to her question in her hand.

'Amy, did you hear what I said? We can read the file now.'

'Yes, pull the file up on the screen and let me see it.'

Robbie sat down and remotely logged in to his computer. He retrieved the Operation Guardian Angel file and opened it. Amy leant over the desk as they both skim-read the file's contents, her eyes displaying her growing disbelief at what she was reading. As she read on, her mind exploded into a vision of pure clarity, like someone had turned on a huge industrial-sized fan to blow away the fog. Now she understood what Adam had meant before he knocked her out, and she could see how everything that'd happened over the last year made complete sense. The puzzle fitted together, and for the first time she understood the reasons for the inconsolable anger and pain Adam felt and had tried to hide from her. Panic flashed across her face as she looked at Robbie who was still reading in silence, the same look of disbelief on his face.

'My God, Robbie, how could I have been so blind? We've got to find Adam and the others, and fast.'

CHAPTER THIRTY-ONE

Peter Berry dashed through the back gate and into the gardens of Number Ten. He was a flustered and dishevelled mess, having fought his way back from the Treasury through the crowds of protesters to the safety of the Met Police's steel barrier that was getting smaller by the minute. A small cut from a stray piece of debris thrown by an angry protester had caught him on the side of his head, and blood was trickling down the side of his face. He took a moment to catch his breath and wipe the blood off with his handkerchief. Before the chaos caused by the Baker Street Five's most damning revelation had erupted, he'd been sent on a very important assignment. Prime Minister Brooks had relented and given into his colleagues' demands to pay the ransom and had ordered Peter to force Chancellor Havering to transfer the entire ransom demand to the account specified. The whole thing was sheer lunacy and Peter knew that paying the ransom would be a futile endeavour. He was proven right. The irreparable damage had been done with that last damning leak and he knew his boss was finished.

However, he was a loyal subordinate and the only thing left on his mind was getting his boss out of London. Bolting and then barricading the garden gate behind him, Peter darted through the garden, noticing that several large bonfires had been set alight by the staff that had no doubt deserted Prime Minister Brooks in droves by now out of sheer fear and dread. The tall flames consumed the reams of questionable documents of the Brooks government years that they considered inflammatory or could possibly incriminate them as complicit accessories in the eyes of the public.

'Traitorous bloody fools. Your fates are sealed and intertwined with ours,' he said under his breath, looking at the fires as he rushed up the terrace stairs and through the now silent rooms and corridors of political history which were strewn with mess from the mass exodus.

Prime Minister Brooks sat slumped in his favourite chair, drinking a rather large glass of pure malt Scotch, in the lounge of the Prime Minister's residence. He appeared to have lost almost all sense of reason and reality, preferring the sanctuary of denial. Not even being told via phone that he'd been removed as Prime Minister earlier that day seemed to have had broken through. The entire apartment was a complete and utter shambles. It looked like a bomb had hit it; furniture, fixtures, appliances and artwork lay damaged and splintered in pieces. On hearing the news that the Baker Street Five had released damning material against him and his cabinet colleagues involved in the Guardian Angel cover-up, Prime Minister Brooks had flown into one of his notorious uncontrollable rages. His sunken eyes, heavily shadowed by dark circles, stared blankly out of the window while the impending chaos outside echoed through the shattered glass panes. His hand shook as he raised the glass to his lips to drink the remainder of his malt Scotch to steady his fraying nerves and contemplate his options. Peter tapped on the door to the lounge, in awe at the utter mess that lay before him all around.

'Where the hell have you been, you stupid fool? It's been hours since I sent you off do a task.'

'I'm sorry, sir, but it took a little longer than I thought.'

'I don't want apologies; I want to know if you've done what I asked.'

'Yes, sir, it's done.'

'Good. Now everything can get back to normal, the way things were before this horrible mess occurred.'

'With respect, sir, it's over. You know it deep down too, and I think—'

'Shove your respect, Peter. How dare you question my actions and my right to be PM? It's not over, and may I remind you that you're not paid to think; you're paid to do what I tell you to do without question, understand?'

'Yes, sir. But we need to think about getting you out of the city for a while. We can't stay here and I don't know how much longer the police are going to be able to hold back the angry mob baying for your blood.'

'You know, Peter, whoever these Baker Street Five degenerates are, they must be feeling very pleased with themselves. They think they've won but they haven't. When this all blows over – and it will, in my favour – I will dedicate my remaining years on this earth to tracking down and ruining each and every one of them.'

Peter suppressed his frustration and tried to remain stoic, but inside he was recoiling at Prime Minister Brooks's chilling and nonsensical ramblings. In his own misguided way he felt pity for his boss, knowing full well he was deluding himself. Perhaps it was his way to cope with his dramatic change in circumstances. In all likelihood they would all be going to prison for a very long time if they were captured, and the fallout from this entire fiasco would be etched deeply into public consciousness.

'Sir, let's worry about that later. Right now, my main concern is keeping you safe. Would you please come downstairs to your office?'

'What the hell for? I'm perfectly comfortable here.'

'I know, sir, but John should be back any minute, and I would like you to be ready at a moment's notice in case the police can't hold back that mob and we need to get you out of here quickly.'

'Oh, for God's sake. Fine, if you bloody insist,' said Brooks, clearly irritated by Peter's incessant nagging. Finishing the rest of his drink in one big gulp, he staggered out of his chair and reluctantly followed Peter out of the residence.

Clasping the stair rail firmly as he descended the main staircase, Prime Minister Brooks was lost in his thoughts as he passed the many skewed and broken portraits of his predecessors that adorned the walls. He couldn't help but smirk with arrogant pride. His strong if somewhat delusional sense of self-entitlement and his narcissistic inability to admit his failings meant that he felt he'd been better than all of them. None of his predecessors or his perceived usurper Tom Phoenix would ever achieve the heights he had or do more for this country than he'd done. One day soon he would find a way to fix Tom Phoenix and his party for good, but for now he'd bide his time to get his revenge. Peter was right about one thing; self-preservation was more important and pressing right now. Reaching the bottom of the staircase, they crossed the main hall and proceeded to the Prime Minister's private office. Brooks produced the key from his pocket and handed it to Peter. Under normal circumstances during the transition of power, the locks would have been changed and the room sealed in preparation for the new PM to take office, but given the dramatic events that were unfolding, this protocol hadn't been carried out.

They sauntered into the antiquated office, and Prime Minister Brooks sat down at the desk with his arms folded while Peter stood watch at the door, waiting for John to return. On the desk in front of him, Prime Minister Brooks noticed some letters that had been delivered and decided to go through them to pass the time. Anything was better than the monotony of being stuck in the office twiddling his thumbs. As he sifted through the mail, his eyes widened and his face contorted as he looked down upon a large crisp white envelope emblazoned with the logo of the Baker Street Five.

'Peter, have you or John let anyone into this room against my wishes?'

'No, sir. It's been locked all day. Why, what's the matter?'

'Then what the hell is that on my desk? Why wasn't I told those bastards had sent me a response?' Prime Minister Brooks grabbed Peter's tie and yanked him down as he pointed to the Baker Street Five envelope.

'I'm so sorry, sir. I've no idea. It must have got missed in the chaos after   '

'Never mind now, you idiot, it doesn't matter. This must be the location of where they've stashed the remainder of our precious goods.'

Releasing Peter from his grasp, allowing him to breathe again, Prime Minister Brooks ripped open the envelope like a man possessed and tipped out the envelope's contents. A king's chess piece broken in half rolled out onto the desk along with a tiny card. He was perplexed; it wasn't what he'd expected. He picked up the card and turned it over. On the other side, written in black marker pen, were the words *Checkmate. You lose, Brooks.* Shaking with anger that he'd been duped and realising the significance of the broken chess piece was a metaphor for himself, Prime Minister Brooks bolted up from his chair and tipped over the antique desk in a fit of rage. He was angrier than he'd ever been. The small vein in his head pulsated wildly as Peter tried to calm him down.

Brooks's other bodyguard, John Cook, burst into the study amidst the commotion. 'Sir, we have to go now. The mob has broken through the police security cordon and are heading this way. I've received word from a reliable source that a warrant has been issued for your immediate arrest.' Brooks remained silent and breathed heavily to contain his rage. He was too blinded by his anger to register the full consequences of what John had said.

'Sir, for God's sake, we need to leave now. My source has also told me we must get you to the safety of Chequers so we can make preparations to fly you out of the country,' John continued.

'What source? Who is he? Can he be trusted?'

'Yes, sir, he's been very reliable and informative. Aree hasn't let me down yet. He said that Chequers is the best place for us as it's out of the way and no one will think to look for us there for a good while, but we need to go now.'

'Shall I contact Home Secretary Jackson and tell him to meet us at the helipad, sir?'

'What the hell for, Peter? He's caused me nothing but trouble. Our deal is off; let him fend for himself. Lead the way, John. Let's get out of here.'

'This way, sir. We'll use the long underground tunnel behind the bookcase in the library. That should give us enough cover to get a good head start.'

CHAPTER THIRTY-TWO

In the exclusive residential area of Belgravia, former Foreign Secretary David Miller, who looked pitiful and an utter shambles, sat at his desk, teetering on the verge of madness. The exposure by the Baker Street Five of his illicit affair and the revelations of his involvement and subsequent collusion in the Unit Six Guardian Angel scandal had almost shattered his already frayed nerves. Prime Minister Brooks had even stopped taking his calls despite his promises to protect him. A swift, earth-shattering slap across his face, which almost knocked him out of his chair, brought him crashing out of his limbo to the screams and anger of his long-suffering wife, Caroline, whose emotionally distraught voice echoed around the study. He remembered they were in the midst of having another blazing argument before he'd zoned out.

'How could you have done this to us? You've ruined everything we ever had, you bastard,' said Caroline, shouting at the top of her voice. Her cheeks were stained with the constant stream of tears that were pouring out of her red-raw hazel eyes.

'Caroline, please, she meant nothing to me, absolutely nothing; it was business. Please forgive me, I'm begging you,' David replied, getting out of his chair to console her.

'Don't touch me. You've no idea how disgusted and humiliated I feel. You and your harpy can go to hell for all I care. And business? Is that what you're calling it? So, was it business when you conspired with your precious Prime Minister and our enemies to murder those poor soldiers last year? How could you have been so depraved, cold and heartless? You're a murderer, David, and a monster.'

'Don't call me that. I'm not a murderer. It wasn't even murder. I acted in the best interests of this nation. Prime Minister Brooks made it very clear to me that to win we needed to sacrifice the few in order to get an advantage from the impossible situation that Afghanistan has become. Conventional conduct in that war is no longer an option.'

Caroline laughed at her husband's arcane justification of his actions. 'You foolish man. You really are lost under his influence. Your precious Brooks is no longer the Prime Minister and you are no longer Foreign Secretary. He has destroyed and abandoned you, David, to take the rap for all of this, and when they come for you I hope they drag you out in chains.'

David lashed out in a fit of anger, backhanding his wife across the face, which he instantly regretted. Caroline let out a small scream as she fell to the ground.

'Caroline, I'm so sorry, I didn't mean that … I—'

'That's the last time you will ever touch me. The man I married is dead. I don't know who you are and I never want to see you again. Get away from me!' Caroline rubbed her cheek as she picked herself up off the floor. She removed her wedding ring, threw it at her former husband and ran past him out of the study.

Sobbing uncontrollably, David Miller felt it hit him like an even sharper punch to the gut – his marriage was over. Of all the horrible revelations and humiliations that had come to light over the past few days, this one hurt the most. He heard the front door close with a bang; she must be planning to drive off. He ran after her and dropped to his knees in desperation on the front doorstep of their house.

'Caroline, I can't live without you. I know I've done bad things, but I can change.'

He felt her look at him, the man she used to love, with complete disdain, hatred and pity. As tears streamed down her face, she stepped into the driver's seat of her Porsche 911, turned on the engine and sped away, the tyres of her car screeching all the way down the road until she vanished out of sight.

David picked himself up, head in hands, completely broken. He sobbed uncontrollably at the smouldering wreck that was now his life.

292

Another screech of tyres caught his attention; a vehicle of some sort was moving fast towards him. As it drew nearer, he realised that it was an SI7 vehicle. He knew they'd come to arrest him and, panicking, dashed back inside and locked himself in his study.

Major Corcoran, accompanied by two of his men, pulled up abruptly outside the former Foreign Secretary's residence and leapt out of the vehicle. He instructed one of his men to go round the back and cut off any other potential exits while he and his other man proceeded through the open front door. After a few minutes' search, Corcoran came across the locked study door and began knocking fiercely. 'Mr Miller, this is Major Corcoran. Please open the door. I've strict instructions to arrest you and take you back to headquarters for your own safety, and I am authorised to use force if necessary.'

'Go away. I'm not going anywhere with you.'

'Sir, I insist you open this door at once, or we will break it down. You've nowhere to run. You must come with us. Don't be a fool,' shouted Corcoran, his fist bearing down on the door. There was no response. 'Alright, Mr Miller, have it your way. Break the door down, Ahmed. That's an order.'

A gunshot echoed from inside the study.

Corcoran's other man burst through the kitchen door and found them still battling to gain entry. After several attempts, Major Corcoran ushered his men out of the way and unholstered his SIG P239 9 mm handgun from his hip. He took aim at the door lock and fired three ear-piercing shots. Several more kicks and the heavy door gave way. They burst into the study to find Miller slumped in his chair with his eyes open. Blood poured from the wound where the bullet had passed through what was left of the back of his skull. A small 9 mm Beretta pistol lay on the floor by his feet. One of Major Corcoran's men rushed over to check for a pulse but it was futile. On the desk was a shakily scribbled note: *I'm sorry for everything. I can't go on. My life is over. I hope God has the mercy to forgive me for my sins.*

A short way across the city, the exterior and grounds of the Home Office looked like a battleground. Shattered glass, debris and torched cars lay scattered and burning following violent clashes between protesters and police officers earlier that evening. Thankfully, the military had finally agreed to lend support to the flagging Met Police officers, who were beginning to buckle, and had driven the rioting protesters back, sealing off the area. Within two hours the military had secured the surrounding area and most of Whitehall to form a base of operations. Everything was a little quieter in this area now, apart from a few fragmentary pockets of violence and civil unrest beyond their perimeter. Driving up Marsham Street towards the Home Office were two more of Major Corcoran's unit. Harris and Kobo drove past the last temporary military checkpoint and up to the shattered glass building. It had definitely felt the wrath of the public's anger; as well as the smashed-in windows, some floors were still smouldering from extinguished Molotov cocktails thrown inside from the street.

The Major's voice bellowed over their radio comms link.

'Attention Bravo, Charlie and Delta teams, this is Major Corcoran. David Miller, the former Foreign Secretary, is dead. I repeat, dead. Be advised targets may have concealed weapons and may be a danger to themselves as well as others. Approach with extreme caution. Over and out.'

'Oh, Christ, that's all we need. I hope the former Home Secretary doesn't cause us any problems; we've got enough to deal with right now,' said Kobo, irritated by the news.

'From what I've heard, Eric Jackson is far too fond of himself to do anything that foolish. The man is a misogynistic, self-entitled pig,' Harris replied as they parked up at a safe distance from the burning vehicles blocking their path. As they got out of their jeep, the soles of their shoes crunched down against the broken glass and debris

strewn across the street. They proceeded over to a small group of
soldiers gathered near the entrance.

'Who's in charge here?' asked Harris.

'I am. Lieutenant Turner. What can I do for you?'

'I'm Harris and this is Kobo.' They showed Lieutenant Turner
their SI7 identification. 'We've orders to arrest Eric Jackson, the
former Home Secretary, and take him with us. Where is he? We were
told he was here.'

'That piece of shit is up on the roof and he's refusing to come
down. Personally, you're damn lucky that my men and I haven't
skinned him alive for what he's done. Part of me wishes he'd jumped
when we first arrived and saved us all a lot of bother.'

'I understand, Lieutenant, but we both know it wouldn't solve
anything.'

'No, I guess not. I know this one has to be done by the book.
I've two good men up on the roof watching him and we've laid out air
cushions along the entire perimeter of the building in case he tries to
cheat justice.'

'Is he armed, Lieutenant?' Harris asked, looking up towards
the roof.

'Not that I or my men could see, but he's a wily one. I'd
approach him with caution.'

'Okay, thanks, we'll take it from here. Have your men on standby in case things escalate, and tell your men on the roof we're on our way up,' said Harris as she and Kobo drew their weapons and rushed into the building.

Eric Jackson stood at the edge of the roof of the Home Office, taking in the pandemonium in the distance that had brought this great city to its knees. He knew that Prime Minister Brooks had betrayed him and left him to carry the can while saving his own behind, yet a small part of him still clung onto the deluded idea that Brooks would keep his word and rescue him at the last minute. His own words that night in the clock chamber of Elizabeth Tower had come back to haunt him. The bell had indeed tolled like he warned Brooks it would, but it had tolled for them all thanks to the Baker Street Five and that useless bitch Agent Amy Johnson, who he held personally responsible for the entire situation he'd wound up in. He swore he would find a way to fix her at some point in the future.

Despite his dire circumstances, he hadn't collapsed into a complete wreck. He was clean-shaven and dressed in his best charcoal-grey suit. He wanted to look his smartest for whoever they sent to collect him, which he knew would happen soon. He took out a silver hip flask from his trouser pocket. It had been a present from the Prime

Minister who'd given it to him in recognition of his long service and dedication to the party, which now meant nothing. He unscrewed the cap and drank the entire contents in one go before throwing it off the roof. He reached inside the top pocket of his jacket and pulled out a large Monte Cristo cigar with his stubby fingers and held it to his nose to smell the rich aroma of the tobacco. He placed it in his mouth. It was likely to be his last cigar for some time.

The fire exit door to the roof sprang open. Two armed officers stepped out and aimed their weapons at him.

'Eric Jackson, I'm Harris and this is my colleague Kobo from SI7,' shouted Harris.

'That's Home Secretary Jackson to you. I do not recognise the authority of SI7, and you can tell that bitch Agent Johnson I said so,' Eric Jackson replied without even turning round to face them.

'I don't care what you recognise and neither does Agent Johnson. You're no longer the Home Secretary, sir, and I will not address you any other way than by your name. We have our orders to place you under arrest. You do not have to say anything but it may harm your defence if you do not mention when questioned something you later rely on in court. Anything you say will be used in evidence.'

Eric Jackson removed the cigar from his lips and turned round to face his two would-be arresting officers. As he exhaled a vast cloud of thick white smoke from his mouth, his eyes showed nothing but contempt. 'Well, this is just the icing on the cake to add to my humiliation … to be arrested by two women. Spare me the bureaucratic formalities; I'm not in the mood for it. I'm not even sorry, you know; not one little bit. I'm proud of what I've done for my country. My only questions are what am I being charged with? And is Brooks in custody yet?'

'Treacherous bastards like you rarely are. But I'll humour you a little. Former Prime Minister Brooks is still being sought but don't worry, he won't get far; and as for you, you're being charged with corruption, gross misconduct in public office, conspiracy to murder, and treason.'

'How very colourful those trumped-up charges are; but no matter, I'll have my day in court and you will see me walk away a free man. And another thing, you won't catch Brooks. That bastard's too crafty. He's probably already out of the country by now.' Jackson jumped down from the ledge of the roof and held out his wrists to be handcuffed.

'I doubt that, and I suggest you shut your mouth and don't utter another syllable, otherwise Kobo and I will be more than willing to hand you over to Lieutenant Turner and his men for a few minutes. They're all itching to give you a piece of their minds.'

Outraged at Harris's threat, Jackson opened his mouth to say something clever in rebuke but thought better of it. He could see in Harris's eyes she wasn't bluffing and decided to remain silent. He only had to look into the eyes and faces of the other two soldiers who'd kept him company on the roof for the last few hours to know they were longing to have their pound of flesh.

CHAPTER THIRTY-THREE

Albert Ball airfield near Aylesbury in Buckinghamshire was a former RAF base that had fallen into disrepair following nearly fifty years of neglect. After some considerable negotiations, the fifty-two-hectare airfield, which was named after one of Britain's greatest World War One flying aces, had been acquired by a private company called Mercury Air Logistics for a cool five and a half million pounds. This shell corporation had been set up by Adam Knight over a year ago through a hidden line item in Knight Technologies' research and development budget in preparation for this moment. All was quiet inside the perimeter of the airfield, which was surrounded by high barbed wire fencing and a state-of-the-art anti-intruder detection system. The only thing stirring was the grass that was being blown around by a light breeze of wind, creating a cascading wave effect. It was a stark contrast to the chaos sweeping London and other parts of the UK. A few metres from the old administration buildings in the north-west corner of the airfield were four large corrugated aluminium hangars that once housed repair workshops for the RAF aircraft. Now they were empty, except for one that had a streak of light coming through the partially open hangar doors. Adam was waiting for Aree to answer the phone and give him one last update.

'Aree, at last. I've been trying to get hold of you for half an hour,' said Adam as he paced back and forth.

'Forgive me, Adam, but I'm a little preoccupied. It's not exactly a quiet night with the powder keg you ignited earlier. We're trying to contain the fallout here in the city and around the country.'

'Alright, Aree, my apologies. I know you've got a lot on, but I need this information. Where do we stand on Prime Minister Brooks's arrival time at Chequers?'

'It's well in hand. I've been keeping a close but informal acquaintance with one of his men and feeding him a few titbits of useful information here and there. I've told him that he and his colleague must get Prime Minister Brooks out of the city, and that the only safe place for them right now is Chequers. You know, out of sight is out of mind.'

'Did he take the bait?'

'Oh yes. I'm very sure he'll do what I've told him. He sounded quite desperate and a little frightened of being set upon by angry protesters.'

'Excellent work, Aree. How long will it take for them to reach Chequers?'

'I spoke with him over an hour ago, so if they managed to run the gauntlet and make it to Battersea heliport, where a helicopter was waiting for them, I'd say they'll be at Chequers very soon. Are you all set to go at your end?'

'Yes, I'm all set, but what about Amy?'

'Don't worry about Amy; she and I will be at Chequers in time for the final crescendo.'

'Good. I'll see you at Chequers very soon.'

Adam hung up with a big smile on his face and walked back into the aircraft hangar. In the left corner stood a small brick building which housed various tools along with a small office, and at the back was a small fuel dump comprising ten barrels of jet fuel. Taking up most of the hangar's space was Adam's beautiful black Bombardier LearStar jet, designation AK-797. Adam headed towards the plane where Cormac, dressed in his dark navy-blue pilot overalls from his days in the RAF, had stepped out of the cabin and down the small metal stairs to make his final checks of the aircraft. Adam's mind wandered as he stared up at his jet. In one respect he felt a great sense of accomplishment at having come this far. Very soon he would be thrusting the final nail into Prime Minister Brooks's coffin, which gave him no end of gratification. He was also thankful to the invaluable help of his loved ones, content in the knowledge that they'd soon be escaping the ever-closing net of Agent Amy Johnson and the other authorities to the safety of Switzerland, where he'd made provisions for them to live comfortably for the rest of their lives without hindrance. Yet the feeling was bittersweet. He felt tremendous guilt that, like him, they'd had to sacrifice so much – a debt he knew he'd never be able to repay.

There was also the issue of a small deceit on his part that weighed on the back of his mind. He'd told the others that he would meet them in Zurich a couple of days after his final confrontation with Prime Minister Brooks, but the truth of the matter was Adam intended to go further in ensuring Brooks received his dues. He had murder in mind, and he'd been contemplating it from the moment Colonel Monroe had told him the truth that horrible storm-ravaged night. His evil deed would be a burden he, his conscience and his soul would face alone and in all probability take to the grave as he didn't expect to survive – a course of action the others would never let him undertake if they knew, but the hatred and animosity he felt and had suppressed this past year was too overpowering for him to consider anything else.

'Is everything ready to go?' Adam asked, coming out of his thoughts as Cormac approached him having finished the last of his checks.

'Aye, she is. Our flight plan's been approved through an old contact of mine and we've got enough fuel to get us to Zurich. LJ and

Calypso are in the cabin doing some final checks and getting changed into their outfits.'

'Good. And you all know your roles?'

'Yes, we've all got our forged documents and are ready to play our parts when we reach Zurich. It'll be interesting to see how Johnny plays the son of a wealthy diplomat.'

'I'm sure he'll be fine. Speaking of Johnny, where is he?'

'He's around here somewhere; he took his bike out to do a quick patrol of the perimeter. I think he's anxious and I've noticed he's also acting a little strange. I suspect he wants to stay with you, Adam.'

'I was afraid this might happen when it came to the crunch, but don't worry, I've prepared for that eventuality. If Johnny is planning on announcing something like that, I need you to do something for me which will require you not to ask questions. I need you to be ready to go into the cabin, pull out your tranquilliser gun and sedate him.'

'Adam, that's—'

'There's no other choice, Cormac. Please, do this last thing for me only if it becomes necessary,' said Adam, placing his hands on Cormac's shoulders. LJ and Calypso emerged from the cabin and caught both Adam and Cormac's attention as they descended the small steps, looking smart in their bodyguard outfits.

305

'You can put your eyes back in your sockets, boys. We just came to say that everything's ready and we're good to go,' said LJ, turning to Calypso.

Calypso's phone let out a loud ping. 'Hey Adam, I don't believe it. Prime Minister Brooks coughed up the entire one hundred million pounds into that Swiss account. What do you want me to do with it?'

'Transfer it all to our various charities, including the St Georges Foundation, in the usual way. I'm sure Kerefese, as my interim replacement as CEO of Knight Technologies, will be thrilled that the foundation's finances will be secure for the foreseeable future,' Adam replied, swelling with immense pride. This was an added pleasure; he hadn't expected Brooks to cough up the money when he sent that final note with the broken king chess piece to him. Calypso tapped away on her phone, making all the necessary transfer arrangements.

With the last bit of business concluded, it was time to say their goodbyes. Adam hugged LJ and Calypso and kissed them both gently on the cheek. He shook Cormac's hand and they embraced each other as Johnny walked through the hangar doors. He clearly had something on his mind and wanted to get it out in the open.

'Johnny, there you are. Hurry up, now, son. The others are ready to leave.'

'I'm not going,' Johnny replied, his voice full of defiance.

LJ and Calypso both looked stunned. Cormac walked past them and climbed up into the cabin. Adam remained silent as he and Johnny stared at each other.

'Can you give us a few minutes?' The girls nodded and stepped inside the cabin.

Adam turned back to face Johnny and took a few steps towards him. 'Get on the plane, Johnny. I need you on there and the others need you to fulfil your role.'

'I don't want to leave you. I've as much right to see the end of this as you do, Dad. You've looked after, loved and accepted me for who I am, and I love you and the others just as much, if not more. Please let me stay and help you. I don't want to lose any more of our family,' Johnny replied, his words broken up by emotion as he fought to hold back tears.

'Come here,' said Adam, embracing him tightly. 'You'll never lose me, Johnny. We may not be related by blood, but you'll always be my son and I'll always be your father in every other way,' he continued, releasing Johnny a little to look into his sad eyes and tear-streaked face.

Adam gave Johnny another reassuring smile and embraced him once more, moving him into Cormac's line of sight. He knew what had to be done to get Johnny on the plane and he hated himself for having to do it. He turned and looked up at Cormac who was waiting by the cabin door, tranquilliser gun in hand, and gave him the signal. Cormac took aim and fired. The dart hit Johnny in the back, making him flinch in shock.

'Dad, no, don't do this ...' Johnny fell to the ground. His eyes closed and his head fell onto Adam's chest while the rest of his body went limp and unconscious in Adam's arms. Tears fell from his own eyes as he tenderly kissed Johnny on the top of his head and caressed his light blonde hair.

'I love you, son, with all my heart, but what I'm about to do you can have no part in. I hope you will understand and forgive me one day,' he whispered into Johnny's ear.

Outside the hangar on the refurbished runway, Cormac pushed the throttle of the LearStar jet into full gear and taxied down the runway. As he reached the appropriate speed for take-off, he pulled back on the yoke and the plane lifted off the tarmac with a thundering, whooshing sound, passing over Adam who was standing by his Silver Ford GT, waving goodbye. Cormac tilted the wings of the plane to acknowledge him and ascended into the clear night sky to begin their journey to Zurich.

With a final wave goodbye, Adam stepped into his car and started the engine. It purred into life thanks to Cormac and Johnny's excellent mechanical skills. He took out his phone and placed it on the hands-free clip on his dashboard in preparation to call Tom Phoenix. It was time to uphold the last part of their agreement. Slipping the car into gear, he pressed the accelerator to the floor and shot off with speed through the main airfield gate, ready for the final act of his plan at Chequers with Prime Minister George Brooks.

CHAPTER THIRTY-FOUR

Ever since Tom Phoenix received the first phone call from the man claiming to be the head of the Baker Street Five, three questions had been burning away in the back of his mind. Who was he? Was he trustworthy? And what were his true motives? He felt some shame at having played a small part in following and aiding this man's unpredictable agenda, which had led to the chaos and madness that was now engulfing the nation, to forward his own. For better or worse, he'd been thrust into the most powerful job in UK politics and he had a duty to the British people that far outweighed his guilt. Tom was feeling the full weight of the burden and privilege of what it was to be Prime Minister.

As parliament was still out of action and Downing Street overrun and compromised, Dóchas House had now become the temporary seat of the British government. The building was overflowing with members of the Phoenix Party who'd braved the chaos to come and lend their help and support to their leader and their country in its hour of need. Every room inside this unique building was now in use, each with a specific purpose: communications, intelligence, military command, security and public information. The security services and the military had sealed off the surrounding streets, which extended from Birdcage Walk to Palace Street to Victoria Street and Broad Sanctuary, thus encircling and protecting the acting Phoenix government in a ring of steel. In other parts of London and around the country, emergency security hubs had been set up to enable communications and orders to be sent back and forth. It was vital to prove that there was still a central command structure in place despite all the chaos. The most important order Tom Phoenix had initiated since taking office was the enacting of the Civil Contingencies Act of 2004 – an act which granted any government in office emergency temporary powers to establish a clear plan of action and response, in the event of a local or national emergency, to restore or keep order.

Emerging from the party's main conference hall after having chaired another meeting of COBRA with his new cabinet, the Chief of the Defence Staff, security services and first ministers of Scotland, Wales and Northern Ireland via video uplink, Tom was beginning to show small signs of fatigue and stress; hardly surprising given the extreme circumstances he was working under. Khalil had known him long enough to recognise the signs. He needed a break, even if only for fifteen minutes to grab a coffee, something to eat or gather his thoughts before throwing himself back into the action. Cutting through the queue of people surrounding him with papers to sign and further orders to give out, Khalil dragged Tom away, telling the crowd that the Acting

Prime Minister would be back in quarter of an hour to attend to their enquiries and needs.

'Khalil, this is ridiculous. I'm fine and I don't have time for a break right now.'

'Well, you're going to make time, Tom. You've been going for hours without a break and you need some time to breathe and gather your thoughts,' replied Khalil. Tom knew he wasn't going to take no for an answer.

'Yes, but these aren't normal times, Khalil, and I have a million and one things that need attending to,' said Tom, trying to get past Khalil who blocked his path.

'No, sit down. You've a very good team around you and they can manage on their own for fifteen minutes. You can't hold their hands all the damn time; and besides, what good are you to them if you are too tired or too stressed to make the important decisions?'

Realising he wasn't going to win this argument, Tom sat down at his desk. Khalil poured them both a large cup of hot black coffee.

'Thank you, Khalil, I appreciate this.'

'Do you want to talk about how you're feeling?'

'No, I'm fine, honestly; maybe a little overwhelmed but as you said, we've a good team around us and we're making gradual progress.'

'Yes, the reports coming in are positive. At least we have half the country back under our control. The other half will come before this night is out, thanks to our security, emergency, military and volunteer personnel. When everything's back under control, you'll need to hold another press conference and address the nation. The public need reassurance, and you need to show them they can trust you and your new acting government. It will not be an easy task to accomplish after so much bad blood.'

'I know, and that's why I'm glad I have you and the others around supporting me, and I know I can leave it to you to make the necessary arrangements when the time comes. God knows what I'm going to say to the public, but hopefully the right words will come to me.'

Tom's private phone rang out. 'No rest for the wicked, hey, Khalil?' said Tom, reaching for the receiver.

'No, I'll get it. You finish your coffee.' Khalil picked up the phone. 'Acting Prime Minister Phoenix's office. Who's speaking, please?'

Tom looked across expectantly.

Khalil held his hand over the receiver. 'Tom, it's him, our mysterious friend,' he said, passing the receiver over.

'You son of a bitch. Do you have any idea the damage you've caused? What you've unleashed with your games and revelations?'

'Calm down, Prime Minister Phoenix. I never said the road to power was going to be an easy one; and besides, if anyone can restore order to the country, it's you. The people will listen to you.'

'It's Acting Prime Minister, and what makes you think they'll listen to me, let alone trust me, when my corrupt counterparts have shown them how low the Westminster establishment will sink?'

'They'll listen because you laid yourself and your records bare for all to see. Now, combine that with your morals, values and vision for this country and I assure you that the people will come to accept you.'

'That is yet to be seen, but I suppose you want a thank you, do you?'

'No, I want you to listen as you have been doing. I want you to come alone to Chequers by any means necessary. When you get here, you'll find what I promised waiting for you.'

'Are you mad? I can't leave London. Surely you realise that, given the circumstances.'

'If you want to keep the keys to the kingdom, you'll find a way.'

The line went dead. A sense of curiosity, uncertainty and ambition swept over Tom as he took the phone away from his ear and stared into the distance. What to do? How could he leave his position without it being noticed when the country needed him the most? Questions swam around his head, making him feel nauseous. Khalil's muffled voice started to crack through his train of thought, repeatedly asking what their mysterious friend at the end of the telephone had to say.

'Khalil, I need you to hold the fort. I have to go to Chequers.'

'What? No, Tom, that's insane. You can't leave; you're needed here. And besides, it's far too dangerous. You're the Acting Prime Minister of the UK and Northern Ireland, and you have responsibilities here. Let me go instead.'

'No, my friend, he was quite clear; it has to be me and only me. I need you here to keep things under control while I'm gone. I've never trusted this man but my gut instincts are telling me, given recent events, to go on blind faith.'

Tom took out a pen and paper, scribbled a few lines and signed it at the bottom. 'Here, this paper should help. Congratulations! I've made you my temporary Deputy Prime Minister, and you have my full confidence and authority to carry out my orders while I'm away dealing with an important issue,' said Tom, handing the paper over to Khalil.

'This won't sit well with everyone downstairs, Tom. What will I say when they ask me where you've gone?'

'Tell them I've gone to deal with an urgent matter. Under the current circumstances, they'll have to accept that answer, and I'll be back as soon as possible. I'll be on my phone if you need me.'

'Then may God go with you, my good friend, and please be careful,' Khalil replied, shaking Tom's hand.

'Thank you. When I get back, I expect you to have the press briefed and waiting for me to address the nation. Now, go get me my chief of personal security and tell him to come upstairs right now.'

CHAPTER THIRTY-FIVE

The sound was deafening as the MIL Mi-34 helicopter descended from the night sky and hovered a few feet above the grounds inside the Chequers estate, the official country residence of British prime ministers since 1921. Having escaped from London after holding the frightened pilot at gunpoint, former prime minister George Brooks and his two aides Peter Berry and John Cook leapt from the helicopter onto the damp muddy ground, caking their shoes and suits, already ravaged in a scuffle with a crowd of protesters during their escape to the helipad, in mud. As the frightened helicopter pilot ascended back into the cold night sky, thankful to still be alive, the three of them trudged their way up to the deserted mansion which was shrouded in complete darkness. They reached a side entrance and, having no keys, Peter and John kicked in the door with brute force, damaging the lock and surrounding frame. Looking even more dishevelled, Brooks pushed them aside and proceeded into the dark confines of the mansion towards the study, unaware that within that darkness, hidden from view, Adam Knight was watching and waiting for them, having set up his final trap.

The study was decorated in the traditional style of a bygone era. Wooden panelling covered the floor, walls and ceiling,

encompassing bookshelves, paintings and cabinets. A black marble
fireplace stood as the central focal point of the room. A fifty-inch
plasma screen television hung above the mantelpiece. Surrounding the
fireplace was a three-piece suite with side tables which sat on a large
and intricately woven Persian rug. At the far end of the room by the
summer doors which allowed access to one of the gardens was a
beautiful hand-carved antique desk accompanied by a dark red leather
captain's chair. Peter and John switched on the low ambient lights to
secure the room whilst Brooks headed straight over to the antique desk
like a man possessed. Grunting, he forced open one of the top desk
drawers with a large letter opener and accessed a secret false panel
which he'd used to hide his emergency papers in the event he ever
needed to get out of the country in a hurry.

A cold realisation swept over Brooks, as if someone had
placed a large lump of ice on his chest and was pressing down hard. His
breath became shallow, as if he were having a panic attack, and he was
overcome with a sensation of fear and vulnerability he'd not felt since
the days when he'd started his political climb. He held out his hands in
front of him and watched as they shook uncontrollably. Disgusted with
himself at succumbing to his fear, his eyes darted to a cabinet
embedded in the wooden wall panelling where he knew a large
selection of alcoholic beverages was kept. He licked his thin lips and

made a beeline over to the cabinet, flung open the door and took out a crystal decanter containing a thirty-year-old Highland Scotch. He poured a generous amount into a glass tumbler.

'The room has been secured, sir,' said Peter.

'How long before the reserve Range Rover in the garage is fuelled and ready to take me to the airfield?' asked Brooks, draining his glass of Scotch.

'About fifteen minutes, sir. Try to remain calm. You'll be on that plane and out of the country within the next hour.'

'Good. Get on with it, then.'

Brooks lifted the decanter and emptied some more Scotch into the crystal tumbler, his tremoring hands creating the vibrating sound of glass against glass. Peter and John looked at each other with concern but continued with their orders and vacated the study, closing the double wooden doors behind them. Brooks closed his eyes to savour every last drop of the Scotch and steady his fraying nerves, and let out a deep sigh.

The sound of two muffled shots rang out beyond the double wooden doors, followed by two large thuds. Brooks spun on his heel to face the doors.

'Peter? John? What's going on?'

The lock on the double doors clicked violently from the outside and the low ambient lighting in the study flickered, causing Brooks to drop his glass and the decanter, smashing and spilling the contents all over the polished floor. 'Who's there? Come out and face me,' said Brooks, his voice cracking as his eyes darted in every direction.

The large fifty-inch plasma TV above the fireplace burst into life. A blinding white light took Brooks by surprise, knocking him backwards into the drinks cabinet as the ominous logo of the Baker Street Five flashed up on the screen, illuminating the entire study. A series of images of Colonel Arthur Monroe and the members of Unit Six flashed across the screen, the words *You Murdered Us* written in bold red letters. The images rotated faster and faster as Brooks watched on, dumbfounded and paralysed by fear, until they stopped on the image of the young lieutenant in charge of the unit at ground level.

The lights flickered back on and an ear-piercing gunshot broke the silence. Brooks cried out as he fell to the floor, clutching his knee as blood began pouring out from the wound. Through tear-soaked eyes and horrific pain, he peered up at the approaching figure. As the haze from his eyes cleared, he could see Adam Knight towering over him, pointing his gun.

'Knight, it's you,' he said through gritted teeth as he looked into Adam's cold, unsympathetic eyes that burned with hatred.

Five miles away, an unmarked black Alfa Romeo sped down the dark deserted country lane, its headlights guiding the way to the Chequers estate. Agents Amy Johnson and Robbie Ellis had sat in total silence since they'd left London. Robbie glanced over at Amy, who was staring out of the front passenger side window in a dreamlike state. Robbie knew that the revelations they'd learned from the Guardian Angel file and the evidence they'd uncovered were troubling her.

'It's not your fault, Amy. This case has had so many twists and turns; we were bound to get caught up and tangled in its web,' said Robbie, breaking the awkward silence and Amy out of her thoughts.

'How could I have been so blind? I should have realised from the start what was going on. All the evidence was there staring me in the face and I still couldn't see it.'

'We can't change what has happened but we can affect what happens now.'

'I know. How much longer until we reach Chequers? And by the way, who gave you the tip-off that Adam and Brooks would be here?'

'We'll be there in about fifteen minutes. And before you blow
up, it wasn't a source; it was Adam Knight himself.'

CHAPTER THIRTY-SIX

Adam thrust Brooks's face into the drinks cabinet, making him cry out in pain as the shattered crystal glasses and bottles of alcohol cut into his battered face. Adam was determined to hurt Brooks and make him feel the same depth of pain, anguish and hatred that he'd caused him. Now all that pain, anguish and hate he'd suppressed for so long was bursting out of him like poison being drawn out from a wound.

'Why are you doing this to me? What have I ever done to you?' said Brooks, struggling to break free of Adam's grip.

Adam remained silent. He pulled Brooks out of the cabinet and launched him across the small table that stood against the back of a sofa, knocking over the art deco lamps and breaking several antique trinkets as Brooks rolled over the sofa and crashed onto the floor. The bullet wound in his knee bled out onto the beautiful Persian carpet as he clutched it in his blood-soaked hands. Brooks looked helpless and terrified as Adam glided round the sofa towards him to deliver more punishment.

'Do you recognise him?' replied Adam, pointing at the giant image of the young lieutenant.

'Of course not, you bastard! Why the hell should I?' said Brooks defiantly, wincing in pain as he glanced up at the screen.

Adam's anger exploded once again at Brooks's insincere and ignorant remarks. He rushed at Brooks who'd backed himself up against the black marble fireplace in a futile attempt to get away, and pressed down hard on the injury with his foot, making him scream out in pain.

'Don't play games with me. Look at the screen. Take a good look, you son of a bitch.'

'Alright, he's one of the soldiers from Unit Six who was killed last year. So what?'

Adam released the pressure on Brooks's knee and took a step back.

'That young soldier was Lieutenant Jamie Andrew Knight. He was my son and you murdered him. You sold him and his friends out to that extremist slime of humanity Al-Kabir and then destroyed the life of my good friend Colonel Arthur Monroe by framing him for your crimes.'

'No, it wasn't like that … it wasn't my fault. It was all Richard Ashworth, David Miller and Eric Jackson's idea to go through with it. They're to blame, not me.'

Adam pulled out the gun again from his jacket pocket and aimed it at Brooks. 'You disgust me beyond words, Brooks. They're as guilty as you, but I've already taken care of them. You're the last. You took from me one of the most precious things in this world that I truly loved. So, I've taken everything you love: your money, your power, everything … except your miserable, pathetic life.'

Brooks quivered with fear as he lay against the fireplace, his bloodied face drained of colour as he stared fearfully down the barrel of Adam's gun. Adam looked down at the pathetic and crumpled form cowering before him. This was it, the moment he'd waited for, that he'd dreamed of for the past year. One gentle squeeze of the trigger and it would all be over. Tears rolled down his cheeks and he cocked the hammer back on the gun.

'I want you to feel hopelessness like my son must have felt, abandoned and alone with no means of escape; and I want you to feel fear like you've never felt fear before as I kill you and the devil places his hands upon what remains of your rotten soul.'

Two loud gunshots rang out as the double wooden doors to the study splintered and burst open, and Agents Amy Johnson and Robbie Ellis rushed in with their weapons raised. Adam grabbed Brooks and pulled him up from the floor to use him as a human shield, pressing the barrel of his gun into Brooks's neck.

'Agent Johnson, thank God. Shoot him. He's trying to kill—'

'Shut up,' said Adam, pressing the gun harder into his neck.

'Amy, you're not going to stop me now. I've lived, breathed, dreamed,

planned and sacrificed everything for this moment. I have to do this.'
Adam peered out from behind Brooks to look straight at her.

'Adam, calm down. I understand now what you've been
through, I do. I don't want to shoot you but I will in order to stop you
doing something you'll regret,' Amy replied, assuming a defensive
stance.

'No, you don't understand. You've little comprehension of
how it felt to look at what was left of my son after those butchers had
finished with him. Shall I tell you what my son's loyalty and devotion
to his country earned him? Betrayal by his own government,
ingratitude, and a coffin draped in the Union flag with telegrams of
empty words of comfort from filth like this sack of shit.'

'I know, but that still doesn't give you the right to be judge,
jury and executioner, Adam.'

'I realise you've a job to do, Amy, but I'm more than prepared
to die for this. Despite our mixed feelings for each other, you leave me
little choice but to play my last hand. You've got my back, haven't you,
Aree?'

Amy was stumped by Adam's words. What had she missed?
Then she heard a gun hammer being clicked back. She glanced
sideways to see Robbie pointing his gun at her. Shocked and sickened,
she felt angry at herself for being so slow on the uptake.

Aree ... or RE.

The name of their mysterious informant had been Robbie using his initials all along. It was so obvious. She hated herself for not seeing it or being able to see through Robbie's duplicitous nature. In a fit of rage, Amy turned her gun on Robbie to fire, but it was empty. Frustrated, she realised she hadn't bothered to check whether her weapon was loaded. Robbie must have given her an empty weapon when he'd fetched them from the SI7 armoury.

'You absolute bastard. How could you do this to me?'

'I'm sorry you had to find out like this, Amy. Aree was a pet name for me when I was stationed in Northern Ireland during the troubles. It was easy enough to use that nickname and turn it into a separate and false identity that Adam could use to our advantage. Now drop your weapon and kick it over towards me.'

Robbie's response was a monstrous betrayal of their friendship and trust, and it hurt her deeply. One last thing was now clear, though; one of the last mysteries of this case. How was it possible that Adam and his Baker Street Five had left no concrete trail of evidence? Now she had the bitter answer. Robbie had been first on the scene almost every time. He would have had enough time to ensure that Adam and the others were never compromised.

'Robbie has been an invaluable asset and instrumental in helping my plan to succeed, Amy. Try not to judge him too harshly,' said Adam, throwing Brooks back onto the floor and pointing his gun at him.

'Tell me, Robbie, how much is a Judas kiss worth these days to betray your country, your colleagues, your service, and most of all, me?' said Amy, shaking with anger.

'It wasn't a decision I made lightly, and I didn't do it for a price. This was personal. I know you won't believe me but I never wanted to hurt you. I had to do it for Colonel Monroe. He was my friend and a former colleague, and he was wrongfully accused and murdered. When Adam presented me with the facts that you yourself have seen as our independent witness, I had to help in any way I could. You have your part to play in this too, Amy, because now that you've seen everything and know the truth, I know when you come to make your report it will justify everything we've done. Adam, whatever you decide to do, I will support you in your decision.'

Amy's mind was racing. She couldn't take in that they'd made her party to this insanity, but she needed to find a way how best to resolve this volatile situation. She looked over at Adam staring down the barrel of his gun at Brooks, who was cowering on the floor. His emotional state was a chink in his armour and a way of getting through to him. Despite her anger and bitterness towards him and Robbie, she was still an SI7 agent and she still had her duty to perform.

'Adam, please listen to me. If you pull that trigger, Brooks will win. What he's done to you and this country is criminal, perhaps unforgivable, but as I said, it doesn't give you the right to be judge, jury and executioner. Revenge isn't justice, and I promise you now that Brooks and his conspirators will be punished for their crimes in accordance with the law if you put that gun down.'

Adam let out a little laugh. 'Our justice system is a joke. He'll just slither away like they all do and still end up on top with a book deal or some peace envoy post in the Middle East. Why should I let him live? He showed no empathy or shred of decency when he robbed my son and his friends of their lives for his own selfish interests.'

'Adam, I know you're hurting, but look at your son up on that screen,' Amy replied, imploring him to see reason. Adam looked up at the screen as tears continued to stream from his eyes.

'Jamie would never make you a murderer, and nor would Colonel Monroe for that matter. Deep down, you know they'd never agree with what you're thinking of doing right now, and if you truly felt something for me, you won't do it, because this isn't justice and it's not who you are deep down.'

Adam paused for a moment, his gun still shaking in his hand and still pointed at Brooks's head. Wiping his tears, he continued to look at his son with obvious deep affection and love. Amy's compassionate words had clearly penetrated. Looking back down at Brooks, still cowering with fear, he reluctantly clicked the hammer on his gun forward, lowered his weapon and broke down, collapsing to his knees. Amy breathed a sigh of relief and, ignoring the weapon that Robbie had aimed at her, rushed over to Adam to console him.

'It's alright, Adam, it's alright. Please give me the gun,' she said, placing her hand on his shoulder as tears formed in her own eyes for reasons she couldn't understand. She was conflicted now more than ever, and she couldn't understand why, after everything Adam had done and put her through, she still cared.

A cold, menacing mixture of painful laughter emanated from Brooks, who'd found his voice again.

'What's so bloody funny?' said Robbie, training his weapon on Brooks.

'Well, it's just I can see why your son died, Knight. He wasn't a man, he was a coward; and like your son, you lack the courage to do what a real man and father would've done.'

Amy looked at him in utter disgust.

Kevin G. Robinson

Brooks's vindictive words crushed what was left of Adam's restraint. He picked himself up from the floor, raised his weapon and fired three shots at Brooks before Amy could stop him.

A cold silence fell over the room.

Breathing heavily through gritted teeth, Adam walked across to Brooks's crumpled body. He was still breathing but crippled once more by fear. The three bullets had missed his head by inches and were embedded into the marble behind him. Adam picked him up by his lapels and shoved him hard into the mantelpiece. Brooks winced in subdued pain.

'My son was more of a man than you will ever be,' said Adam defiantly as he pistol-whipped Brooks hard across the face, splitting the bridge of his nose open and rendering him unconscious as he slumped back down on the floor in a bloodied mess. Adam dropped his gun and turned back round to face Amy and Robbie in quiet resignation to whatever fate awaited him next as the sound of wailing sirens started up in the distance.

'That'll be our back-up arriving. I'll go and wait for them,' said Robbie, rushing out to the front of the house.

'Don't judge Robbie too harshly, Amy. I know you're deeply hurt by his – our – actions, but he's a good man at heart, and in time I

331

know you'll see that and forgive him,' Adam said as she watched Robbie vacate the study, a foreboding look on her face.

Amy remained silent. Her head was awash with how much this entire case had cost her professionally as well as personally. In her ten-year career at SI7, never had a case left her feeling so lost and questioning everything she thought she knew.

'I know you've every right to arrest us both, and I won't stop you from carrying out your duty if that's what you choose to do. I realise I've no right to ask you this, but there are a few things outstanding we need to discuss right now before your back-up gets here – if you're willing to hear me out?'

Amy was at a standstill, unsure of how to go forward. In fact, she wasn't even sure how to process everything that had happened. Her head and heart weren't in the same place and she fought to hold back her own tears. She felt totally conflicted and compromised. Turning round to face Adam, she looked straight into his eyes and wondered what should she do? Where should she go from here?

CHAPTER THIRTY-SEVEN

Agent Amy Johnson walked out of the front door of Chequers and onto the gravel driveway, holding the silver briefcase which Adam had handed over to her. The entire house and grounds were swamped with emergency and security service personnel from various intelligence branches including SI7, who were in the process of surrounding the perimeter of the mansion. But it would do them no good. Prime suspect Adam Knight had already flown the proverbial coop, having escaped through a series of secret Cold War tunnels that ended about a mile and a half away from the mansion. The conversation that had taken place between Amy and Adam had lasted for ten intense minutes, and Amy had decided to keep their discussion secret for the time being.

'Is everything okay, Agent Johnson? We've been trying to get hold of you for over an hour,' said Major Corcoran, running over to her with several of his men following behind.

'Everything's fine, Major. I'm sorry for not responding to you. In the rush to get here from London, I forgot to bring my radio. Did you complete your assignment as I instructed?'

'Yes, we did, and to be honest, most of the people on your list came without a fuss. I think they were relieved to be in protective custody. We're holding them all at various SI7 safe houses. However, there is one point of order. I regret to inform you that the former Foreign Secretary, David Miller, took his own life before we could detain him.'

Amy let out a deep sigh. 'That's regrettable, but I can't say I'm surprised. What's the overall situation looking like now?'

'Things are moving fast, but the latest reports suggest there are only a few pockets of discourse and unrest left to deal with, but we're confident they'll subside in the next twenty-four hours or so.'

'That's good to hear. I'll have your full report tomorrow afternoon on my desk at 1400 hours.'

'Of course. Do you have any further orders for me and my men this evening?'

'Yes. You'll find former prime minister George Brooks unconscious by the fireplace in the study. He's in urgent need of medical attention. See that he gets it. You'll also find his two subordinates outside in the corridor. They've both been tranquillised but are coming round. When they're fully lucid, please arrest and detain them all and don't let them out of your sight for one minute. Is that understood?'

'Yes. I'll personally see to it that they're properly detained,' replied Major Corcoran, turning round to his men. 'Right men, get inside on the double.'

Amy walked down the gravel driveway towards Robbie, who she'd spotted in the distance talking to a smart and casually dressed man in jeans, a black turtleneck and jacket. She recognised the man immediately as Tom Phoenix. So Adam hadn't been joking when he said he'd be here. As she got closer, she felt a surge of anger towards Robbie for his betrayal, but now wasn't time for personal recriminations; there would be plenty of time for that in the coming days.

'Prime Minister Phoenix, what are you doing here, and with no protection?' she asked, interrupting Robbie's report.

'Ah, Agent Amy Johnson, isn't it? Delighted to meet you. Don't worry, I'm perfectly safe. I've a small security attachment with me. I was just explaining to your colleague Agent Ellis my circumstances for being here. I believe a certain mutual friend of ours has left something for me?'

'Yes, sir, he wanted you to have this with his compliments. Unfortunately, he didn't hang around to hand it over to you personally.'

'Have you opened it, Agent Johnson?'

'No, I haven't. But it's evidence, sir, and we will need to have it back.'

'I understand. Thank you. Now, I know you've had a tough night but I need every available security officer working overtime.

Things have started to simmer down but we still have a long way to go
to restoring complete order, and I must address the nation with the
other first ministers when I get back. So, you can give me your full
report tomorrow.'

'Very well, sir, I'll head back to SI7 right away and help out in
any way I can. If you'll excuse me?'

'Agent Johnson, one more moment please.'

'Yes, sir?'

'I assume you know our mutual friend's identity?'

'Yes, sir, I do.'

'Who is he? Where is he now, and why didn't you and Agent
Ellis arrest him on sight?'

'That's a long story, sir, but everything you need to know
about him, I'm told, is all in that briefcase. As to his current
whereabouts, he could be anywhere by now.'

'I see. Well, for what it's worth, Agent Johnson, our mutual
friend isn't a saint, and his methods are and were questionable and
dangerous to any democracy; but a part of me admires his actions to
some degree. I may not understand them fully yet, but perhaps people
like him are needed to remind us all that our values, and the systems we
use to implement them, need a shakedown from time to time so that

complacency and rot don't get a chance to set in and destroy what we hold dear.'

'I think his actions are a very grey area, sir, but I will agree with you that he and his accomplices are definitely not saints,' Amy replied, glancing at Robbie for a moment. Turning on her heel, she made a beeline for their SI7 vehicle. Robbie excused himself as well to catch up with her.

'Amy, wait, I want to talk with you about—'

'You don't get to talk to me right now, Robbie. Leave me alone. I need some time to get things straight in my head. If and when I'm ready to talk to you, I'll let you know.'

Amy got into the driver's seat of their Alfa Romeo, slammed the door shut and started up the engine. As she pulled away, her eyes glazed over with tears. Had she made the right decisions? Could she live with the decisions she'd made and the ones yet to come and still continue as an effective SI7 agent? Those questions and many others would haunt her for a long while.

* * *

Tom Phoenix opened the briefcase he'd been given, keen to satisfy his curiosity. Inside the lid was a mini hard drive mounted in foam, with a note explaining that it contained a digitised copy of the compromising information the Baker Street Five had taken from the vault, along with the location of where the original documents were hidden. The bottom half of the briefcase contained the red leather-bound ledger from the vault detailing which safety-deposit boxes had belonged to which parliamentarians and additional information concerning the boxes' contents. On top of the ledger lay a crisp white envelope engraved with the Baker Street Five logo, addressed to him personally. He took a deep breath and opened it.

> *Dear Mr Phoenix,*
>
> *If you're reading this letter, then everything I've set into motion over the past year has near enough played out as I intended. I've at best escaped the custody of the authorities or at worst paid the ultimate price with a bullet. Either way, my life in this country is over. I won't lie to you any longer, and I've no doubt that Agents Johnson and Ellis will fill in the blanks over the coming days. I know you want to know why I did this, and my answer is simple: I did it for revenge and to right an injustice done to me and many others.*
>
> *Yet, in carrying out my plans, and despite the chaos I've caused, I've also given you a remarkable opportunity. Contained in this briefcase is almost everything you will need to sweep away the old politics and restore the public's faith that our nation doesn't belong to*

criminals and the corrupt. It will be a mammoth task to accomplish, and one I'm sure you're more than capable of carrying out. The people deserve a better class of representatives in parliament who will truly put their needs and concerns before personal ambitions.

I realise I have no right to ask anything of you, but I hope you will at least give serious consideration to a cause that is close to my heart and deserves you and your new government's attention: our armed forces. They fight and sacrifice themselves for us so that we may continue to live in a free democratic country, which we are all guilty of taking for granted. These men and women never ask to be thanked, and it's about time politicians stopped playing political chess games with their lives.

My son, his comrades in Unit Six and their commanding officer, my good friend Colonel Arthur Monroe, weren't so lucky. Their trust was betrayed, and they died as a result of Prime Minister Brooks and his government's treachery and double dealings with our enemies. I hope you'll make sure this can never happen again and that the colonel and his men, including my son, are all remembered honourably, and that Colonel Monroe's wrongful conviction and dishonourable discharge is expunged. He deserves to be posthumously reinstated and buried with full military honours next to his beloved unit.

I live in hope that you'll be a different kind of leader for this country, and I implore you to ensure that our brave servicemen and women serving at home and abroad don't die in vain. Give them the tools and equipment they need to get the job done; but also, and more crucially, make sure we look after all of them and their families when they come home, and treat them with the compassion, dignity and respect they deserve. It's only right that we as a nation give back to those who have given and sacrificed so much for all of us, and to whom we owe a debt of gratitude that can never fully be repaid.

Live up to your name and make a difference.

Sincerely yours,

Adam Knight

Tom was taken aback to learn the identity of the man he'd been chatting with all this time. At long last he could put a name to the voice, and it wasn't one he'd expected. He reread the letter several times and was profoundly touched by Adam's words and sentiment. Despite their differences and for reasons he couldn't explain, he decided he would take on board what Adam had said. He slid the letter back into the envelope and placed it inside his coat pocket. Closing the briefcase, he watched in the distance as Major Corcoran and his men brought out the former prime minister on a stretcher, along with his two subordinates in handcuffs.

CHAPTER THIRTY-EIGHT

Eighteen months later

A cold and overcast morning gripped the city of London, but it wasn't the only thing gripping the British public's minds. Today marked the end of the high-profile but closed cases, sensationally dubbed 'The Clean Sweep Trials' by the press, of the former Brooks government and various corrupt and former parliamentarians. Outside the Old Bailey, a strong police presence lined the perimeter of the courthouse as large crowds of the public, along with domestic and international press, waited with bated breath to hear the verdicts on former prime minister George Brooks and the last of his former cabinet colleagues. Inside Central Criminal Court One, having put up a very feeble defence of their actions, the jury had found each of them guilty on multiple counts of corruption, treason and conspiracy to murder. After their sentencing, they were taken down one by one to their respective prison transports to be transferred to the new Tartarus Maximum Security Prison.

Former prime minister George Brooks was the last to be taken down to his transport following sentencing. His head was bowed like a man taking his final steps towards oblivion. He appeared unshaven and more dishevelled than he'd ever looked before. Escorted out by two prison officers, Brooks took a slow walk with a slight limp; a constant and painful reminder not only of how far he'd fallen from his lofty tower of power, but also of the man who'd given and left him his new permanent affliction as a memento in retribution for his crimes. As he arrived at his respective transport, Brooks looked up and saw his rival and successor, Tom Phoenix, impeccably dressed in a beautiful light grey three-piece suit with a long charcoal-grey overcoat, staring at him with a smug smile on his face.

About a month after Brooks and all those involved had been arrested, a snap general election had been called; and a month after that, in an unprecedented election victory with one of the highest voter turnouts for over twenty years, Tom Phoenix and his party were officially elected to government by the British people. Rage swirled in every fibre of Brooks's being as he tried in a futile attempt to break free of his restraints and lash out at Tom Phoenix to wipe that smile off his face.

'What the hell do you want, Phoenix?' said Brooks, his voice full of anger and hate. His face turned a deep shade of red as the prison guards pinned him to the side of the van.

'I couldn't let you go without saying goodbye,' Tom Phoenix replied with a wry smile. Brooks tried to kick out at him but it was hopeless; the prison guards had him pinned tight against the van.

'I don't know how you did it or who you paid off, but you deliberately sabotaged my trial. We both know that Adam Knight was the one who shot me and was behind the Baker Street Five.'

'I've no idea what you're talking about. As I understand it, you alleged without any corroborating evidence that one of our top defence technology moguls, Adam Knight, a man whose son you murdered, was behind the Baker Street Five and that he tried to kill you. It's a very fanciful story, and it's also disgusting that you would make up such a fabrication as Adam Knight is also one of your victims. However, I'm pleased to say that the jury saw right through it thanks to the countering testimonies and evidence presented by Agent Amy Johnson and her colleague Agent Robbie Ellis. They maintain they went to collect you for your own protection, and in your disturbed, drunken state you resisted by pulling a gun on them; whereupon Agent Johnson shot you in the knee and you fell right on your face, knocking yourself out cold.'

'That's not what happened, and you damn well know it.'

'Have a safe journey to prison, Brooks. I doubt we'll be seeing each other again.'

'Your day will come too, Phoenix, mark my words. You and I aren't so different, and it wouldn't take much to push you out of the light to make you like me,' Brooks replied through gritted teeth as a huge cheer erupted from outside the front of the courts. Tom Phoenix raised his head to the sound of clapping and jubilation.

'That'll be your verdicts being read out to the public and the world. You'll have to excuse me now as I've a press statement to make and a country to run. And by the way, in answer to your question, you and I are nothing alike. I may bend the rules but I never break them, and unlike you, I actually give a damn about this country and the people who live in it. They've given me their trust, and I intend to honour that trust because I consider the role of serving in elected government and as Prime Minister a privilege and an honour, not a birthright.'

Brooks remained silent, unable to respond as he watched Tom Phoenix walk off to address the public and the press. His humiliation and downfall complete, he resigned himself to his fate as the prison guards marched him into the back of his prison transport.

* * *

Adam Knight drove through the open wrought-iron gates and into the grounds of War Memorial Park Cemetery. The journey back to the UK had been a tricky and arduous affair but having travelled for over two days under various aliases and laying down false trails, he'd at last made it back for the anniversary of his son and Unit Six's deaths.

In the distance, row upon row of white stone crosses of fallen heroes glistened like diamonds from the icy glaze that Jack Frost had covered them with the previous night. The park was quieter than normal; not a sound stirred except for the occasional tweets from the swallows which had nested somewhere in the grounds, and the light, cold breeze which blew against the pristine cut grass and the tall trees. Adam was dressed in his best suit and long black overcoat and was wearing a pair of dark sunglasses which he removed as he walked to the semicircle memorial of white crosses where he and the other parents from the St Georges Foundation had laid their children from Unit Six to rest. He surmised that Kerefese and the others must have been up earlier from all the flowers and notes that'd been laid down. In Adam's eyes this spot was the most beautiful in the whole place, and he took a moment to pay his respects to his old friend Colonel Monroe, whose court martial and wrongful conviction had been overturned. He was now buried alongside his unit, whom he had loved and had given his life for, with full military honours.

'Thank you for everything, old friend. I got lost in my own darkness for a while, but I hope I did you justice and that your faith in me was well placed,' he said, patting his hand gently on the colonel's white stone cross.

Adam sidestepped across to Jamie's grave. Kneeling down, he ran his index finger over his son's name, which had been engraved into the cross. Tears of sadness and subdued joy ran down his cheeks. 'I wish I could hold you in my arms one more time. I miss you so much, Jamie, as does your little brother. I know I still need to make amends with Johnny, and I hope he'll be able to forgive me one day. I have to go away again for some time and I don't know when I'll be back, but I hope you're at peace, wherever you and your friends are, and that you're as proud of me as I am so very proud of you.' He leant forward to tenderly kiss the top of Jamie's grave.

'Oh, I almost forgot. I finally finished our last chess game. The final move you wrote in your last email had me over a barrel. You always were the better chess player, and I thought you'd like to have the winning piece.'

Adam pulled out the contemporary silver knight's chess piece he'd been carrying around since the moment he'd been told Jamie had been killed and placed it lovingly on top of Jamie's cross. Following a moment's reflection, he closed his eyes and pictured Jamie standing in front of him in his best dress uniform, so close he could almost reach out and touch him. Jamie said nothing but stared lovingly back at his father with his cheeky smile; a sign that the nightmares that had plagued Adam for so long had finally been purged and laid to rest.

Standing up, Adam wiped away the trickle of tears and replaced his dark glasses. At last, he felt something he hadn't felt for a very long time: internal peace and curiosity as to what the future held, as the warm sunlight broke through the cracks in the dense cloud cover to lay its warm, heavenly glow upon the whole of the park.

Kevin G. Robinson

About the Author

Kevin G. Robinson was born in Surrey, England. He has always had a fascination with crime and espionage. *Knight's Gambit* is his first foray into the world of the crime thriller.

In his spare time, he can be found researching famous and infamous true crime and espionage stories as well as indulging his passions for history, politics and classical civilisations in museums and galleries in London and abroad. He also loves to travel at every available opportunity and immerse himself in different cultures and ideas while enjoying a cocktail or two.

Printed in Great Britain
by Amazon